WORLDWIDE
ADVENTURES
IN
LOVE

Also by Louise Wener

Goodnight Steve McQueen
Big Blind
The Half Life of Stars

WORLDWIDE ADVENTURES IN LOVE

LOUISE WENER

HODDER &
STOUGHTON

First published in Great Britain in 2008 by Hodder & Stoughton
An Hachette Livre UK company

1

Copyright © Louise Wener 2008

A CIP catalogue record for this title is available from the British Library

ISBN 978 0 340 832462

Typeset in Plantin Light by Palimpsest Book Production Limited,
Grangemouth, Stirlingshire

Printed and bound by Clays Ltd, St Ives plc

Hodder & Stoughton's policy is to use papers that are natural, renewable and
recyclable products and made from wood grown in sustainable forests. The
logging and manufacturing processes are expected to conform to the
environmental regulations of the country of origin.

Hodder & Stoughton Ltd
338 Euston Road
London NW1 3BH

www.hodder.co.uk

For F, with all our love

'Adventure is worthwhile in itself.'
Amelia Earhart

I

Edith's house interested us from the beginning; there was never any sunlight inside it. Every window and doorframe was heavy with fabric, greyed chenille curtains so darkened by time they may very well once have been red. When we visited as children my sister, Margaret, and I would dare one another to go upstairs. Beyond the safety of the kitchen the house tightened then spread, careering off in all directions like a maze. Rooms split into one another, doors led to more doors, cupboards turned into flights of stairs and four storeys up, as close to the sky as we could imagine, sat an attic room populated by ghosts.

'Listen,' Margaret used to say. 'I can hear something.'

'What do you hear?'

'People's lives.'

We became friends with Edith by accident. It was a Sunday in June and like all Sundays in the seventies there was nothing whatsoever going on. My father was pottering, my mother was washing clothes, and everything good was closed on account of God. Margaret and I were playing in the street, daring one another to climb on the neighbours' cars.

'Come on,' I said to Margaret. 'Climb up here on the boot. You can see Mrs Dunn making gravy.'

'Who cares?'

'Looks like she burnt it. Mr Dunn looks like he might be about to wallop her.'

'Is she going to throw his plate out of the window again?'

'Quick. Get up here or you'll miss it.'

This was good stuff. The row was in full flow but we couldn't quite see into the window. We advanced to the roof of a car parked on the opposite side of the street.

'Come on,' I told my sister. 'Give me your hand. Put your foot up here on the windscreen.'

My sister wasn't sure, she was bothered by heights. I egged her on just for the sake of it.

'I'm going to fall,' she said, suddenly. 'Jessie, don't make me. I'm slipping . . .'

My sister lay on the ground in an odd shape. She'd fallen face down on the kerb and the cut on her forehead was bleeding so hard it turned my skin cold to look at it. She had her eyes closed. She wasn't crying. I had killed her.

Edith just happened to be there. She picked my dead sister from the pavement in her bony arms and carried her inside without asking. In her kitchen, a room brash with tiles and echoes, she bathed my sister's cut with salt water until the blood stopped running and the cut beneath looked reasonable. After that she waved a glass bottle under my sister's nose, which woke her from her faint like a magic spell and made her gag so hard I thought she might be sick.

'What were you thinking, child?' Edith asked her. 'Climbing up over a car like that.'

'Jessie made me,' said my sister, still woozy. 'Have I died, are you an angel? Is this heaven?'

'Idiot girl. There's no such thing.'

★   ★   ★

After Edith saved my sister's life Mum made each of us write her a thank-you letter. I used the new Parker ballpoint I'd got for my birthday and worked closely with my sister on her opening lines. She wrote:

Dear Mrs Edith,

Your house smells of mouldy biscuits and dogs and is very much dirtier than ours is. It reminds me of the house on the drama serial *Upstairs Downstairs* except not nearly as nice. Thank you for saving my life. My mum could lend you some Mr Sheen polish if you'd like.

Very sincerely yours,

Margaret

Mum asked us to deliver the letters in person but our plan was to drop them through the letter box without knocking and run away. Edith had other ideas. Her door opened just as we reached it and she told us we had better come in. She didn't thank us for our notes or bother to open them and I felt tongue-tied, which was unusual for me. The only thing I could think of to say was something my mother might have said.

'What a nice street we all live on,' I told her. 'Very good standard of people.'

'Philistines,' Edith said quickly. 'Philanderers, hypocrites and cuckolds. I ought to take a bull whip to the lot of them.'

I didn't know the meaning of the words but I knew they weren't complimentary. I tried again.

'It's the Queen's Silver Jubilee next year, of course,' I said. 'I hope you'll be coming to the street party. My mother is responsible for cups.'

'I'll be helping with the bunting,' Margaret said.

Edith coughed and said, 'Parasites.' From this I surmised she was a Communist.

There was a lull after that while Edith looked at us with

something approaching pity. When the silence became too much she relented and asked if we'd like to explore the house. Margaret said we very much would.

I'd walked past Edith's house twice a day, every day, in the three years since I'd started at senior school. Hers was one of the few Victorian houses in our suburb that hadn't been flattened during the blitz or bulldozed when the new estates were put up in the fifties. It was ramshackle and unkempt and the front garden was large and overgrown. Most of the neighbours, including my mother, referred to it as the dirty house. Margaret and I had talked about it often, in between discussing our horoscopes and arguing about which Charlie's Angel we'd rather be, and had inflated ideas of what it might be like inside.

It was more fantastic than we'd imagined, larger and darker and wilder. The building had old bones that creaked and ached with every step, and layers of dust that got deep into our noses. We spent an hour in a room with no furniture, just books, and another in a room filled with leather trunks. I found an empty box labelled *Bullets* and Margaret found a collection of jewellery stuffed inside the portion of a violin case where the cloth and the resin might usually go. There were necklaces inside, tangled gold and silver chains, loose pearls, single earrings and a golden bracelet wrapped in tissue paper and etched with strange letters, only big enough to fit a child's wrist. It had red stones in it that I thought were probably rubies. It killed Margaret not to take some of it home.

After that we visited Edith once or twice a month. We took her chocolate, which she liked, and she sometimes baked us a sponge cake that tasted of violets. We grew used to the smell and the mess; I'd even say we came to appreciate it. Our own house was tidy and regular and small, and everything in it was beige or brown. Being with Edith was like stepping into a parallel universe. Each time her front door clicked shut behind us there seemed the real possibility that the outside world might be gone for good.

There were notes and papers strewn everywhere, the kind of things most people throw away: bills, train tickets, time-tables, theatre programmes and newspapers that dated back years. The walls were a mass of patterns and delights, a back-ground of pastel-coloured paper the texture of velvet, lined with bookshelves, portraits and maps. There were strange ornaments on every table and shelf: statuettes of black, naked people; pieces of seal fur and a whale bone; hunting knives in cases; perfume bottles with crystal tops so intricate and brightly coloured they might have been out of *The Arabian Nights*.

Some things we struggled to identify. The wooden paddles in the bathroom that looked like tennis rackets turned out to be snow shoes. The carving behind the dresser with faces that gaped open like they were hungry or screaming turned out to be a totem pole. When we asked Edith where she found all these things she simply replied, 'On my travels.'

There were no photographs of people in Edith's house and we wondered if she had any family. Margaret once asked her if she had children and Edith said children were noisy, thoughtless, ungracious and cruel and that she'd never had any time for them. That's when my sister began calling her Aunty Edith. My sister was clever like that.

We knew her less than a year. We visited her two dozen times at most. We got on with our lives and she featured in them both significantly and insignificantly, like postcards from Antarctica or the moon. We were too young then to realize how exceptional she was or how little use we had made of her. She was Edith. She was old. She was the lady at the end of the street.

One spring day Edith had a visitor. He arrived in a beautiful car. He wore a silk coat and polished shoes and carried a bunch of lilies in his hand. He left an hour later with his head held down, the flowers still carried in his hand. It was somewhere around this time that my mother started laughing about things that weren't funny and Edith's house burnt to the ground.

2

On the day of the fire my family and I were at my second cousin Wendy Hillier's wedding. Wendy is from the rich side of our family on account of her father going into the coat-hanger business and my father going into the civil service, which my mother always called the mug's business.

The wedding party was held at the Royal Garden Hotel in Kensington and cost the Hilliers six thousand pounds, which was everything my father earned in a year. There was a champagne reception with smoked salmon canapés, followed by a sit-down dinner with flower arrangements on every table. We ate mushroom soup with garlic toasts, which nobody liked, followed by roast chicken breast and duchesse potatoes. There were profiteroles with chocolate sauce for afters followed by coffee and petits fours on a silver tray.

After the chicken, Wendy's groom, Anthony, made a speech in which he thanked his in-laws for welcoming him into their family and treating him like a second son. By this I think he meant that he wouldn't have to work as a taxi driver any more and could instead look forward to a secure financial future in coat hangers. He complimented his bride on her dress and her taste in men and told the bridesmaids they looked beautiful, which they didn't. Wendy's father stood up then and told us all he'd booked the newly-weds on a two-week honeymoon to Italy where they would be staying in the best hotel in Sorrento. Everyone clapped.

The atmosphere had begun while we were getting ready. Mum was putting on the flouncy chiffon dress she'd bought from Dickens and Jones and Dad was giving her a ton of grief for buying it. She had driven herself half mad in choosing it, picking it up and putting it down a dozen times. This dress was the most expensive piece of clothing she had ever owned. Her hands had shaken when she paid for it. She looked pretty in it. It was green. Dad wanted to know who she was trying to impress and what was wrong with the pleated trouser suit she had worn to the last two weddings and the Cohen boy's bar mitzvah.

My mother ignored him and tried to get on with things. She put matching green eyeliner on her upper and lower lids and applied a peach-coloured lipstick and gloss. After that she sprayed her cleavage with perfume and let Margaret and me have a decent squirt behind our ears. She struggled with her zip and asked my dad if he would help her but he tugged at it too hard and made a meal of it. She finished the outfit with a string of amber beads that were longer than she usually wore and seemed a little bit young for her. None of us had seen them before.

My father got ready then, changing into the dinner suit he'd grudgingly hired from Moss Bros. It had tapered legs instead of wide ones, which was the fashion, and against my mother's strict instruction he'd saved himself the extra two pounds fifty by deciding to forgo the satin cummerbund. His shirt fitted him badly, puffing out over the waistband of his trousers and making him look like he had a paunch, which he didn't.

When they had finished dressing my parents stood in front of the full-length mirror in the hallway with disappointed expressions on their faces. Mum worried that she looked done up like a dog's dinner and Dad said what was the point of spending six thousand pounds on a wedding when half the guests would be wearing rented suits that didn't fit them. Margaret and I wore the lilac peasant-style dresses we'd worn to the Cohen boy's bar mitzvah. Neither of us liked them, but they were tried and tested and in every other way un-contentious.

The drive up to the West End was miserable. Every traffic light was red and apart from my father shouting 'Pillock!' at a man who cut him up on the Mile End flyover, no one spoke. Mum pursed her lips because she didn't like Dad's driving and Margaret buried her head in her library book. It bugged me that my sister was able to read in the back of the car without feeling sick and that she'd rather do that than talk to me. She was reading a book on the polio virus. When I asked her what she liked about it she said the stories about the people in the iron lungs.

At the reception Margaret and I were seated away from our parents on the younger persons' table next to the musicians' stage. The guests there included Wendy's younger brother, Gavin, who was in my class at school, and assorted cousins and friends. There was a box of cigarettes next to the flower arrangement – black with gold tips – and Gavin tried to get me to smoke one. I refused in such a way as to make him think I was above that sort of thing rather than that I'd never smoked one before. Gavin lit one anyway, even though he was under age, and Margaret said, 'I hope it gives you cancer.'

After the wedding speeches there was a supper dance. Sandwiches and cakes were laid out for anyone who was still hungry and a six-piece band called Mixed Emotions played unusual arrangements of popular songs. Margaret and I drank snowballs with maraschino cherries in them and danced to a bossa nova version of 'Hey Jude'. We talked about our own weddings in the future. Margaret said she wanted to have a white dress just like Wendy's, with a train as long as the aisle. I said I planned to get married in a registry office and avoid the expense and the fuss.

We caught fleeting glimpses of our parents throughout the evening. I saw Dad smoking a cigar on the outdoor terrace with the good views over London and saw Mum talking to a man called Jeremy who she told us was a friend of a friend. He looked like the kind of man that read thrillers. He was wearing a cummerbund. He was telling her a long involved story about something or other and as he waved his hands to emphasize the punchline he bumped his elbow into a woman who was eating a slice of wedding cake. Ordinarily Mum would have been mortified but instead she laughed out loud in an embarrassing way and went to fetch a serviette.

At the end of the evening the band played a tune called 'The Gay Gordons' and the dance floor filled with people making arches with their arms and twirling their partners with their hands. Mum and Dad weren't twirling with anyone and neither of us wanted to twirl with Gavin Hillier, who was drunk, so we decided to see where they'd got to. We found their name tags on a table at the edge of the room, populated by geriatrics and the recently bereaved. When I asked the woman who was sitting next to my parents' place names if she knew where Mr and Mrs Lester had gone she said she didn't think she had met them. She followed this up by saying her late husband had been a tailor all his life and that our dresses were very poorly made. Margaret named theirs the table that time forgot.

Our parents turned up on the mezzanine level, drinking Tia Maria at the bar with Wendy's mother. Dad was rocking on the balls of his feet, which was something he did when he was trying to look important, and Mum was pursing her lips and holding her balloon glass too tightly.

'*Girls!*' she said, when she saw us. 'Goodness, you look tired. David, we should think about getting them home.'

Neither of us was tired and I for one could have gone for an extra round of snowballs but Mum was speaking in her phone voice and using words like 'goodness' so we knew she was angling to leave. I yawned on cue, a little overdramatically, and Mum smiled like she wanted to hug me.

The drive home was better. Among the night's gossip was a rumour that the Hilliers' coat-hanger business was in trouble. They had gone into hock to pay for the wedding and had only afforded the Royal Garden Hotel after borrowing up to their eyeballs. I hadn't seen Dad look that happy in ages. He went on about it most of the way home. He used words like 'Tory' and 'capitalist' and phrases like 'kick up the jacksie'. Margaret joined in by making a funny comment about the mushroom soup and garlic toasts that no one had liked and I said I'd heard Sorrento wasn't all that nice. Mum said Jeremy had told her an amusing story about trade unions, which seemed to me to be a contradiction in terms. I think I was the only one who heard her say it; the rest of them were distracted by the flames.

3

Edith's house was on fire, angry and wide awake and shaking its fists at the night. Our neighbours had gathered on the street; some of them were in their slippers and night clothes. My mother said, 'Look, it's the dirty house,' and Margaret said, 'Jessie, it's Edith.'

Dad held our hands as we made our way towards the crowd and we stood close together, the four of us, watching the fire take shape. In the time it had taken us to walk a hundred yards it seemed to have doubled in size. The flames spat and cursed and waved their arms at us, and we wondered if Edith had got out yet. Fire engines came with their sirens peeling; they sang, 'Be calm now, don't worry, we'll save her.' Men jumped out with hoses, wearing oxygen masks that made them look like aliens or astronauts and everyone seemed to be running and shouting.

The noise separated us from one another and it was difficult to listen or speak above the din of it. The roar of the fire, the rush of the water, the grind of the hydraulics as they raised a high platform to Edith's roof. Dad helped fetch buckets that nobody had any use for and tore his dinner jacket on a sharp point on Edith's gate. Someone said they had seen her wave a hankie at her bedroom window and that's when Mum tried to take us home. She didn't want us to see it. The smoke was so thick, the fire was too far gone, she expected they'd be pulling out a body.

The end came suddenly when part of the roof collapsed causing everyone to gasp and run in different directions. The house seemed to crack and yawn open and the firemen screamed at us all to keep back. The flames simmered after that and the crowd reassembled. The fire sputtered out some minutes later.

It was one of those moments when your heart lags a way behind your head. We were caught up in the adrenalin, high from the wedding party and the cheerful drive home and the excitement of seeing a real blaze. It wasn't until the fire surrendered, until the building was smouldering and dripping in water, that we realized someone had died. We stood there helpless in our coats and posh frocks: Mum in her chiffon dress, forever saturated with smoke fumes; Dad in his ruined suit that he'd have to pay for.

The noise fell away gradually, replaced with the familiar suburban hush, and in the aftermath we finally saw our neighbours. Some of the men wore vests with no shirts and a few of the women were in curlers. I could see who was fat without their Playtex eighteen-hour girdle and who was bald without their toupee. I noticed who looked ugly with no make-up on and who slept in their underpants and socks. They didn't look so clean in their housecoats and slippers; their weakness and dirt were on show. Mrs Dunn had forgotten to put her dentures in and when she took her hands away from her mouth, where they'd been while Edith's house was burning down, it looked like her face had caved in.

'Old dear probably left her fan heater on,' someone said. Another said it might have been a loose fuse.

'She was senile, of course,' Mr Rosen said.

'No,' Margaret said to him. 'She wasn't.'

My sister screwed her face up and lifted her fists like she

wanted to punch Mr Rosen in the stomach. He had a smart coat on over his pyjamas and the outside of him looked respectable while the inside of him looked all askew.

'She's upset,' said my mother, explaining. 'The girls knew Mrs Burton, they used to visit her.'

Mr Rosen just shrugged, and as the four of us walked home I told Mum how Edith had described the people on our street.

'She was right,' my mother said, which surprised me.

The evening got the better of all of us and by the time we reached our front gate Margaret had begun to cry. Mum dried her tears on her smoke-stained dress sleeve and Dad tried to comfort her by saying something clumsy about heaven.

'There's no such thing,' said Margaret.

'We don't know that,' said my dad.

'Yes, we do,' Margaret said. 'Edith told me. And she'd been absolutely everywhere, so she'd know.'

4

Greenland

To take:

Jaeger camel-hair suit and skiing helmet
Jaeger flannel trousers and coat
Four windproof blouses with hoods
Five pair sealskin gloves, lined with puppy skin*
Four pair woollen inner mitts
Silk underwear
Woollen underwear
One pair deerskin moccasins
Leather gauntlets
Snow glasses
One pair Salvoc yellow goggles (*Theodore Hamblin Ltd, Wigmore Street*)
Two pair bearskin trousers and jackets
Six pair woollen socks
Two pair blanket slippers (*Hudson Bay Company are best*)
One Eskimo anorak (windproof) made of seal's stomach
(* The gloves ought to have two thumbs, so that when one is wet the other can be used.)

9a, Cavendish Place,
Fitzrovia,
London,
April 6th 1933

Dearest Broo,

What a week it has been already. Supplies arrived
yesterday from Blacks. Three packing crates containing
Primus stoves, bedding, field instruments, tents and all the
rations. We are to live mainly on a substance called
pemmican, an unpalatable mixture of dried beef and fat
compressed into tough little cakes. To this we will add
supplements of margarine, cocoa powder, cubed sugar
and sledging biscuits, as well as some Quaker oats, milk
powder, pea flour, lemon juice and tea. Just sniffing the
pemmican in its tin made me long for one of Mummy's
roast chickens or a plate of the delicious crab we ate in
Cornwall last summer. Nevertheless, it felt reassuring to
have it all finally and I allowed myself a moment of relief.

Andrew Linton had advice for me this Sunday, while I
was up at Rochester, which made me think I was a
million miles from ready. I had planned to wear fur on
the flight up to Melville but Andrew said I must not even
consider it. In the event that we have to make a forced
landing (God forbid!) skins will be too cumbersome for
walking and he suggests windproofs with layered woollens would be best. Fur collects snow that cannot easily
be brushed out and instead will thaw and wet the whole
garment. When the garment is removed (and I confess I
found this funny instead of fearful, which was his intention), the entire thing will freeze solid.

When he'd finished, I thanked him heartily and kissed
him on both cheeks and he blushed a little then, which
seemed astonishing. One would imagine that after all his

adventures and escapades a kiss from a girl would be as nothing. Perhaps he has spent too long with his beloved Eskimos. Perhaps he has never met a forthright girl! In any event I was immensely grateful that he had taken the time to speak to me and I have made separate notes of his best recommendations regarding frostbite.

As I was leaving he made the kindest gesture, donating to me his own copy of *Baffin's Ice Navigation with Sledges*. He was even sweet enough to inscribe the inner leaf with a good-luck note. It made interesting reading for the train journey home but weight is so tight on this trip I doubt I'll have room to pack it and may be forced to commit the best of its chapters to memory. The part on building snow houses is exemplary and the section on crevasses has a way of settling in one's mind.

Just under a month now, can you believe it? How I wish you and Frederick could be there to see me off. At night I dream of nothing but the ice. Andrew says the sight of it is quite incredible. He met Amundsen once, did I tell you? I tried not to seem too impressed when he mentioned it but am afraid I hardly managed it.

It will be my downfall, Broo. I know it. I must give more effort to keeping my emotions in check. Only yesterday I could hardly get to sleep for the excitement and tossed and turned for hours even though I was tired. This morning when I woke, the cherry trees were coming into blossom and the whole world felt so vivid and alive. People are saying it will be another good summer in England. I thought, Edith, my darling, you must be mad.

With love,
Your sister,
Edith

5

The street awoke as if from a hangover, slowly and lazily, weary from a night of vivid dreams and unrewarding sleep. Edith's house was gone and in its place was a gaping hole. From our bedroom window it looked like a rotten tooth had been pulled from a row full of perfect ones.

Margaret and I dressed quickly and went to look at the mess before breakfast. It seemed far worse in the daylight. We could see right through from the pavement to her back garden and everything in between was a mass of charred wood, brick and cinder. We stood for a while, scuffing our plimsolls on the ground, feeling awkward and searching for words.

'The snow shoes,' I said.

'The bullet box,' said Margaret.

'The old-fashioned globe.'

'The ruby bracelet.'

These were our favourites, the things we would have saved, but our naming of them felt inadequate. The regret was larger than that. Our friend was gone and our treasure trove had burnt to the ground. Our playground was lost with all its magic. We felt it keenly and selfishly.

The wreck was surrounded by a cordon and a sign had been put up which said 'Keep out'. I could feel Margaret itching to get past it. Her eyes scanned the wreckage, dipping up and over the ruins, planning her route back inside. I felt her edging forward, inch by inch, and reached out to grab the back of her jacket.

'It's not safe,' I said. 'Let's just leave the flowers and go.'

Margaret threaded the flowers she'd picked – irises and daffodils – through the ironwork on Edith's front gate. She took her time, mixing the colours the way she thought best and fixing them so they wouldn't fall out. I was relegated to the role of chief assistant, passing the blossoms to her stem by stem. Some of the neighbours wandered by while we were doing this, including the Lightfoots, Jack and Joni. Jack and Joni Lightfoot had long hair and wore ethnic clothing and were roundly disapproved of by almost everyone. The rumour was they smoked marijuana and held séances in their garden at full moon. To add insult to injury they weren't actually married so, if you wanted to be pedantic about it, they weren't really the Lightfoots at all.

'What an awful thing,' Joni said.

'We ought to light a candle,' said Jack.

Others arrived then, including Mr Rosen, who Margaret refused to speak to, and Mum's friend Barbara Hill from next door. Barbara was nice about it, saying things like, 'Lovely flowers, girls,' and 'Chin up, Margaret,' and 'How terrible about Mrs Burton.'

The neighbours gossiped about the blaze, their loose lips moving in circles as they marvelled at the firemen on their ladders, and complained about how badly each one of them had slept. It wasn't too long before one of them got onto whose job it would be to demolish things and clear it all up. Edith's house was a stain on the environment and there was something in their click-clack conversations that suggested they were almost happy to see it gone.

Margaret and I left them to it. We kicked our way home

through the debris that littered the pavement and ran our fingers over the film of ash that coated the red-brick walls and identical iron garden gates. The brightness had gone from the street and men washed their cars and women brushed their driveways, vigorously trying to reignite it. Early spring blossom was falling from the trees. It felt to me then like things were changing.

For breakfast Mum had laid out a plate of buttered toast and poured out cold milk for our cornflakes. She looked tired. She had gone to bed in her make-up and her eyes were still ringed with green liner. Dad padded into the kitchen still dressed in his pyjamas and asked for tinned prunes and boiled eggs. Mum stopped for a while. She held the kettle in her hand as if she might say, How can you wander in here as if nothing happened last night and ask me for prunes and boiled eggs? Dad held his arms out in an expression that said, What? and in the end she just laid out an egg cup and said, 'One or two?'

'How does it look?' Mum said, as we ate.

'Bad,' I said. 'There's stuff all over people's lawns.'

'It looks like a bomb went off,' said Margaret, pouring sugar on her toast and folding it over to make a sandwich. 'Maybe Edith was bombed by the IRA.'

Dad looked up from his newspaper and smiled. He couldn't resist it. He sheared the top from his second egg and, for the hundredth time that year, regaled us with the story of the Christmas toe socks. The story had passed into family folk-lore and was usually told something like this:

Early last January Mum had received a mysterious package with a northern Irish postmark on the front. Somehow or other she'd convinced herself it was a letter bomb. She'd picked it up from the door mat with salad tongs, rushed it to the end of the garden and locked it in the shed behind the Flymo. With enormous restraint she'd resisted calling the bomb squad – even though she'd sworn she could hear it ticking – and Dad had been made to hurry down there and examine it after work.

The package wasn't a letter bomb at all, of course. It was a box of brandy-snap biscuits, a pair of hand-knitted toe socks and a recipe for flourless chocolate mousse cake cut from a copy of *Woman's Realm*. It was a lost Christmas present from Nanna that had gone missing weeks ago, been forgotten about and sent from pillar to post. Somehow it had ended up in Belfast and someone had been kind enough to forward it.

We joked about it frequently after that. We made fun of Mum's silly paranoia, and the story bent this way and that until Dad became the rational hero of the piece and Mum seemed the hysterical fool. Nobody mentioned that Dad's hands had shaken when he'd cut the brown string away or that at one point he'd suggested that Margaret should call 999. Mum was good about it mostly, laughing at herself when required to, but you could tell it annoyed her when Dad brought up the story ad infinitum at family gatherings or repeated it in front of the neighbours. I think she knew it was one of those things we'd still be making fun of when she was old and grey and Margaret and I had children of our own.

Later, when she left us, I worried that our joking and siding with Dad might have had something to do with it.

6

When my cousin Gavin Hillier showed me his penis I felt nauseated, and that's before he asked me to put it in my mouth. It was pale like a worm, droopy and pointed, and looked nothing like my father's, which I'd seen once by mistake when he was getting out of the bath.

'Put it away, why don't you.'

'Come on, Jessie. Touch it.'

'You're revolting, Gavin Hillier. You're sick in the head. No one is going to touch your penis as long as you live.'

'You're scared of it. You're scared of my dick.'

I was incredulous.

'It's small, Gavin. Look at it, it's puny. Do you want me to tell everyone I've ever met in my life all about your puny, worm's penis?'

He looked hurt, he genuinely did. I almost felt sorry for him for a moment. That's when he asked me to put it in my mouth. That's when I charged him with my book bag and knocked him over.

Something strange happens to a person on a Monday morning, especially on the Monday morning after a family wedding. A person can be a little jumpy. A person might act a little out of character. This was Gavin Hillier's defence. He knew he should have urinated in the toilet block and not on the library wall; he didn't know what had come over him. He was sorry I'd walked by at the wrong moment and caught him at it. My mouth gaped wide open at the lie.

The headmaster bought it hook, line and sinker. It was easy, it was clean. It meant he didn't have to phone either one of our fathers or engage in an uncomfortable conversation about under-age sex. In his fucked-up logic I think he blamed me. He didn't say as much but in his closing argument he dwelt heavily on the fact that I had head-butted Gavin in the chest, winding him badly, rather than the fact that when they'd picked him up off the ground his penis was still poking through the zip hole of his slacks. Gavin's behaviour had been 'inappropriate', but mine had been 'unladylike'. Gavin was to use the toilets at all times in future and I was to avert my eyes and find a teacher if something like this ever happened again. We were both given a week of detentions. My form teacher said we were lucky not to get the cane.

It took me until lunch break to get over the injustice of it all and even then I had trouble eating my sandwich. My best friend, Rebecca Witt, said it was a typical male response and that I could probably sue Gavin for sexual harassment.

'The woman is always to blame,' she said, indicating that she'd finish my sandwich if I didn't want it. 'For leading them on. No matter what happens, it always ends up being the woman's fault.'

I wondered how much I'd get if I sued the Hilliers for sexual harassment now that their coat-hanger business was in trouble. I wondered if Rebecca was turning into a feminist and if she might stop wearing a bra soon. I spent the whole of the afternoon cross-examining myself to see if there was anything at all in my demeanour that had led Gavin on or made him think I might like to touch his penis.

★   ★   ★

Margaret was waiting for me after detention.

'Everyone's calling you a weirdo,' she said. 'I'm the girl with the weirdo for a sister.'

'I didn't do anything.'

Margaret shrugged.

'Well, anyway,' she said. 'Everyone's saying you're a slag.'

I felt bad for myself, but arguably even worse for Margaret. She'd been subjected to a nasty bout of bullying the term before on account of winning the school geography competition with her project on the life cycle of the cocoa bean. It couldn't do her lack of popularity any good to have an older sister who was getting a reputation for herself.

I put my side of things to her on the short walk home and she wasn't entirely unsympathetic. She offered the odd word of consolation here and there, and when I mentioned Gavin's name for the fifth and final time she screwed her face up in a way that would have scared him had he seen it.

At Edith's house we stopped still in front of the gate, mesmerized by the violence of the wreckage. Together we removed the flowers that had shrivelled fast and died, and brushed away the petals that had fallen like stale confetti on her step. As Margaret reached up for the last of the daffodils she asked if I wanted to go inside.

'There might be something left.'

'Not a chance.'

'You owe me.'

'For what?'

'You know what.'

I wasn't in the mood. I knew there'd be nothing worth saving.

'It's not safe,' I said.

'I'll bet it is,' said Margaret. 'You're just chicken.'

The pair of us got right down to it then. We took off our

blazers and rolled up our sleeves and walked in through the gap where the wide bay window had been. Margaret gasped. You could see all the way to the attic: four storeys of air with little platforms jutting out at every angle which were all that remained of the landings.

We made our way left, to the space where the kitchen had been. The floorboards moaned in pain beneath the gentlest pressure from our feet, giving way here and there to jagged holes. At one point Margaret stood still and refused to move, convinced she'd fall through to the basement if she took another step. I promised her she wouldn't but, when I saw where she'd got herself, I honestly thought that she would.

Everything around us was blackened and if it hadn't been for the light pouring in through the ceiling and walls it would have felt like we'd dug underground to a cave. It smelt bad in there. Not the rich, autumnal scent you get after a bonfire, more like the sickly, decaying smell you get when you catch a strand of your hair in a hairdryer.

'Look,' Margaret said. 'By the pantry.'

My sister pointed to a scrap of wall beneath the burnt coving. A section of wallpaper was untouched even though everything around it had been scorched. It was perfect. It looked dazzling and blood red in the midst of all the darkness and ruin. You could still see the pattern, still make out the wings on the birds.

We stumbled our way across the width of the ground floor, our eyes scanning the walls and floors for signs of life. Everything was turned to junk and rubble. Piles of it. Heaps of it. Fallen rafters we had to climb over, bent metal, powdered brick, soaked carpet, and segments of fabric that turned to charcoal when we rubbed them between our fingers. From time to time we'd stumble upon something we thought we might recognize from its shape. Could that be the velvet hatbox with the silver clasps and pearl inlay? Could that be her ivory walking stick? Was that damp patch of ground the place where the walnut dresser once stood, or the spot where Edith lay down and died?

Margaret and I knelt on something that might have been a chair leg and picked up a scrap of something that might once have been a curtain. We stared up at the roof, now open to the wind, and felt the weight of the house on our shoulders.

'It's like this all the way, isn't it?' Margaret said, sadly. 'I bet it's like this all the way to the top.'

We agreed that it was. The house was dead and empty and Edith hadn't left so much as a ghost.

7

Ilulissat
Greenland
September 12th 1933

My dearest Broo,

I have died and gone to heaven. We are properly warm
for the first time in months and I can hardly begin to
describe the joy of it. We are under real shelter at last, a
wooden shack of sorts that even has beds and a stove.
Last night we dined on whale meat, hot in a broth. It
was the finest meal I have ever tasted.

The setting for this shack is quite exceptional, situated
as it is directly on the bay of Ilulissat Icefjord. We are in
direct sight of the glacier. It towers over us, full of
menace, yet is the colour of sweetest peppermint. As I
write the most incredible bergs are moving out into the
bay. Each shears off from the glacier, which is its parent,
then glides magnificently to the ocean. They are
monsters, Broo, the size of mansion blocks or entire
towns. In the warmth of the sun they fissure and crack
and emit the most piteous roars. Our Inuit barely
notices them but I am shaken to the core each time I
hear one, as if the devil himself were at my ear.

Last afternoon the gang went hunting for seal. The tactic is to wound the animal from some distance since they are notoriously difficult to approach. When they are hit they dive down to their ice holes and the trick then is to wait until they surface for air and harpoon them again at close range. Cooper found two with his shotgun, wounding one in the flank and blinding the other. It took half an hour for the poor things to surface and by then Cooper's hands were close to frostbite and so our Inuit had to finish them off. We trudged back to camp in the most ferocious wind that froze the saliva on our lips. It is brutal out here, unimaginably so, but the scale and serenity is like nothing else. I know why Andrew called this place a magnet. I am in love with it and can't imagine I won't see it again in my lifetime.

I am happy to report the expedition looks to have been a success; in any case all correspondence from the Royal Geographic has been favourable. It will take some weeks yet to collate all our research but it seems we have charted an entirely new sub-oceanic mountain ridge and this is causing some excitement back home. It stretches for some hundred miles, between the islands of Bear and Jan Mayen, and I long to point it out on a map for the boys when I return. The two of them would have adored our little boat. I can just see them now, tearing about the deck like proper captains. We sailed right to the edge of the pack ice and photographed whole colonies of seals and families of delightful polar bears. At times they came so close I felt I might reach out and shake their paws or stroke their backs.

Of course I'm misleading you, for it has hardly all been so romantic. Our weeks on the ice cap were murderous and there were hours so unforgiving and desolate I thought I might collapse and give in. Some days I felt my lungs would explode if I took another breath, or my legs would buckle if I walked another step. I am thin as a whippet, all muscle and bone, but have discovered reserves I thought unimaginable.

Last month we were closed in for ten days at a stretch, unable to leave the shelter of our tents for fear of being blown to the Pole! The elements were out for us and Cooper later confessed there were moments he thought we might perish. I have never felt so alone, nor so pitiably small. But when the storm broke, what a glorious picture it was: the blue sky stretching out to infinity itself, the ice so innocent and still. For mile after mile the landscape smiled back at us and all that had gone before it was forgiven. There is sunlight all day here, can you imagine? No sunset, no dark, no day's end.

Thank God we are done with our sledging. We began our crossing of the sea ice with twenty-seven dogs of which ten remained to the end of our journey. Their number was reduced as our load grew lighter, the dogs in the worst condition being killed and fed to the others. It is harder than you might think to see them go, but a comfort to have them finished off humanely, which is more than they could expect from the Greenlanders. In any case I shan't miss their cries; they howl all the way through the storms.

The cold has a knack for grinding the spirit down. It has the instincts of a sadist and behaves as if it were a living thing. It claws through every piece of your clothing, which seems as nothing in the freeze, as if one is wearing a coat made of paper. Cooper has permanent frost damage to his nose and Hanson may yet lose a part of his toe from wearing his boots done up too tightly. He is being terribly good about it but the smell of the rot when one notices it is quite revolting.

I know you think it madness I should be here and how much you prayed this trip would be the end of things, but I am loathe to admit I fear the reverse may be true. I am bitten by the bug and plan on using my share of our inheritance to fund more travels. Don't feel badly towards me. The circumstances of our fortune will always be wretched but I cannot feel guilty for having choices. I am the first English woman to set foot on these islands and I confess it feels thrilling to know it. I wonder were I a brother and not a sister to you, Broo, if you wouldn't admire me just a little.

I must finish and hurry to sleep. We have an early start next morning and will begin the long march up to Baffin Bay where the ship will meet us to begin our journey home. Pray she comes early for us and that we don't get iced in through the winter. The timings will be tight but we dearly hope to be in before Christmas. I am longing to see you. I miss green England. I miss you and my darling nephews, with all my heart.

All my love,
Edith

8

For a while I wondered if it was our coming home late from school that afternoon that tipped her over. Our mother was often waiting for us. She'd be standing at the window most teatimes and she'd wave when she saw us coming and we'd wave back. The day we went exploring at Edith's burnt-out house no one was waiting at the window. Our door was open to the street. The house was in an uproar.

'Your mother is having a nervous breakdown,' my father announced, succinctly. 'Don't take any notice.'

'That's right, David,' my mother said, in a voice I'd never heard her use before. 'Don't take any notice.'

Mum was in a state. Her eyes were red from crying, her face was puffy and her cheeks were stained with streaks of waterproof mascara that had turned out not to be water-proof. There were clothes scattered all along the stair rail. Her coat was by the door, half in and half out.

'What's wrong?' Margaret said. The obvious question.

'I told you,' Dad said. 'I thought I'd made it clear. Your mother has gone completely mad.'

Mum let out a sigh and motioned for Margaret to come towards her. She hugged her too tight, squeezing her ribs and pulling her hair slightly as she stroked it.

'How was it?' she asked Margaret, as calmly as she could. 'Did you have a good day at school?'

'It was OK,' Margaret said, gamely.

'I'm glad,' Mum said. 'I'm so glad.'

She motioned me over then and gave me similar treatment. She ruffled my hair too roughly and enquired about my day with her watery eyes. I kept things short. I thought that was best. I didn't tell her anything about the events surrounding Gavin Hillier's penis.

'Is Dad right?' Margaret asked. 'Have you really gone mad? Are they going to send you to Claybury?'

Claybury was the mental asylum a couple of miles from our house; you could see its red-brick chimneys from our bedroom window. It had given us nightmares when we were little. This was the place where they electrocuted the 'schitzos'. This was the place where they imprisoned sane people by mistake and kept them doped up to the eyeballs. It was the place our neighbour Mr Benson had gone when the syphilis he'd caught as a teenager had rotted his brain in old age and turned him mental.

'No, darling,' Mum said, sobering up a little from her own breakdown. 'They're not going to put me in Claybury.'

'Are you sure?'

'Yes, darling. I'm sure.'

Dad gave the door to the under-stairs cupboard a bit of a kick then and you could tell he was thinking that putting Mum in Claybury wasn't an entirely inappropriate idea.

'Why are you sitting on a suitcase?' I said. 'Are you going on holiday?'

'Yes,' Mum said. 'In a manner of speaking.'

Our parents sent us to the kitchen for crisps and squash and when we came back they sold it to us like this: Mum was tired; she'd been working very hard for a very long time and she needed a bit of a rest – not from us, who she loved very much, but from her life here in Inderwick Road. She was feeling unhappy and wanted to spend some time thinking about things at Nanna's. She was going there now. She would speak to us every evening and whenever else we liked, and we could go and see her at Nanna's at the weekend.

Margaret and I both felt she was hazy on the details of what exactly she was unhappy about.

I said, 'Are you and Dad getting divorced?'

'Don't think about that now,' she said. 'Let's just get to the weekend.'

'Who will cook dinner?' Margaret said.

'Dad's going to come home early from work. He'll look after you. It'll be fun.'

My sister and I exchanged looks. Dad smiled in a way that made him look deranged.

'I'll pick you up from school in the car,' he said. 'We can all go to Rossi's for ice cream.'

'I like Coke floats,' Margaret said.

'You can have one every day if you like.'

My sister smiled even though she wasn't supposed to.

Dad tried to put a positive spin on things. He stopped talking about Mum going mad and having a nervous breakdown and began saying things like, 'The best way to make Mum feel better is if we give her some time to herself and let her relax for a little while.' I didn't think these were his own words. Nor did Margaret.

For most of the next hour we pretended that everything was normal. Mum unpacked our school bags and asked more details of our day and Margaret went to watch the end of *Screen Test*, her favourite TV quiz. When it had finished Mum put her coat on and called a taxi. She ordered a black cab instead of a minicab and I think that's because she felt the gravity of the situation warranted some extra level of extravagance. She reminded Dad that we were running low on toilet roll and told us not to cry because if we did it would only make her cry and that wouldn't do anybody any good. I waved from the door in my school uniform as she went and it felt like someone had punched me.

On the evening Mum left us Dad cooked frozen chicken pie with no vegetables and we ate it on our laps watching a television programme called *The Good Life*. *The Good Life* was a sitcom about two suburban couples, the Ledbetters and the Goods. The Ledbetters were wealthy and lived a traditional life. The hen-pecked husband, Jerry, worked in the city and earned all the money while his wife, Margo, stayed at home and spent it. The Goods were a different kettle of fish. They'd turned their back on the rat race and were living a life of self-sufficiency in which they grew their own food, made their own clothes, kept their own chickens and would never have to work another day in an office again. Tom and Barbara were unconventional for the time. The idea was that they were equals.

All of us liked the programme for different reasons. Margaret liked it for the animals. I liked it because I thought the Goods were rebellious and appreciated the way they didn't give a stuff what other people in their street thought about them. Mum liked it because she half fancied the idea of self-sufficiency herself and Dad liked it because he fancied Felicity Kendal, the actress who played Barbara Good. Everybody's dad fancied Barbara Good. She was sexy but in an unthreatening way. She always looked pretty. Even in dungarees. Even when she was knee-deep in pig shit.

The Good Life was shown every Monday night at seven and Mum used to tease Dad while they watched it.

'You fancy that woman,' she'd scold him.

'Don't be so silly,' he'd say.

'Oh yes, you do,' she'd say, frowning.

'Well, you fancy Tom, then,' he'd reply.

After that Mum would go to the kitchen to put the plates in the sink and fetch us all some afters; rice pudding with a teaspoon of jam in it which we'd stir until the pudding went pink, or perhaps a Birds Eye frozen chocolate mousse.

There wasn't any afters that evening and Dad said it was because Mum hadn't been shopping. He said we could have bread and jam if we were still hungry but Margaret pointed out that we only had Marmite, which was savoury. Dad said Margaret couldn't have anything anyway because she hadn't finished her pie yet. Margaret went quiet and after a while she said her pie was still frozen in the middle. I felt it was hard for her to tell him this. She hadn't wanted to upset him.

My sister laid her plate on the floor, the dinner my father had tried to cook for her half eaten. As the gravy began to congeal I thought to myself that life was becoming strange and that Mum and Dad hadn't joked about who did or didn't fancy Tom and Barbara Good for a very long time.

9

Nanna lived in a bungalow that smelt of the overripe bananas she bought every Monday and left to go off in her fruit bowl for the rest of the week. It was near the seaside, a bleak stretch of coast that wasn't really coast and was in fact a river estuary. When you bathed in the sea near to Nanna's house you came out dirtier than when you went in. There wasn't any sand at the bottom, just layers of sticky silt and mud that seemed to devour your toes, a sensation that made you feel sick until you got used to it. Dad said there were turds in the water and that's why he never went in. Mum used to go in up to her knees from time to time but she kept a careful look out all the while.

Rumour had it that Nanna had been tall and leggy in her youth, but in old age she'd shrunk to the size of an adolescent on account of having no calcium in her bones, which were now all but powder. I was fairly sure Nanna had once had a neck but she didn't seem to have one any more. Her chin began where her bosom ended and her legs looked even shorter than they were since she had no discernible ankles. The point being that Nanna was the correct size for her bungalow, as was all of her furniture: the two-seater couch, the round fold-out table, the old person's armchair and dinner chairs. Mum looked like a giant in it, like she was living in a gingerbread house.

The second thing I noticed, which almost made me cry,

was that Mum wasn't sitting on her suitcase. I'd assumed we had come to collect her. Even though she hadn't once promised it on the phone it was clear in my mind that the sole purpose of this visit was to bring our mother home. On the doorstep Nanna asked me did I want to take my coat off and I let out a short, snappy 'no'. I could hear the kettle boiling for tea in the kitchen and the sound of its hiss and gurgles made me cross. Nanna seemed not to notice. She directed us to the front room and offered us a choice of two cakes – coconut or lemon curd – which made me inexplicably angry. We weren't there for cake, thanks very much. We wouldn't be staying long enough to eat it. The sooner we were out of there and back to our own house the sooner we could put this episode behind us and pretend our mother's leaving had never happened.

'Lemon curd,' Dad said wearily. 'I might like some coconut,' said Margaret. I sat down next to Mum and turned my back on them, traitors both.

On the settee Mum wrapped her arm around my shoulders and I inhaled her soap-powder scent. It was as much as I could do not to yank her by the hand and forcibly drag her to the door. It's dark in here, I wanted to yell at her. It reeks of bananas and dying flowers and – hadn't she noticed? – Nanna's dress smells faintly of wee. We've tidied up our rooms for you, I wanted to say, and washed our hair on a week night. We're neat as pins. We're good as gold. We're wearing our peasant-style dresses.

'What are you wearing?' Mum said, looking at Dad. 'Why did he put you in those?'

How to answer this question? We'd chosen the dresses ourselves. We'd pulled them off their hangers, ironed out their creases and spot-cleaned the chocolate sauce stains left over from the Hillier wedding. She'd been gone less than five days and already we'd forgotten how to please her.

It had been the strangest of weeks and I wondered if its oddness showed on our faces. Could Mum tell that we'd been living on Coke floats, tinned food and Nimble low-calorie bread, and that Margaret had been eating cream of tomato soup for breakfast? Did she know we'd been staying up late every night and that Dad had let us watch Alex Hailey's *Roots* – about the history of slavery – even though the last time we'd seen it Margaret had suffered nightmares after watching the character Kunta Kinte get part of his foot chopped off?

We had run out of toilet paper on Thursday evening and I'd had to go next door to Barbara Hill's house to borrow a roll. She'd called me 'poor thing' and sent me home with a six-pack of Andrex in an avocado-green colour that jarred with the pink tiles in our bathroom. Our house had come loose since Mum left, like it had been shaken. All its bits and pieces were out of place.

We stumbled through the next few minutes. Everyone tucked into their cake and I began to regret not having some. Nanna baked everything from scratch and favoured a sweet iced sponge or a fruit-based product, whereas Mum favoured shop-bought chocolate biscuits. The coconut cake looked especially good and there was a moment when I could have changed my mind and asked for a plate but I managed to hold my ground and get past it.

'Girls,' Mum said, laying her fork down. 'Why don't you put your coats on and go for a walk with Nanna? Your dad and I need to talk.'

'It's cold out,' Margaret said. 'It's drizzling.'

'Come on, now. A short one. Just to the sea wall and back.'

Nanna walked so slowly I wanted to hit her. The sea wall was less than half a mile from her bungalow and left to our own devices Margaret and I could have been there and back by now. She had trouble getting up the hill. She gripped our wrists awkwardly, stopping every tenth step or so to catch her breath and to point out local landmarks that weren't really landmarks at all. The woman whose lawn *that* was had a husband with Alzheimer's disease. The man whose car *that* was had a son on a kidney machine. Over there was the council building, full of layabouts and hippies who wasted every penny of her rates money digging up the roads but did nothing about the glue-sniffers in the bus shelters or the plague of unmarried mothers who were taking over the town.

Her laments were doom-laden and typical Nanna. She was the kind of person who woke up on the twenty-second of June and phoned everyone she knew with a joyless shiver in her voice to inform them the nights were drawing in again. The summers were too hot for Nanna now. The winters were far too cold. People today had no back bone or moral fibre and the world itself was going to pot. Nothing was like it had been when she was a young woman. Chicken didn't taste like chicken any more. Potatoes didn't taste like potatoes.

By the time we reached the sea wall the tide was going out and the sight of it did little to lift our spirits. We stood together on a narrow strip of shingle and watched the dishwater-coloured waves retreat over the mud, exposing tin cans, tyres and doll parts, and pea crabs that scuttled back and forth. We could see Peter Pan's Playground, closed after the winter; its wheels, roundabouts and rickety rides were shapeless under layers of grey tarpaulin. Our parents had taken us there last summer. Dad had laughed at his reflection, long and thin in the hall of mirrors, and Mum had held everyone's bags and coats while we went on the ghost train.

The drizzle had turned to rain and the wind whipped it hard against our umbrellas, forcing us to huddle under their nylon like clams beneath their shells. In the midst of the storm

I wondered if I should ask Nanna what was going on. She'd been with Mum every day, she had to know. I could find out right now, this very second, if Mum was coming back or staying put. The pitying look she'd given Dad when we arrived made me wonder how bad things really were and whose side Nanna would be on if it came down to a matter of taking sides. In Nanna's world there could hardly be a reason for a wife to desert her post for half a day, let alone a whole week. Dad wasn't the kind of man to have affairs or hit his wife and, in any case, there would be a part of Nanna that would think it was the wife's job to put up with it.

'Is Mum leaving Dad?' Margaret asked, suddenly.

The wind seemed to gasp. It snatched Margaret's words and tossed them out with the tide so Nanna couldn't hear them or was able to pretend that she hadn't. In any case she didn't answer my sister's question. She peeped out at the horizon from the shroud of her umbrella and looked almightily sad. I wondered what she was most sad about: us, or her daughter, or her son-in-law. Or people's degenerating moral fibres in general.

'Of course, you know what your granddad would have said about all this nonsense?'

We waited for her to fill us in.

'What the country needs now,' she said, turning back for home, 'is a World Cup or a damn good war.'

10

I had only seen Nanna cry once; it was after my grandfather's funeral. She kept her face plain all the way through the prayers and didn't even cry when they sent the coffin behind the curtain for its final journey. What made her sob out loud, what struck her down with grief was the caterers forgetting the sausage rolls. Nanna had never used caterers in her life and had planned to do all of the cooking herself, but Mum and Aunty Jean wouldn't hear of it.

Granddad had liked sausage rolls. Nanna made the pastry with butter.

The women from Party People had done their best. The trestle table was heaving with mini-quiches, pork pies, vol-au-vents and sherry trifles but Nanna acted like her mourners might starve. How could they have forgotten them? What kind of people were they? Had they no respect for the dead? She collapsed on her chair with the pain of it and the kitchen filled up with her cries. I remember that Aunty Jean had to steady Nanna's shoulders with both of her hands to keep her upright.

The second time I saw Nanna cry was that afternoon when we got back to the bungalow.

'Stop it,' Nanna said. 'Just *stop* it. Both of you, think of the children.'

Mum and Dad had gone into battle. They stood in front of the cuckoo clock, their faces inches from the other, like cats in heat ready to explode.

'I needed to do this.'

'It's not about *you*.'

'Why not? Why isn't it about me?'

'Fifteen years. For nothing. For *nothing*.'

'It's my turn, David. It's *my* turn.'

'You think it was easy for *me*? Doing that job? Coming home to you every night?'

'It's not a competition.'

'Isn't it? *Isn't* it? I thought that's exactly what it was.'

They didn't make much sense to me. They were halfway through an argument that had started a decade ago and wasn't due to finish until Margaret and I left home. It had to do with work, love and money, and my mother living her life as an unpaid drudge.

'It's not enough any more.'

'I've done everything I could for this family. What more did you want me to do?'

'Nothing. *Nothing*.'

'Tell me what you wanted me to *do*.'

I felt my father's plea was genuine, that he really wanted her to tell him, but my mother simply said, 'I don't know.'

'Liar,' Dad said. 'You're a liar.'

'Go home, then. Why don't you just go?'

Nanna snapped at that moment and cried out and Margaret threw the cake tin at the wall. She was over by the window, still standing with her coat on, her hair dripping rain water down her neck. She grabbed the tin from the table, sending teacups to the floor, and propelled it with all her force towards the hearth. It struck above the mantelpiece sending crumbs and ornaments and pictures of dead people flying, and the suddenness of its impact made me jump. The five of us stopped still for a moment. There was quiet in Nanna's bungalow and all you could hear was the cuckoo clock ticking and the seagulls complaining outside. This is what it sounded like at night, when Nanna was sleeping.

'Tell them the truth,' Dad said softly. 'Why don't you tell them the truth?'

Our parents were splitting up and the long and the short of it was that Dad wouldn't be leaving or giving up the house because he hadn't done anything wrong.

'What has Mum done?'

'Do you want to tell them? Or shall I?'

I held my breath. I thought I knew the answer. It had something to do with that man at the Hillier wedding, the one with the jokes and the velvet cummerbund.

'Are you sleeping with Jeremy?' I said.

'Who's Jeremy?' Mum said.

'That man at the wedding. The one who was making you laugh.'

Dad looked at Mum as if to say, *Are* you? Are you sleeping with that son of a bitch *too*?

'Please, David,' Mum said. 'Don't do this now. I need to explain things to them properly.'

Dad seemed to think this was a fine idea. She could come round on Wednesday. He wouldn't be there. Her belongings would be waiting in the porch.

'You know you can't do that.'

'Can't I? Watch me. Girls, get in the car. We're going home.'

Something odd happened then. I waited for Mum to stop us, but she didn't. She stood stock-still in the hallway. She breathed quickly and evenly like an animal that had broken free from its cage unexpectedly and had no idea where to go or what to do. Her fingers tugged at the cuff of her blouse like she wanted to tear it off and replace it with a new, thrilling garment that none of us had yet seen or imagined. Dad looked superior and bullish, the last time he would for many months. He smelt a victory of sorts – one that would prove to be short-lived – and read Mum's excitement as panic.

'Girls, don't you worry,' Mum said, bending down to hug us. 'Things will be all right now. I'll be back before you know it. I promise.'

I pressed into my mother's soft body. I thought about a film I'd recently seen where a man was able to travel back and forth in time and alter the sequence of events. I wanted to make the day start all over again; to enter Nanna's house at a different hour from a different direction to see if things would turn out another way.

Dad tried to hurry us forward to the door, pushing hats and umbrellas into our hands, and Margaret, who seemed not to have understood much of what was going on, grabbed Mum's arm and said, 'Mum, are you dying?'

'Don't be silly,' Nanna said, rubbing at the spots of cake icing still spattered on her cardigan. 'Your mother's not ill. She's an adulteress.'

11

The policeman knocked on the door while we were having breakfast. Dad was spreading toast with margarine because we'd run out of butter and Margaret was having a bowl of cold baked beans. She was eating them in a peculiar way. She'd poured them cold from the tin and was eating them one by one with a plastic toothpick. When she got bored of doing that she began sucking the juice from the leftover beans until each of them was naked and all that was left was a neat pile of flesh-coloured ovals.

'Is Mum coming today?'

'No, I told you. Wednesday.'

'Are you taking us to school?'

Dad nodded, yes.

'I need my PE kit.'

'Where is it?'

'It's dirty.'

'Why didn't you say so last night?'

Margaret speared one of her beans. Then another. Then another. Then another.

Dad answered the door in his dressing gown, expecting to find the paperboy or the postman, or a neighbour who wanted him to move his car. He stuttered when he saw who it was. Dad was awkward in the face of authority.

'Mr Lester?'

'Oh . . . yes. Why?'

'No need to worry, sir. We're talking to a few of the neighbours, regarding the fire up at number eleven.'

My sister slipped off her bar stool and went to the porch.

'Do you know how it started, yet?' she asked him.

'No,' the policeman said. 'Not exactly.'

Dad invited the policeman into our kitchen, which was a mistake. Mum would have known to ask him into the front room which we only used for special occasions like Sunday lunch or Christmas dinner or home visits from the doctor or the Avon lady. I wondered if I was the only person to be embarrassed by the state of things. The sink was full of washing-up. The leftovers from last night's dinner were clammy on the breakfast bar and the neck of an empty whisky bottle was protruding from the top of the swing bin.

'Is Mrs Lester home?' the policeman asked.

'No. No. Well, she isn't.'

'Can you tell me when she will be?'

'Oh . . . well, then. We don't know.'

Dad began to lose focus. He suddenly seemed to notice the disorder all around him and I wondered if perhaps he'd realized the extent of his kitchen mistake. He stared down at his slippers, which appeared to make him sad, and his eyes began to redden as he excused himself. Margaret said, 'Dad, are you crying?' I asked the policeman if he might like to have a cup of tea.

Nanna always said that drinking alone had the tendency to made a person maudlin. Drinking moderately in public, in a pub or at a party, did you no end of good, but drinking on your own was a slippery slope. Granddad was a fine example of this. He had two pints of stout every night of his life at the Two Brewers in George Street, which suited her fine, but if he drank as much as another drop when he came home to her, he was a beast. When he woke the next morning he'd be regretful and clingy and made of memories, and you'd think that the blitz was only yesterday. It would be as much as she could do to force a prairie oyster down his neck – tomato juice with a raw egg cracked into it – and pack him back off to bed for the rest of the day.

Dad had ignored Nanna's stringent and useful rules on drinking. He'd put a brave face on things after we'd got home from seeing Mum but as soon as we'd finished dinner he'd sidled over to the drinks cabinet and announced to no one in particular that he needed a drink. Our drinks cabinet had a smoked-glass front which opened with a key and it contained exactly this: one bottle of Gordon's gin; one bottle of scotch; one bottle of Martini Bianco; one bottle of Dubonnet, which Mum liked; two bottles of Cava that the Hills had brought us back from Spain; some salted peanuts in a bowl; a calendar from the local Chinese takeaway; a tub of maraschino cherries; a bottle each of tonic water and cream soda; and a bottle of Advocaat – it must have been five years old – for making Christmas snowballs for me and Margaret.

Dad had settled directly on the scotch. He'd poured a small glass and drunk it down in one go, then poured himself another which he'd nursed in front of a documentary about the recent death of Elvis Presley. The narrator said the King had died alone on the toilet. He'd been lonely, obese and full to the brim of drugs and pills. His favourite food was deep-fried peanut butter and banana sandwiches. His coffin had weighed more than nine hundred pounds.

The policeman drank his tea out of a 'World's greatest Mum' mug while Dad went upstairs to refocus and stop being maudlin. He took out his notebook and asked us questions which made us feel clever and important.

'You knew Mrs Burton?'

'We used to go to her house and look at her things,' I said. 'Once or twice a month, maybe more.'

The policeman wanted to know what kind of things were in the house. Were they antiques, was anything valuable? We weren't sure of the value but we told him there were papers and map books and strange ornaments from around the world, and that everything was interesting and old.

'Did she seem forgetful to you? Confused?'

'No,' Margaret said. 'Definitely not. She wasn't senile, if that's what you were thinking.'

'Some of the neighbours seemed to think she was,' the policeman said. 'She didn't talk to many of them, did she? Kept herself to herself?'

'She couldn't be bothered to talk to them,' Margaret said. 'All of our neighbours are philanderers.'

The policeman coughed and tapped his pencil on his notepad.

'Did she speak about her family?' he said.

We told him that she didn't.

'Did she mention any friends?'

We told him no.

'Was there anything she gave to you? Something from the house, perhaps? Something that might help us find a relative?'

I shook my head, no, and Margaret half opened her mouth to say something then closed it up tightly again.

'There was a visitor, once,' I said. 'A few days before the fire. He drove an expensive car, the one with the flying lady on the bonnet.'

'A Rolls-Royce?'

'Yes. He brought her flowers. But he took them away when he left.'

We couldn't remember much of what he looked like or

what he wore bar the shine of his shoes and the hour he'd spent inside the house with Edith. The policeman didn't seem to mind the gaps in our recollection and studiously noted these fragments down.

Dad came in presently, looking better. He'd splashed water on his face and changed into his good clothes. A pair of nylon slacks, a clean shirt and beige tank top, and the brown corduroy jacket with patches on the elbows that he kept for going to parents' evenings at our school. He hadn't had time to shave but he'd dabbed on some of the cologne that Margaret and I had bought him from Woolworths for his birthday.

'You look nice, Dad,' Margaret said.

'Well,' Dad said, and left it at that.

The policeman didn't stay much longer. He thanked us for his tea and assured us we'd all been very helpful.

'We know so little about her, that's the problem. There's no family so far as we can tell.'

'Poor old girl,' Dad said, as he walked him to the door. 'Can't have been easy for her, can it? All alone in that big house. No friends to speak of, no family.'

'No,' the policeman said. 'It's a pity. I doubt it was much of a life.'

'Idiots,' my sister said, going back to her beans. At least, I think that's what she said.

12

Dearest Broo,

I am in my element. The South of France is warm and
such an antidote, and Monte Carlo is the most amusing
place. We welcomed the new year in with all guns
blazing, playing cards with a Russian Prince and a
charming group of New Yorkers who had words to say
about Wallis Simpson. We drank rounds of gin and It,
and rather too much champagne but it seems the inebri-
ation helped my luck. At five minutes to midnight I won
a hundred guineas and the entire table stood up and
cheered, declaring me to be their lucky charm!

It appears I am something of a celebrity. Since that
article in *The Times* people are calling me the Polar Girl
and even the Americans, who had no knowledge of
exploration – or much of geography come to that –
professed to have heard of me. I hadn't expected to be
met with such a fuss but in truth I am relishing every
minute. There is talk now of an award from the Royal
Geographic but I must not let my pride get the better of

me. The honour will be shared among all of us and I am committed to letting Hanson be the one to collect it, since he is predictably furious at my picture appearing in the paper in place of his.

We are staying in a terribly good villa to the west of Nice on Cap Ferrat and are guests of the Stauntons, who you know. I am here with Yolande Morris and her brother, Edward. She is more beautiful than ever, of course; head to toe in haute couture and full of jokes about my callused fingers and dismal wardrobe. She insists we stop over in Paris coming home so she can dress me in the manner of a newly chic and worldly woman!

Andrew Linton arrives on Friday with the Snowdons and the plan is to take a yacht down as far as the bay of Naples and Capri. I am looking forward to seeing him. It will be a tonic to discuss the Arctic voyage fully at last and to swap observations with a person who can appreciate them. It's not that people don't want to hear about it, but they limit their enquiries to trivia about marine life and climate, and how I managed in the company of so many men. They are barely interested in the science and my attempts to instil in them the sheer poetry of the glaciers and ice fields are more often met with shivers than with smiles.

Yolande has taken on the role of social secretary for our group and tomorrow has organized a visit to a perfumery in Grasse. The men are off on a pheasant shoot and when I suggested that it might be fun if we all joined in the hunt Yolande sulked and stifled the idea. She is such a generous girl usually, full of sweetness and charm, but I'd forgotten how dull she can be on occasion. There is a growing traditionalism among some women since the depression, have you noticed? A feeling like the shutters are coming down. The fashion is all waists and long hems again and I wonder what Mummy would have made of it. I long for that boldness her women friends had: Hilda and Meredith holding court in the drawing room and lecturing their men on economics. Mummy with her slick bob and cigarettes, teaching the two of us to Charleston. She was such a vivid girl, Broo. I miss her terribly, as you must too, and daily wish she could have been here for all this.

Again, my apologies for not staying with you longer; the house was so restorative, as was the Norfolk air and the hearty food. It was a joy to see the four of you looking so jolly and so well. The boys grow more like their father every day. They are terribly handsome and clever and will doubtless break hearts all over Europe.

Hoping to see you for Easter, dear sister. I have stories and presents for you all.

My best and fondest love,
Edith

13

I don't know why I chose to share my family's problems with Gavin Hillier; on paper he was the last person I should have trusted. But there was something about his manner which brought it out of me that morning and, besides, I felt the time was right to try a drag on his cigarette.

'Your mum's been bonking someone, then?'

Mum. Bonking. The thought repulsed me and made my head spin. Perhaps it was the nicotine.

'It's supposed to be men who have affairs, not women.'

'Is it?' I said.

Gavin shrugged.

'Your mum's OK-looking, though. My dad would probably bonk her.'

Two girls from my class walked by then and one of them shot a fake wink at Gavin.

'That was my best wink ever,' I heard her say. 'Show me your best wink, Maxine.'

Maxine's effort was more of a squint than a wink and on an ordinary day I might have leapt up in a spirit of competitiveness and showed them what kind of wink I could do. I didn't, of course. It seemed ridiculous. Who cared about stupid things like winks?

'My dad's going bankrupt,' Gavin said, exhaling a pin-thin

plume of smoke from his lips. 'I was going to get a skate-board for my birthday but I'm not any more. Mum says we have to sell the house. We'll most likely end up living in a caravan.'

'Christ,' I said, and I liked the way it sounded in my mouth.

'I was going to get a pocket calculator.'

'We were going to go on holiday to Spain.'

'The cheque for the wedding dinner bounced.'

'Dad put Mum's underwear in the porch.'

'He got caught smuggling cash in from the Channel Islands in a suitcase.'

'She's going to go mad when she sees the mess.'

'It's taxes mostly. He might go to jail. We should have emigrated to Australia when we had the chance.'

'She's living at my Nanna's. Dad's drinking at night. Margaret isn't eating any food.'

'I hate him,' Gavin said. 'I hate my dad.'

'Me too,' I said. 'I hate my mum.'

I hardly meant it, not even for that second, and when I heard it said out loud it felt so poisonous I thought my heart would stop. I waited for God's thunderbolt to strike me down. It didn't.

On the way back to class I noticed Margaret deep in conversation with Ian Warrington. Ian was a strange boy. He was tidy and fat, with a high-pitched voice and a pale and powdery skin. His mother was overprotective and prohibited him from doing sports or watching television, or leaving the house without a jumper, even on warm days. He knew and used words like 'megalithic' and 'Palaeolithic' and had an encyclopaedic knowledge of dinosaurs and Iron Age man. He wore patent shoes and socks in the summer time and knew nothing at all about pop music. He hadn't a single enemy or friend. He'd been strange for as long as anyone could remember.

I made a face when my sister spotted me. It was the kind of face that said, What are you doing with him? Get away or his odour will taint you. It was a moment before I realized she was giving me a version of the same look. Gavin Hillier was standing next to me and we looked like friends. No, I mouthed, shaking my head. You don't get it, you don't under-stand. Gavin's sort of all right, he's only a cretin because his family is going through a mad time. I don't like him, it isn't like that. My sister dropped eye contact. She stood up with Ian and walked away.

Gavin and I could only go so far together. At the doorway to our classroom he shuffled and grinned, then lumbered off towards his desk. Gavin sat in the back row with his own friends: the clowns, the spectators and the troublemakers. In the back row they turned their pocket radios up loud and laughed about the world, not because they found it funny but because they held it in contempt. The girls wore tight skirts and had wide-open mouths, dumb and doughy with chewing gum. The boys wore loose ties and tucked-out shirts and had digital watches on their wrists. The headmaster knew each of them by name and every once in a while the teachers threw blackboard rubbers at their heads.

At the front of the class the wink girls gossiped and hummed and applied sticky lip gloss to their mouths. Their gloss came in tubes etched with flowers, in flavours like bubblegum and very cherry. Their skirts flared past their knees and their eyes were ringed with dark kohl and pity for the non-wink girls. I took my place in the centre, neither wink girl nor trouble-maker, next to my best friend, Rebecca.

'Shelley's selling those lip glosses, did she tell you? I might buy one off her, I reckon?'

'Yeah. Suppose.'

'I don't want tutti frutti, though. I'd rather have the mint.'

'Mint. Good.'

'Or cola. Cola's OK. Cherry is the best but she hasn't got any cherry left.'

'Shame.'

'What's wrong with you?'

'My parents are getting divorced.'

'Right. I heard. Sorry.'

Rebecca glanced at the wink girls as she took out her maths book and I sensed in her a subtle shift in spirit, as if she'd rather be sitting with girls who liked lip gloss than someone with difficulties, like me.

'Are you coming to youth club tonight?'

'Can't, my mum's coming round.'

'Maybe they'll make it up.'

'Yeah . . . suppose.'

Rebecca disapproved of my look. She was a great believer in positive thinking. She already knew she would never get cancer because she was a positive thinker. If she ever did get cancer she would beat it via positive thinking.

'I asked my mum if she knew,' Rebecca said.

'Knew what?'

'You know, if she knew who your mum was . . . you know.'

'Bonking?'

Rebecca sucked her pencil.

'She thought it had been going on for a while, that's all. That's all I'm going to say.'

I wanted to gouge her eyes out. I wanted to gouge them out with her pencil and fill up the holes with cherry lip gloss.

'Well, she's coming tonight. So I'll find out.'

'It's OK if your parents split up, anyway. It makes you more interesting in later life.'

'It's horrible. It's making me depressed.'

'I get depressed before my periods. Mum says it's pre-menstrual syndrome.'

'I couldn't even sleep last night.'

'The only way to stop it is to go on the pill.'

'I can't believe she did it. It's disgusting.'

'Or the menopause. But then you get the hot flushes. Which are shit.'

'I just saw Margaret talking to Ian Warrington. That can't be good, can it?'

'Double maths. What's the point of maths? What more do I need to know about friggin' isosceles triangles?'

I gave up on Rebecca at that moment. One day, quite soon, I'd shift my desk away from hers and take my place in the back row of the class.

14

Dad left at a quarter to seven and Mum arrived at ten minutes to. I had the feeling she had been there for ages, watching the house from the street, waiting for Dad to take his leave. She was an early person, a *leave home with an hour to spare* person. Her hands were frozen.

'I'm sorry,' I said.

'Don't be silly,' she said, 'it's not your fault.'

I was apologizing for her clothes being left in the porch and for my failure to stop Dad from leaving them there. It was a sad place to put a person's clothes. Our porch was cold and draughty and the lino had any number of holes. Mum's clothes sat there shivering like rejects in their plastic bags: her skirts, her bell-bottoms, her knickers.

'There aren't any shoes.'

I wondered what my mother meant by this. Was she worried for the whereabouts of her shoes or hopeful that Dad's not consigning them to the porch was a good sign?

'They're in the shed, mostly.'

Mum said, 'Oh.'

She walked into our house with the awkwardness of a stranger. She seemed not to notice the mess. She stopped by the glass table in the hallway and ran her fingers over a china ornament, a statuette of Cinderella getting out of her coach.

'I hate this thing,' she said blankly. 'What possessed me to pay good money for a thing like this?'

It was a good question.

'Have you had your dinner yet?' she said, like she'd just remembered to ask.

'We had frozen pie and packet mash.'

'Was it nice?'

I told her it wasn't as good as when she made it and she nearly lost it then; her bottom lip started to wobble.

'What are you having at Nanna's?' I said, to settle her down and also for something to say.

'Oh . . . well. Your nanna made a nice roast at the weeken—'

'You're not eating there, are you? You're eating with *him*. At *his* house.'

Margaret was stood at the top of the stairs, her eyes fixed bullet-hard on my mother's.

'Margaret, come down here. It's OK.'

'It isn't, though, is it? It's *not*.'

Mum tried as hard as she could to coax her out. She spoke quietly and evenly. She laughed and she begged. She offered incentives but got nothing. Downstairs, defeated, we sat together on the settee in the living room while Mum searched for a packet of Tic Tacs in her handbag.

'How long has she been like that?'

I didn't know how to answer. I didn't know what she was like.

'Has she said much? About all this.'

'Not really. She's been . . . OK. She's been quiet.'

I thought about telling her that Margaret had made friends with Ian Warrington, but I wasn't sure if she would get the significance.

'What's going to happen?' I said. 'What's going to happen to us?'

Mum moved her lips up and down without answering, as if she were going through a mental list. First up was Margaret and how she was coping, second up was why she was leaving Dad.

'He made me feel invisible,' Mum said, offering me a sweet and pulling a tissue from her bag. 'Is that something that you can understand?'

I wasn't sure. She seemed clear and present to me. Her hair was wide and hard in its coating of Harmony hairspray. Her face was slick and shiny from its layer of Max Factor panstick. She wore her new string of amber beads and a striped cheesecloth blouse that I'd never seen before, but in every other way she looked exactly like herself.

'I wanted to get a job. I didn't . . . it's silly.' She wiped her nose. 'But your dad, he wouldn't have liked it.'

I watched her fiddle with her tissue. Her hands were rough and dry, with busy fingers. They were the kind of hands that wrote out shopping lists and to-do lists and filled in competition slips on the back of cereal packets on rainy afternoons. They could pick up whole joints of meat, fresh from a roasting tin, and move them to a serving plate without flinching. They were the kind of hands that stroked your face when you were ill or sad, or cross about something you didn't know you were cross about.

'You don't like Dad any more, do you?' I said.

'No, Jessie. It's not . . . We've grown apart.'

She went on at length then, repeating some pre-prepared statement. She talked about life stages and missed opportunities and the world changing its mind about the way things had to be. She'd married very young. She'd wanted different things back then, and Dad and she wanted different things now. Take going on holiday, for instance; Mum had wanted to try a villa holiday in Spain, whereas Dad had been happy with another year on the Isle of Wight. Mum wanted to get a fitted kitchen and a washing machine whereas Dad was happy with separate cupboards and Mum trekking to the launderette three times a week. Dad had never liked the idea of her working or learning to drive even though we were clearly short of money and Mum would have liked to have used the car from time to time. Dad didn't like reading books or going to the cinema and preferred watching the television night after night, whereas Mum herself was sick of television.

She seemed to think her speech was going well, but at times she didn't sound like herself. She used words like 'self-discovery' and 'empowerment' and said things like 'someone's daughter, someone's mother, someone's wife'. When she got to the end she paused and twiddled with her beads, relieved that she'd made her way through it.

'What about him?' I said. 'You haven't mentioned him . . . Isn't he what this is all about?'

'Well,' she said, raising her head as the doorbell rang. 'I've known him a while now, his name is Ray.'

Barbara Hill swept into our kitchen, rearranging chairs and plates and pulling mugs off the mug tree and using the kettle as if it were her own.

'I was worried about you. I rang the doorbell twice. I thought goodness knows what might have happened.'

'I was talking to Jessie. He's gone out.'

'Of course. That's right. So you said.'

She made my mother tea. She put sugar in her mug even though Mum didn't take sugar.

'I suppose you saw the bags?' Mum said, looking for biscuits.

'Well,' Barbara said. 'I didn't think it was your washing in the porch. If he thinks you're taking all that with you, you should tell him he's got another think coming.'

'I'll take what I need. If he throws anything away he'll have to pay for it.'

'That's right.'

'I've got as much right to be here as he has.'

'It's *your* house.'

'I know I've hurt him, Barbara.'

'Of course. Of course.'

'But he's only got himself to blame.'

The two of them nodded as if this went without saying.

'Mum was just going to tell me about Ray,' I said. 'So you'll probably want to stay and hear about that as well, or you may want to help yourself to another five of our biscuits.'

'Jessie, don't be so rude.'

'It's all right, Joy. It's completely understandable.'

The two of them went about their business. They boiled more kettles, opened more biscuits and twittered on about divorce and custody and women's lib and rudeness until I thought their reedy voices would drive me mad.

'I've been chief cook and bottle-washer for twenty years, Joy. Believe me, I know how you feel.'

'He wouldn't discuss it.'

'Of course not. They don't. They never do.'

'I feel like it's passing me by.'

'Well, this is it. Where was I in the sixties? Smoking a joint with my knickers round my ankles? Was I heck?'

'Marijuana? I never even tried it.'

'I *am* still here, you know.'

'Ever wear a miniskirt?'

'My father would have killed me. I went straight to maternity smocks.'

'God, what's the point?' I said, exasperated. 'I might as well go upstairs and sit in the dark with Margaret.'

'All right,' Mum said firmly. 'I'm ready. Let's get this over with.'

'What does he do?'

'Ray is a writer. He writes books.'

'Self-help manuals,' said Barbara, helpfully.

'I went on one of his morning courses at the arts centre.'

Mum? On a self-help course? It seemed more unlikely even than the affair.

'What was it called?' I said, bitterly. 'How to destroy your entire family's entire life?'

'*The Wings of Change*, wasn't it?' said Barbara.

My mother confirmed that it was.

'You've left Dad for a *Moonie*?'

'He's not a Moonie, Jess.'

'A hippy, then? He sounds like a hippy.'

'He's not a hippy,' Mum said. 'He's alternative.'

Alternative to Dad.

'Where does he live, then, this hippy?'

'Not far. Between here and your nanna's.'

'So Margaret's right, you are living with him. The two of you are living in *sin*.'

I don't know where it came from, this sudden rash streak of morality. I don't know what made me fold my arms. I wanted her at home in her Marks and Spencer's cardigan, filling her Co-op stamp book with Green Shield stamps. I wanted her watching *The Good Life* with a fish and chip supper balanced on her knees while Dad moaned about the soggy batter and the lack of vinegar. I didn't want her dressed up in beads and a cheesecloth blouse, going on courses and sharing Nanna's steak and kidney with a hippy.

'Jess, this is difficult . . . for all of us. I wasn't expecting . . . at my time of life . . .'

'You're nearly thirty-six,' I said. 'You're very, *very* old. You should be *ashamed* of yourself.'

Barbara, who had celebrated her fortieth birthday at least five times to my knowledge, sucked her teeth.

'This is real life,' Mum said, taking hold of my arms. 'You're old enough to understand things like this now. It's going to be hard for a little while yet, but we're going to have to deal with it as best as we can. We have to embrace our new horizons.'

Real life? New horizons? Where did she find these expressions?

'I should have left your father years ago. I haven't been happy for a long time.'

'We've made you unhappy? *Us?*'

'Now you *mustn't* ever think that,' said my mother, looking panicked. 'I love you and Margaret. Don't you know that?'

She pulled me to her then and stroked my face, and even in the midst of this hurricane I felt sleepy and wanted to lie down. I vowed there and then to ruin things for Mum and the hippy. She could leave Dad if she wanted to, but there was no way in the world she was leaving us.

15

Margaret let me in after Mum left. She was sitting on the bedroom floor peeling pith stalks off some orange segments and looking up foreign cities in her pocket atlas.

'Monte Carlo is in the South of France,' she said, pointing to France. 'Capri is part of Italy. But it's an island.'

'Don't you want to know what happened?'

'I'm going to go there one day. I'll probably arrive there by boat.'

'Mum's going out with a hippy! It's really very serious. I think she's been brainwashed or something.'

'After I've been to the North Pole, of course. I'll definitely want to go to the North Pole first.'

'Margaret!'

'What?'

'She wants us to meet him.'

'No. Uh-uh. There's *no* way.'

The seriousness of the situation seemed to hit home for her then and she closed her pocket atlas.

'What's on the radio?' she said.

'How should I know?' I said.

'Let's listen for a while, can we?'

Margaret hit the power switch on our music centre and its coloured dials flickered with happy light. The two of us lay back on the carpet while ABBA sang 'Money, Money, Money' – Benny, Björn, Agnetha and Frida, blissful in a rich man's world – and Margaret closed her eyes and mouthed along to the notes while I studied the Artex whirls and eddies on the ceiling. Every ceiling in our house, and some of its walls, were coated in thick layers of Artex. The points were so jagged that if you rubbed your bare arms against them by accident they could draw blood from your skin.

'Why?' Margaret said, as the song drew to a close. 'Why is she leaving us?'

'She's not leaving us. She's leaving Dad.'

'She's not here, though, is she?'

'She'll be back.'

'When?'

'On Friday, she said.'

My sister huffed and puffed. We both knew that wasn't what she meant.

'Where will we live?'

'Nanna says most likely Mum will get the house. So probably Dad'll move out.'

'And *he'll* move in?'

'Not a chance.'

'Why not? Why wouldn't he?'

'Because.'

'Mum will let him, though, won't she?'

'Don't *bug* me, all right? I don't know.'

My sister absorbed my frustration.

'What are we going to do, Jess?' she asked, when she thought it was OK to ask.

'There's only one option,' I said. 'We'll have to find a way to split them up.'

Margaret sat bolt upright then and turned the radio down, which pissed me off slightly because it was The Boomtown Rats.

'How will we do it?' she said squarely.

'I don't . . . I'm not sure. We'd need to find a way—'

'We could poison him,' she said, her eyes lighting up. 'We could spike his drink with acid. It makes you have hallucinations and you think you can fly. Perhaps he'd jump off a tall building.'

'You want us to murder Mum's hippy?'

She thought for a second.

'OK, I see, we could get caught . . . But even if he didn't jump, Mum might think he'd gone mad. It would put her right off him, I reckon.'

The idea of poisoning Mum's hippy appealed to me at that moment but I couldn't admit as much to Margaret. Instead I said, 'Who told *you* about acid?'

'Ian Warrington,' she said, as if it were obvious.

'You ought to stay away from him,' I said.

'Why should I?'

'He's strange.'

'You can't make me.'

'I'm only saying—'

'Well, don't. Don't you bother. You're not Mum.'

In the end it was Dad's key in the door that stopped the two of us from bickering. We heard him wipe his feet and put his keys down on the glass hall table. He went to the kitchen first and turned the kettle on, then seemed to think better of it and turned it off. I wondered if he'd seen the dirty cups and empty biscuit wrappers? Should I tell him that Barbara Hill had come round too? If I didn't, how would I explain the fact that we'd finished off a multi-pack of custard creams all by ourselves? He might think the hippy had come round and eaten his biscuits. That wouldn't go down well at all.

'He's putting the telly on.'

'He's having a drink.'

'How do you know?'

'I heard the cabinet open. It squeaks.'

'Should we go down, do you think?'

I thought that we probably should.

I expected Dad to grill me but he didn't.

'She didn't take her clothes,' he said.

'No,' I said.

'She'll take them next time, then?'

'I suppose.'

And that was that, no more questions. It turned out Dad wasn't much of a talker.

That night as I was trying to sleep I wondered what I would have said if Dad had cross-examined me about the visit. If he'd wanted to know Mum's side of the story how would I have sold it to him, exactly? In the end I imagined I'd have told him the same thing I told Margaret. On the question of Mum falling out of love with Dad it mostly had to do with kitchen cupboards, the launderette and the Isle of Wight.

16

Dearest Broo,

What an island this is, a jewel with the sweetest heart
and the finest bones. Capri has everything going for it:
sunshine, history, a true and regal beauty, not to
mention its fair share of sexual deviants. On Tuesday
Peter Staunton caused a furore when he invited Yolande
on a walk to Anacapri, which is rumoured to have been
the site of a lesbian colony. Poor Yolande's face when
Peter explained the joke. She'd imagined they were off
to visit penguins!

On the Riviera, all was old families and faces we know
from the usual crowd, but out here we are surrounded by
an altogether more unusual set. At lunchtime the squares
fill with the chatter of artists, poets and bohemians whose
lustre gets under one's skin. Last evening I met a poet
called Sumner who is on his way to Marrakech to see out
the remainder of the winter. He wore a peacock feather in
his hair this morning at breakfast and amused everyone
with stories of reefer-smoking with the Arabs in the Atlas

mountains. He is mad as a spring hare, but I find his spirits gay and amusing.

We have been lucky so far, outrunning the mistral and finding mostly fair winds and mild weather. I write in shirt sleeves at the plainest café, where the air is a perfume of salt and lemons. Just weeks ago I had to keep my inkwell on a stove top to prevent it from freezing solid, and had to breathe on the nib to squeeze a word or two from my pen. It seems so distant now, all that coldness. Of course, dear sister, you will have seen through me by now, for I don't write to tell you about inkwells, nor artists nor lemons. Instead I find something immensely more intriguing to report.

Where to begin, without sounding like a naive school-girl? My inclination is to start with Andrew Linton's arrival, our talk, and our group's first dinner at the Palace Hotel – the views over the Bay of Naples are breathtaking, all tragedy and romance – but my patience is low and so I begin with our swim.

Yesterday the ten of us took a motorized boat from the port of Marina Grande to visit the famous Blue Grotto. To begin with I had been less than keen to go, since the visiting of attractions has always struck me as provincial and hardly interesting. Nevertheless I was persuaded and off we went with our cameras on straps.

Some yards from the attraction our gang was separated into little row boats and I found myself thrown together with Andrew. The grotto's opening is notoriously hard to breach at this time of year and the trick is to make one's approach as the swell rises up and to grab a rope there which will pull the boat inside. The weather was stern and the waves unsympathetic and after several bad attempts by Peter and Yolande, the mood was to pull back and accept defeat.

Andrew was having none of this, of course, and since I was keen to risk it we took our turn at the mouth of the cave. It was stirring stuff. Our little boat heaved and reared, fit to be dashed to pieces, but on our fourth good try we were in. It was quiet inside and so very pretty, the narrow entrance yawning open to reveal the widest, most perfect oval. The ceiling is rounded and from its entire surface it distils fresh water, which fell on us like the first drops of a rainstorm.

The two of us spoke only little, all talk of our travels and my recent adventures taken care of that first night at the hotel. It was the kind of silence that is open and generous and not in the least bit inhibiting or uncomfortable. After a while Andrew suggested that the two of us take a swim, and though neither of us was dressed for swimming, I said yes.

How cold it was in that water, Broo, and how little I noticed it or cared. We swam to all edges of the cave and felt both its smoothness and its roughness. Our clothes sat idly by on the side of the boat, watching us with all their stiffness and prurience while we broke the water's surface with our bodies. When finally we kissed, as you must have guessed we would, I felt elated and resigned to the water. It was more than I could have hoped for. Gone was the blushing boy I'd experienced at Rochester and here was the essence of the great man he is, distilled into a physical act. I felt in him the strength both of lover and protector and allowed myself a moment of such uncommon fragility that I will keep it secret to the grave from all but my closest and dearest friends.

You will say I am overreacting, no doubt, and indeed it was all done with in a flash, as if our embrace were an accident. But I am certain, Broo, that this is the start of something wonderful. He held me with such tenderness and for the first time in such a long time, perhaps since Mother and Father went, I haven't wanted to turn around and run. I have liked him since we first met but had feared he considered me brash and outspoken, and that his ego might not stand the notes of my recent celebrity. It seems that I had him pegged wrong. 'What a woman you are, Edith,' he told me as we kissed. 'There is no one to hold a candle to you. No one.'

Cross your fingers for me, darling.

Walking on cloud nine.

Your sister,
Edith

17

We visited the Lightfoots' house to begin our research into love and divorce in the case of hippies. Margaret took a notepad and a freshly sharpened pencil, and I took a pet rock in a gift box that I thought they would like. Joni Lightfoot was wearing a patchwork skirt and cooking lentils when we arrived, which Margaret and I considered textbook hippy behaviour.

'Why don't you eat meat?' Margaret said.

'Because it's cruel,' Joni said. 'And vegetables are better for you.'

'How is it cruel?'

'Have you ever seen a pig butchered, Margaret?'

Margaret didn't think that she had.

'They don't stun them, of course. That's a lie. It's awful what they do to them, the way they keep them.'

Joni stirred her lentils and as she reached up for her ladle I caught a glimpse of her thickly hairy armpits.

'Are you a lesbian?'

'*Margaret.*'

'What? I'm only asking. Dad said lesbians were hairy.'

'I'm not a lesbian, Margaret. I just choose not to shave my armpits or my legs.'

'You're a feminist, then?' I said.

'Yes, I am.'

'Is that another form of sexual deviance?' Margaret asked.

Joni covered the lentil stew with a saucepan lid and sighed. It was the kind of sigh that said, What am I doing in this stale provincial suburb; how did I end up in the midst of these people; how are these children so ignorant? Joni's bookshelf was heavy with books on philosophy, literature and biorhythms so it seemed clear that she was more sophisticated in her thinking than the rest of us.

'Feminism is about women's rights, Margaret,' Joni said. 'It's about women being equal with men.'

Margaret's mouth fell open. Not at the concept of female equality, which she was all for, but because Joni had sat down cross-legged on the floor and exposed the full hirsuteness of her shins. If you'd been inclined to comb them, you could have combed them.

'What do you want to be when you grow up?' Joni said.

'She wants to be a veterinary nurse.'

'No, I don't any more.'

'That's what you told me.'

'Well, it isn't what I want any more.'

'Let me guess,' Joni said. 'Pilot?'

'No.'

'Surgeon?'

'No.'

'Architect?'

'No.'

'Prime Minister?'

Margaret paused at this but said, 'No, I'm going to be an explorer. I'm going to be an explorer and discover a whole new part of the world.'

'That's quite an ambition to have,' Joni said. 'Better than veterinary nurse, I should say.'

My sister smiled.

'Edith was an explorer,' Margaret said. 'The lady on our street whose house burnt down. I'm going to go on adventures, just like her.'

'We don't know what she was,' I said, worrying that Margaret's propensity to make things up would put Joni off us. 'She travelled a lot. But neither of us knows what for, exactly.'

It seemed that my sister's imaginings hadn't put Joni off us; indeed they had hardly dented her interest at all. Instead of asking another question about Edith, Joni began to rub her feet – clad in the kind of socks that looked like they itched dreadfully – and sank into some private travel reverie of her own.

'San Francisco,' Joni said. 'That's where I'd like to live. By the sea in the Californian sunshine.'

'Why don't you?'

'It's not that simple, Margaret. Our jobs are here, mine and Jack's. And in any case we couldn't get a green card.'

'I thought you were hippies,' my sister said, reminding Joni of what she was. 'It's well-known that hippies don't work.'

'Is that what you think we are?'

'You are, aren't you?'

'Margaret, Jack and I are accountants.'

'Can't accountants be hippies?'

'Oh no, not fully. I don't think so.'

Over a bowl of the lentil stew – which tasted how I imagined boiled slippers might taste – the three of us got down to brass tacks. We explained that our mother was having an affair with a hippy called Ray who ran self-help classes at the arts centre, and that we considered Joni and Jack our most likely hope of insight.

'Well,' Joni said, 'I'd heard the rumours, of course. But your mum never struck me as the sort.'

'What sort?' Margaret said.

Jack came in then, wearing a Jimi Hendrix T-shirt and bell-bottom blue jeans. He had a beard and brown hair that was straggly at the back and fell past his shoulders, and I wanted to ask him if it was permissible for accountants to have long hair and whether or not he had to tie it up in a ponytail for neatness when he went to work. He looked like the man in the illustrations in the book *The Joy of Sex* and might very well have modelled his image on him. Later I thought about sharing this observation with Margaret but I wasn't sure if she had read it.

'Your mum's really left, then?' Jack asked, helping himself to food.

'Not for good,' I said protectively. 'She's coming back soon. The problem with it all is this bastard, Ray.'

I felt it would be OK to swear in front of Joni and Jack and indeed they didn't flinch or reprimand me for my language, they just smirked indulgently at one another.

'Is he married?'

We didn't know.

'I'll bet he is,' Joni said. 'They always are.'

'She'll be his mistress,' Jack said. 'He'll have promised her all sorts.'

I wanted to know what kind of sorts but I thought it improper to ask.

Once up to speed, Jack had plenty to say about my mother and Ray. In Jack's view marriage was nothing more or less than bondage and domestic servitude for the woman and one long holiday for the man. Once the woman had been foolish enough to succumb to this outdated moral orthodoxy, however, she was duty-bound to stay faithful to her husband.

'That's why Joni and I will never marry,' Jack said. 'If you make your bed, so to speak, you should lie in it, shouldn't you?'

Margaret and I were unsure whether we should or we shouldn't.

'If you need society to legitimize your relationship,' Jack continued, holding up his fork for emphasis, 'then you can't turn round and complain if those same people seek to judge you once it's over. And anyway, divorce is one thing, but walking out on kids your age, that's not on.'

'Why not?' Joni said.

Jack forked stew into his mouth. He looked like he wasn't going to answer her.

'No, really,' Joni said to him. 'Why not? If their dad had been the one to leave, you wouldn't have raised an eyebrow?'

'It's different.'

'Different how? How is it different?'

'She's their mother,' said Jack, like it was obvious.

It struck me then that people, the neighbours, were talking about my mother behind her back. If someone like Jack disapproved of her, which he certainly seemed to, I could only wonder what the others might be saying.

Jack filled his cheeks up with lentils and mopped at his sauce with some bread.

'This stew is good,' he said. 'Better than last week's, I'd say.'

'Well, I think your mother's brave,' Joni said, looking at Jack as though she were faintly repelled by his style of eating. 'Divorce should be easier than it is. A woman should be able to walk out whenever she wants to.'

'Don't marry, then. That's what I'd say to that,' Jack said. 'Joni or I can walk out any time that we like. We're not tied, you see. Our commitment isn't based on something spurious like religion or social convention.'

'What is it based on?' Margaret wanted to know.

'Love,' Jack said, as Joni took his plate away.

★   ★   ★

We left with hardly any more knowledge than when we'd arrived, other than a suspicion on Jack's part that *The Wings of Change* self-help series was based, in part, on the healing power of pyramids. We carried this information home like an awkwardly shaped package, unsure how we ought to unwrap it.

That night as we ate I watched Margaret pick every piece of bacon out of the bacon and egg flan Dad had reheated for our dinner.

'What's wrong with those bits?'

'I'm not eating meat any more. I've become a vegetarian.'

'Since when?' Dad said.

'Since now.'

'Why?'

'Have you ever seen a pig being butchered?'

Dad set his fork down as if his flan disagreed with him suddenly.

'Margaret, you need to eat,' he told her.

'I am,' my sister said. 'I'm eating the egg bits.'

'Are you sure?'

'Yes, look. You can see.'

In truth it was hard to determine what she had and hadn't eaten since her plate was a mess of bacon bits, discarded onion and piles of mashed-up and broken pastry. I worried then that Margaret would starve since it seemed to me that a prerequisite for being a vegetarian was a liking for vege-tables and to my knowledge my sister didn't enjoy a single one. I worried, too, what with news of her becoming a vegetarian, that Margaret had decided to follow in Jack and Joni's footsteps and become some kind of hippy herself. On this guess, at least, I couldn't have been more wrong.

18

Seeing a bald eleven-year-old was as surprising and shocking as seeing a bald cat or dog. There was definitely an air of cruelty about it even though it was Margaret who had done the shearing herself. To be fair, she wasn't completely bald since she had left a narrow strip of hair untouched. It ran down the centre of her head and was exactly two inches long (except in the parts towards the back where she had misjudged it), as demonstrated by Margaret holding sections of her remaining hair up against a ruler. In her defence my sister said the whole effect was marred by not having the right strength of hairspray and that it would certainly look a whole lot better when you could appreciate the extent of her Mohican in all its rigid splendour. My sister wasn't becoming a hippy at all; she had become our suburb's, perhaps the town's, youngest punk.

'Oh God. Christ, you haven't. Oh God!'

Dad said 'you haven't' several more times and I think he half believed that if he repeated it enough it might turn out to be true. This surprising baldness in his daughter would turn out to be an apparition brought on by too much cheap whisky in the evenings and not enough decent food, fresh air or sleep.

In response to my sister's lack of hair, Dad held fast to his own hair, tugging at the uneven strands that grazed his shirt collar and running his hand back and forth across his thinning crown.

'You haven't,' he said, one more time.

'I have,' Margaret said. And she had.

There was a moment then when I thought he might hit her, his eyes and his jaw were set so hard. Our father had only hit us once. We'd spent an afternoon playing trampoline on the settee one summer Sunday and after a particularly daring jump I'd fallen off the cushions and crashed into the wall unit that Dad had recently paid sixty-nine pounds ninety-nine for. Its door was broken off and the hinge beneath was badly buckled. The new hinge Dad fitted never sat right, and the imperfection in this piece of landmark furniture that he'd saved up for and purchased outright – instead of succumbing to the lure of hire purchase – made him angry for months. Almost a year on he would still hurl a dirty look at Margaret or me each time its defective door was opened or closed.

Dad went through several stages after the initial shock. The first thing he did was make me look up hair growth in the Encyclopaedia Britannica, but Granddad, who had been buying the encyclopaedia for us in instalments, had died of a heart attack at around the time letter G was delivered so unfortunately hair growth wasn't covered.

'Half an inch a month,' Margaret said, displaying a knowledge of trichology that I wasn't aware she had. 'But I'm going to keep on shaving it, so there.'

'That's what you think, young lady,' said my dad, fetching a hat. 'Put this on. You'll wear it until it's grown back.'

Margaret refused the woollen hat on account of it being warm outside, and accused Dad of being scared of the neighbours.

'This isn't about the neighbours, you stupid girl.'

'Yes it is, of course it is. You're worried about what they'll think of me.'

This was only half true. Dad wasn't worried about what they'd think of her, he was worried about what they'd think of him.

'His wife's left him, you know. How humiliating. He can't even take care of his girls. The youngest one's become a delinquent.'

I sensed this going round in his head, their scolds and judgements, then suddenly came a thin spark of hope.

'Wait till your mother sees what you've done,' he said, relaxing. 'Let's see what your mother has to say about all this.'

The cause of his relaxing was uncertain to me but I believe it had to do with the idea that Margaret's hair loss might facilitate Mum's return to her senses. At the very least it would provoke an attack of maternal guilt deep enough to cause her pain, which in itself was enough to make Dad happy. He put the woollen hat away and went back to his newspaper and Margaret gave him the kind of look that said, What more do I have to do to cause a storm round here? She fingered the fringe of her Mohican as if she wasn't convinced of its impact or attractiveness any more, and moved to stand next to the wall unit, where she spent the next five minutes opening and closing the imperfect door while Dad ignored her, through closely gritted teeth.

'I didn't know you liked punk rock,' I said to her, when she had finished.

'I don't,' she said. 'I like ABBA.'

19

Sierra Leone

To buy:
Materials for turban and Arab keffiya
Two pair slacks (more comfortable than jodhpurs)
One riding skirt with breeches to go under (one pair
   gabardine; one pair khaki drill)
Dust coat
Silk stockings
Pyjamas (light flannel)
Two dresses (long-sleeved and high-necked for modesty)
Two bush shirts
Two Aertex shirts
Sandals
Felt hat
Leather boots, long-tongued with puttees
Cholera belt
Quinine powders
Hammer, chisel, haversack, collecting bags, clinometer,
   compass, pocket knife, notebook, hard pencils

March 6th 1934

Dearest Broo,

We are just into March and I find myself on board a
ship bound for Morocco. This is most unexpected
since I had planned on returning to England for two
months at least before embarking upon my next set of
adventures. The plan is to journey southwards through
the desert, by truck, then on through the Gambia,
perhaps even as far as Sierra Leone. The Sahara will
be dreadful but there is much talk of diamonds in
Freetown, and so I hope to mix some works for the
Royal Geographic with research for a friend at De
Beers. There is still much to organize but I have been
assured through various correspondences and good
contacts that most of what we need can be found when
we dock in Tangiers.

In the meantime I have more pressing issues to deal
with. I am suffering from seasickness, can you believe
it? I am nauseous and pale with a fever that I cannot
shake, and have never succumbed to such a malady in
all my life. When I explain what has happened you will
say it is down to that, but I think it more likely to be
brought on by the endless diet of rice and dried dates
we are forced to eat. They hide them everywhere, even
in the soup.

First off, let me tell you that it came as some surprise
to discover Andrew Linton had become romantically
involved with Yolande while I was away in Greenland. I
wonder if perhaps you knew about it, did you? Of course
not; you would have told me, I am sure. They announced
their engagement and imminent wedding plans with
much fanfare mere days after mine and Andrew's swim.
He had been distant with me since our afternoon at the

grotto but I had put this down to his natural reserve and some uncertainty towards me, though quite how much uncertainty I could hardly have guessed.

It was during our final dinner at the hotel. It really was a picture: the sun setting low behind our island, casting a glorious fluorescence across the bay. The light was all gold, red and honey, the sort that beds down in one's memory to be drawn upon for sustenance during long winter days in London. The staff had prepared a banquet of a dozen or more dishes but I shan't test your patience by describing the food, other than to say it was quite the most delicious I have ever tasted. The veal was ambrosial and I shall remember it all of my life.

After sunset and liqueurs Andrew began to look awkward. Yolande – who had moved from her usual seat next to Peter – had taken root next to him and was casting him the look of a puppy who is about to receive a bone. After a minute or so of this irritation he stood up and, as if on some cue, two waiters appeared with champagne. I was hardly prepared for what happened next and had expected we were all about to toast one another and our final night on Capri. If only this had been the case.

Andrew was the first to raise his glass. He looked so handsome as he stood, dressed as he was in a dark simple shirt with no tie to speak of; his skin, which usually has the look of a ghost about it, healthily coloured by the sunshine.

'I have an announcement,' he said, with no hint of joy. And so he did. The announcement was this. In England, before our trip, he had proposed to Yolande and she had done him the honour of saying yes. He was sorry to have kept it secret from us, his dearest friends, but Yolande's parents had been abroad and out of contact and they had thought it only fair to be discreet until they had been told.

You should have seen her face, Broo; it was hard like a geisha's or a spy's. Her eyes bore into mine with such victory and contrivance, I could barely hold myself from standing up and slapping her.

When he had finished with his bombshell Andrew made to sit down, but was prevented from doing so by the rush of arms, lips and cheeks that were foisted on him by way of congratulation. In the midst of this tangle I managed to keep my seat and tipped back my entire shot of Limoncello and the whole of Edward's, who was sitting beside me. Andrew's eyes caught mine for less than a second but the pain of it was quite awful. In that instant I could tell he had made a mistake, not with me in our cave, but with her.

She had gone for him, Broo, she had hooked him like a fish, like the biggest, wildest fish you could imagine. No doubt she had slept with him in seconds, as is her way, or perhaps held it back as a lure. I felt such a sadness for us both in that moment and such disappointment in him for choosing her. To the best of my knowledge it is his only act of cowardice. He must know she wants him for his money and that her one good goal will be to tame him. Had he shown the guts to take me it would have been quite different since I wouldn't have tied him for a second. He is the one man I have known, next to Father, who has the daring and the wit to be free.

The evening grew increasingly dismal after that, and I increasingly drunk. Yolande floated on air, all smugness and glow, telling stories of their wedding plans – vulgar and lavish – and their month-long honeymoon to New York. 'We will stay as guests of the Roosevelts,' she told

the gang a dozen times or more, and her coterie of girlfriends cooed like pigeons.

He found me for a moment while I was packing in
my room and asked me where I would go. 'Morocco,' I
said, though I hadn't decided until that very minute and
thought of it only because that poet Sumner was
leaving for there the next day. He said then that he was
sorry and I told him not to be and that I quite understood.

'No, you don't,' he replied and from the way that he
said it I knew at once Yolande must be pregnant.

In this next part I am not sure whether to be proud
of myself or ashamed but I was worn down by alcohol
and despair for him and so truly couldn't help it. I
walked close towards him and let him hold my face and
knew I must say the truth since if I didn't it would
remain unspoken all my life and destroy me.

'I love you,' I said. 'I have loved you from the first
time we met.'

And there it was, and it was said, and it might not
have killed me if he hadn't then said to me, 'I love you
too.'

There was nothing left to do then but to pack up my
things and go, and so here I am with a week left to sail
in which to ponder my sickness and my lot. Do you
believe that two people can be meant for one another?
Of course not, and neither did I. Will it surprise you to
know, then, that I have changed my mind entirely and
that loosing Andrew feels everything like grief? I think of
him constantly, since there is little else to think of, and
my only consolation, if there can be one, is that he'll
grow bored with Yolande in months. One might hope
he'll divorce her, though I doubt it, but, as Sumner
remarked, there is always the role of mistress to

consider. I joke, of course, so don't worry, dear sister. Between bouts of the sickness and the sorrows I have moments of tolerable humour.

Did I mention that I am the recipient of a new research grant and that the monies have just now come through? So you see, Broo, things are looking up for me. If I wanted to, which I very well may, who can say, I could hide out in the godforsaken jungle the entire year.

Yours,
Edith

20

They made quite a pairing, Ian Warrington and Margaret: her with her Mohican and her stubbly head, he with his big belly and patent shoes. He stuck to her like glue from the moment he saw her haircut, convinced as he was – correctly as it turned out – that people would tease them less as a couple, since together they ceased to be merely weird and sad, and had graduated to the darker ranks of scary.

There seemed always to be a circle of open space around the two of them – in the playground, at the dinner hut – an exclusion zone, if you like. Kids Margaret's own age were openly distant while the older ones called her *punk* in an outwardly convivial way that hid a seam of wary fascination. To my mind my sister was incapable of looking in the least bit threatening and was so small and sweetly featured she could have come at me with a machete, howling like a Red Indian, and I would have held tightly to my stomach and laughed my head off. She had always been pretty and delicately made and remained so in spite of her razor rash and porcupine hairdo.

Older people saw things differently again and I suppose you could put this down to the behaviour of the Sex Pistols and Johnny Rotten, who Nanna said were unravelling the fabric of decent society with their spitting and their pins and their tuneless music. The mothers who dropped their children off at school that Friday morning seemed genuinely aggrieved by my sister's appearance. They stared at her like she might devour their progeny at any moment, while Ian Warrington would likely lick their bones. She enjoyed it, I could tell. She had never felt so noticed in all her life. Then the teachers had to steam in and ruin things for her.

They had no right to be disappointed in my sister, but disappointment was most of what they felt. Such a good, lovely girl, such a quiet one. How had she ended up like this? I suppose they imagined it was my fault in some way, since the question they asked of me repeatedly was, 'What did you do to encourage her?' They were united in the self-regarding nature of their response, acting as if Margaret's haircut was a personal affront to them and theirs, and to the hard-won reputation of the school. As their unreasonableness grew, compounded by one another, it was agreed she should face the headmaster. I told Margaret not to worry and that it wouldn't be so bad; but in her case I worried that it would.

'He might be expelling me,' she said, when she came out later, her hands turning circles around each other. There were tears in her eyes and her cheeks were flushed from embarrassment, but the way she said expelling suggested this wasn't the worst of it.

'He wants to see Mum and Dad.'

'Together?' I said.

'Together,' she said. 'And today.'

'What did you *tell* him?'

'Nothing,' she said.

'Not about the splitting up?'

'No, I swear it.'

I felt some relief about this since I had the distinct feeling that if the headmaster knew the intimate details of my parents' recent toings and froings it would somehow count against us.

Mum stood in the playground in a smart skirt and jacket which she must have run out and bought when the call came because all her good clothes were still at the house. The skirt was a bad colour, purchased in haste, and the jacket, which was woollen and heavy, was too warm for a late spring after-noon. Her face was all lines and confusion; my sister stood like an apparition in front of her. Margaret's slim hand, when it pulled the hat away, shook a little with the knowledge of what it would do to her.

'Oh, Margaret,' she said. 'Oh, Margaret. What did you do to yourself?'

She stroked the sides of my sister's head over and over, like the touch of her fingers might bring on the impulse for growth. There were nicks and bumps and cuts here and there and Mum made sure to feel every one.

'Your beautiful hair. You cut off your beautiful hair.'

On Margaret's behalf, I'd prepared a defence of her pos-ition which had to do with the overwhelming popularity of the Sex Pistols and punk rock, and the desire for free expres-sion being just as strong in pre-teens as in teens, but in the end she just couldn't manage it. As Mum tugged at the sticky tendrils of her Mohican my sister lost the battle and started to howl. She wept with as much vigour as she could muster, as much in anger for failing to maintain her cool in front of Mum as in despair for her bloody awful haircut.

'Why did you do this?'

'I don't . . . I don't . . . I don't know.'

'It's OK now,' Mum said gently, like it wasn't that big a deal. 'Don't worry, Silly Billy. It'll all grow back.'

She hugged us both then, which was difficult, because it gave the impression that things were back to normal and that everything would work out all right. Dad arrived presently to find the three of us red-eyed from crying; he looked cheerful about it in a strange kind of way.

'It's your fault, all this,' he said, with no preamble, to my mother. 'I hope you're satisfied now. I hope you're happy.' Mum wiped her eyes and told him that she wasn't.

They went into the headmaster's office together while Margaret and I waited outside. It felt peculiar knowing they were in there, called up like naughty children, just like us. Once when I was in the headmaster's office and he raised his voice particularly loudly, I got a strange feeling like I wanted to pee. I think this had to do with the fear and shame he made you feel even when you'd only done something stupid like writing *fuck off* on the blackboard. I wondered whether my parents felt this too, sitting in front of him in the low green seats, the ones with the cigarette burns on the armrests.

They were out in less than fifteen minutes, their tails securely between their legs. Perhaps he had grilled them on their personal life, perhaps he had gone a step too far. Neither of them would be drawn on what had been said inside that office but our hunger for detail was soon forgotten in the happy news of Margaret's reprieve. She wasn't to be expelled after all, but instead would have to write an apology letter to be read out in school assembly and agree to wear a hat on school premises until her new hair grew back.

'Are we going home with Dad, now?' Margaret said, when they had finished.

'No,' my mother said. 'You're coming with me.'

21

Back then I thought Rossi's ice cream parlour made the best cola floats in all the world. This is highly unlikely since the 'genuine' Italian ice cream they used to make them had a texture like frozen lard, and the cola they used was the generic kind that tasted of saccharine and chemicals and was only made palatable by its abundance of sharp, fizzy bubbles. I was at an age when sugary things still delighted me but I pretended, out of coolness, that they didn't. I'd perfected a look that suggested ice cream bored me and that I'd much prefer a cup of milky coffee or a half-pint of cider and blackcurrant. Margaret had no such pretension and the vision of a cherry float with an extra squirt of cream on top was enough to make her forget her woes entirely. Pleasure for her in those days was as simple as very cold or very sweet.

Rossi's ice cream sodas came in tall, narrow glasses with long metal spoons you could use to dig out the melted remains when you got to the bottom. In a moment of dietary abandon Mum had ordered a vanilla one for herself, and so the three of us sat together clanking spoons onto glass and glass onto the marble table top until one of us could think of something uncontentious to say.

'Well, then,' Mum said, wiping her mouth on a paper

napkin. 'It's been quite a day and I'd thought about doing this step by step, or on a different day, but I think it would be easier if we just did it now.'

We looked at each other, Margaret and I, unsure of where this was leading, but certain in the knowledge that it wasn't good.

'I've asked Ray to join us. He'll be along in a little while. I think it's only right that you meet him.'

Margaret shoved her glass away and we watched in alarm as it slid across the table, coming to a perilous stop half an inch from the edge.

'I won't,' she said. 'I thought I made that absolutely clear.'

'Well, you'll have to meet him one day,' Mum said, grabbing Margaret's glass. 'So in fairness to everyone, I think we ought to get it over with.'

Margaret gave Mum a look of some amazement and I think her incredulity had to do with my mother's use of the words 'in fairness'.

'What about you, Jess? What do you say?'

This was a tricky one to play. I felt a certain loyalty to Margaret on this issue – not to mention Dad – but I had to admit I was curious. In my head it was clear that Mum's fancy man – as Nanna had taken to calling him – was an idiot, but a part of me worried he might turn out to be secretly magnetic and cruel. I was scared about him somehow – though I'd never have admitted it – and felt the only way around this was to face him. On top of that I didn't see how we had any hope of splitting the two of them up until we knew exactly what it was we were dealing with.

'We may as well,' I said, shrugging, to Margaret. 'It's going to happen sooner or later.'

My sister lay her spoon down in protest at my treachery. From that day on she never touched another cherry float.

* * *

Ray's gait, when he arrived, was apologetic, somewhere between a saunter and a slouch. He was dressed in an outfit that looked like pyjamas and wore a long chequered scarf that was decorated on either side with a row of sequins and brightly coloured tassels. The loudness of his outfit jarred with the unassuming quality of him. He was thin to the point of malnourishment, wore John Lennon spectacles with bottle-top lenses, and looked nothing like the Ray I had imagined. On first inspection he seemed devoid of charisma and charm, yet Mum smiled when she saw him in the same way Margaret smiled at ice cream. He said, 'Hi, kids, I'm Ray,' except he pronounced this as if it were a question, as if he wasn't sure if he was Ray or he wasn't.

'How old are you?' I said.

'She's canny, this one,' he said, trying to flatter me, but in truth he couldn't have flattered me nearly enough.

Without giving us an answer to the question of his age, Ray went to order himself an ice cream. He took a long time about it, discussing things with Mr Rossi as if it were a matter of some importance and making him rummage about in the bottom of the deep freeze. He returned with a slice of Arctic roll, which was a bit like Swiss roll except it had ice cream in the middle instead of extra layers of sponge cake and jam. He looked pleased with himself and I could see why. Arctic roll was expensive. It was something Mum brought out to impress people at Sunday lunchtimes, or birthday dinners; she served it in the good china bowls with condensed milk or tinned mandarin oranges. The point being, there was a time and a place for Arctic roll; you didn't just order it willy-nilly. Ray ate his Arctic roll with a fork. Nanna was right. Mum's fancy man was indeed fancy.

The mistake Ray made, apart from getting off with my mother, was in trying to get us to like him. He should have started on the assumption that we would hate him and left it at that. As quietly spoken and unassuming as he was, there was something dogged about him. He pushed away at us in an insistent and sickly kind of way that made me wish I hadn't eaten my ice cream quite so quickly. What sweets did we like? What music? What television? What magazines did the two of us like to read? None of his questions were met with decent answers and by the end of his barrage I was ready to tell him to mind his own business. After failing on all subjects of youth and youth culture he started on about the fire up at Edith's house, a subject which he'd heard about from Mum and seemed to me to be unreasonably interested in.

'It's got nothing to do with you,' Margaret said.

'Of course not. Uh-huh, I understand that,' said Ray with aggravating patience. 'The thing is, events like this can be . . . well, they can be upsetting. Especially when other things in your life are, well, let's call them uncertain.'

I couldn't believe it. The cheek of it. The bastard was trying to psych us out.

'Don't try to shrink us out,' I said. 'It's not going to work. I know what you are. You're a hippy and a shrink and you read people's minds for a living.'

Margaret smiled at this outburst and I felt like I'd regained some valuable ground with her. She felt confident enough to join in with the offensive and said, 'You can't fool us, anyway. We know what you do. Joni and Jack said you sacrifice goats under your pyramid.'

Mum and Ray laughed at this suggestion, which for some reason made me want to slap them. Mum's laugh was high-toned and girlish and she played with her beads while she giggled. I expect she thought this made her seem young but it didn't. It made her seem old.

'Pyramidology,' Ray said, making his thin arms into a

triangle. 'It's really very interesting. And there're no goats involved, are there, Joy?'

'No,' my mother said, unconvincingly.

'The fascinating thing is that pyramids have a quite amazing energy,' Ray said. 'Studies have shown that if you put food under a pyramid structure, it stays fresh for almost twice as long. Razor blades left under one take twice as long to blunt and plants grow more than twice as fast. If a pyramid can alter the molecular structure of a razor, say, or a plant, imagine the effect it could have on a person's well-being.'

It all became clear then. That was how he'd done it. He'd altered my mother's brainwaves and forced her to like him by sitting her underneath a friggin' pyramid.

'How old are you?' I said again.

'Thirty-one,' Ray said.

Five years younger than my mother.

'Is Mum your mistress?' Margaret said.

'Now, that's an old-fashioned word, isn't it?'

'Well, is she?'

Ray answered that he was recently separated from his wife which meant that Mum wasn't technically his mistress. Barbara Hill told us later she thought this was a case of splitting hairs.

'This is hard for you, I get that,' Ray said earnestly, taking Mum's hand in his and squeezing it. 'But I'm not trying to replace your dad here, and it's important that you know . . . that you both understand . . . just how much I love and respect your mother.'

Margaret and I recoiled in horror. We'd never once heard Dad say he loved Mum, let alone that he respected her. Now a stranger was saying it without a hint of embarrassment. Out loud. In public. In Rossi's.

Margaret felt she had no option after that. In response to Ray's dreadful declaration she tore off her hat and threw it down on the floor, leaving her droopy Mohican fringe to flap accusingly into her eyes. Her parting shot as she stomped off to the toilet was – somewhat bizarrely, I thought – 'You're sick in the head, the pair of you. Sicker than a camel in Tangiers.'

As Margaret walked away I absorbed the tuts and the stares of the general public. In some ways I felt you couldn't blame them. You didn't find many people who looked like Ray in our neck of the woods. Joni and Jack were one thing but even they didn't go out dressed in their pyjamas. It wasn't usual to see a younger man declare his love for a giggly older woman while her ill-behaved daughters raised their voices about pyramids and goats, and the bald one ran off to the toilet shouting the odds about camels.

Older ladies blanched and turned their backs on us. Younger children stopped licking their ice cream cones. Men folded their copies of the *Telegraph* extra sharply until the corners were as crisp and sharp as knives. Their message was clear. We were letting the side down, bringing ourselves and the community into disrepute. This is what our mother had done to us. She had turned us into freaks. It was unforgivable.

22

Dad was on the back porch hovering over the chest freezer when the two of us got home from Rossi's. At first I thought he was restocking it with food and that perhaps he'd been to the supermarket to buy a job lot of meat pies and chops. When Mum was in charge, the chest freezer was always stocked to the brim as if in preparation for an ice age or a nuclear war. If the balloon had gone up we could have bunkered down in the house, hiding from the radiation, for a good year at least. She bought a new leg of lamb every time she went to the butcher even though there were half a dozen legs of lamb in the freezer already. She liked to buy everything in bulk: sliced bread, crumpets, Victoria sponges, beef burgers, cheese pasties, mixed vegetables, garden peas, sweetcorn, fish fingers, fish in parsley sauce, fish in cheese sauce, fish in butter sauce, frozen Yorkshire puddings, shins of beef, minced beef, steak and kidney pies, and enough whole chickens and chicken drumsticks to feed a core post-nuclear civilization.

For posh days there was frozen pavlova or meringue cases that we could defrost and fill with squirty cream and kiwi fruit ourselves. As a special treat – and for unexpected guests who never came – there was the prized packet of frozen chicken Kiev. The four of us had yet to try it, partly down to a distinct lack of unexpected guests and partly down to Dad's dislike of foreign foods.

'Have you been to the Co-op?' I said.

'No,' Dad said. Then he said, 'Oh hell.'

We had caught him in the middle of something and I saw then that his hands, or rather one hand, was full.

'What have you got there?' Margaret said.

'Love. I'm sorry. It's Simon.'

Dad turned to face us. He had taken off his tie and Margaret later took this as a mark of disrespect. He had blood stains on the edge of his work shirt and jacket and in his upturned palm was the body of my sister's pet hamster; its mouth was wide open, exuding a yellowish, bloody pus.

'I didn't do anything,' Dad said, guiltily. 'I found him like this. On his wheel.'

'Oh . . . but oh,' Margaret said. 'He was fine. He was fine. He was *fine*.'

My sister took Simon from Dad and stroked his underbelly, which was solid from rigor mortis, and kissed it. He was a nice hamster. He was good at eating nuts and could fill his cheeks with what seemed like an unfeasible amount of sweetcorn niblets. He had chocolate-brown fur and a fluffy cream tail, and as rodents go you'd have to say he was fairly fetching. I'd been known to stroke him myself from time to time when my sister wasn't looking – she was violently possessive of Simon – but there was no way on earth I would have kissed him like he was, all solid and covered in pus.

'How do you know he's dead?'

'Uh . . . ?'

'How do you know for sure?'

'He is, love. He is. Take it from me.'

'I want to take his blood pressure. Where's your thingy?'

Somewhere in a distant cupboard sat an unused blood-pressure machine that Nanna had made Dad send off for from the back of the *Sunday Telegraph* shortly after he didn't have his heart attack. The doctor had said it was indigestion. Nanna had said you couldn't be too careful.

'You can't take a hamster's blood pressure,' I said. 'The cuff wouldn't fit round his arm. You'd have to wrap it around his whole body and inflate it until his heart stopped, which would sort of defeat the whole object.'

Margaret let out a muted sob.

'You were going to freeze him?'

'No. No, I wasn't. I promise.'

'You were, you were going to freeze Simon.'

Of course, this is exactly what Dad was going to do, and I imagine he had the best intentions. He didn't know how late we'd be or how long it took dead hamsters to go off, and he hadn't wanted to bury him without Margaret's say-so.

'I want to bury him.'

'Well,' Dad said then. 'Absolutely.'

'What shall we put him in, do you think?'

After some lengthy discussion involving Tupperware dishes, and the inner tube of a toilet roll, it was decided a miniature cereal box from a breakfast multi-pack would be the best bet.

'Which one, though?' said Margaret, in a way that made us realize the choice was important.

'Sugar Puffs,' I said.

'Rice Krispies,' said Dad.

'Coco Pops,' I said and started to laugh.

We all started then: Dad, me and Margaret, all doubled up and close to tears. We laughed because of dead Simon and his burial and his untimely demise on his wheel. Eventually we settled on a Corn Flakes packet because of Simon's well-documented love of corn.

In the garden Dad dug a small hole by the apple tree, the one whose fruit fell early and was always full of maggots, and lowered Simon's body into the ground inside his tiny cereal coffin.

Margaret said a few words about what a pal he had been through the rough times and we all said goodbye and sang the Christmas carol 'Away in a Manger', which wasn't appropriate but Margaret said she thought Simon would like it.

Inside again and out of the damp evening air, Dad fetched up a big plate of toasted crumpets. He slathered them in the new pack of butter he'd remembered to buy and apologized for the glaring lack of honey or even jam. Margaret took small bites and Dad smiled. He'd done it. It was all OK. We had got through this thing together. Without Mum.

'What shall we do with his cage?' Margaret said.

'Well,' said Dad, 'I've had a good idea about that. How about we go to the pet shop one afternoon after school and pick out a brand-new hamster? You could even get two of them if you liked.'

Margaret stared at him like he was an alien.

'How can you *say* that?' she said. 'You can't do that, it isn't *fair*. You can't just throw one hamster away and love another one. You can't, you know. Not just like that.'

She sloped off to bed then, despite our best attempts to get her to stay. The remains of her crumpet lay sweating butter on its plate and she refused to come down for the dinner of cream of tomato soup and cheese on toast that Dad made for us later. He looked all bunched up about it, like someone had cut his strings.

As we ate soup and toast on our laps, in front of the telly, I felt a new and dangerous atmosphere forming. There were clouds in the room: grey, low and heavy, held up by Dad's twitches and slurping and huffing and puffing.

'What's the sod like, then?' he said, suddenly and tightly, out of nowhere, as the credits to the evening news began to roll.

'Dunno,' I said at first.

'Go on,' he said. 'It's OK to tell me.'

I couldn't breathe for a minute. I had no breath.

'Well, he's a moron,' I said. 'He's ugly and pig-eyed and short. He's definitely not rich, so there's no need to worry on that account, and he goes out in pyjamas and his head is full of all kinds of nonsense.'

'Oh,' Dad said, and I knew in that instant I had made a mistake. If Ray was such an odd-ball and a loser, what on earth did that make him?

Dad folded his toast in half and forced the last of it down his throat like it was made of something painful, like sand-paper. After that he went to the drinks cabinet and poured himself a whisky in a way that suggested he didn't really want one but wasn't sure what else he might do. He didn't speak for the rest of the evening and Margaret was fast asleep when I went up to bed. In her hand was a page of thick creamy paper that looked like a letter from someone, but when I tried to see who it was from she pulled it deep down inside her continental quilt.

23

9a Cavendish Place
Fitzrovia
London
May 16th 1934

Dearest Broo,

I remember one afternoon when we were children. We were sat on the lawn at Middlehurst in July, perspiring in the most unusual heat. It was that long hot summer with the bees when Grandpa said the days had broken records. Mother brought us lemonade and let us take our dresses off and you asked which would be the most disagreeable climate to live in: one that was terribly hot all the time, or one that was terribly cold. After a glass of iced lemonade and some minutes in the shade we agreed the cold would be worst. Let me tell you now how wrong we were.

As you'll no doubt have heard, it was a God-awful mess out there and let it be a lesson to me not to embark on anything like it again in a moment of haste. How I made it to Freetown in one piece I will never know. We would all have died from sunstroke in the first few days were it not for two tremendous gentlemen from the King's African Rifles who pulled us through. They were our angels of mercy in the Sahara, pulling our broken trucks from the gulley where they had lodged and escorting us to an oasis which had a well and two palms, and was the sort that a child might draw. It was hardly more than a mile away, yet to us it seemed more distant than the moon since we had had no notion it was there. The stupidity of it was hardest to take, more so than all the burns and the dehydration. To think we could have died for nothing and in striking distance of safety is almost too much for me to bear.

Our desert angels were kind enough to escort us from the wretched sands and even found time to recommend an exemplary team of porters in Banjul. How we came to be laden with so much gear is still a mystery but I suppose that is what happens when you invite a poet onto an expedition where the lure is a mine full of uncut diamonds.

One might imagine a poet would have simple needs – a pen, some paper and a night shirt, perhaps – but this could not have been further from the facts. One way or another we found ourselves lugging his entire household through the mangroves since it turned out he had put down deep and undisclosed roots in Morocco and, despite his reputation as a wanderer, he proved a rigid servant to his chattels. Along came his poet friends – and a paltry bunch they were – as well as all their clothes, linen, china and crockery and even a sedan chair upholstered in velveteen!

What a poet needs with a soup tureen and a sedan chair in the jungle is beyond explanation and can only be put down to insanity. Even now, I can offer you no reasonable excuse other than his desire to impress his band of merry followers with the kind of man he was.

The kind of man he was was a mad one, and despite all
he suffered subsequently I don't feel in the least obliged
to forgive him for keeping this most vital fact from me.

Our corner of Africa was inhospitable in the extreme.
In Greenland our enemy was singular but in the jungle
it had more faces than a Hydra, with heads that grew
back twice as fast. The heat, of course, was punishing,
but hardly the worst of it. There were endless ticks,
leeches and mosquitoes to contend with as well as the
dreadful tangle of the terrain. We were beset with cuts,
bites and sores that refused to heal in the humidity and
gave way to infection in minutes if they weren't properly
dressed up and bandaged.

When the insects were at bay we turned our attention
to the reptiles and mammals: crocodiles, lions, rhinoceros,
all of whom regarded our gang as delicacies of the finest
order and were liable to attack at once if one ventured
from camp for a second. William, a friend of Sumner's,
was lost to a river crocodile when the two of them took
a walk unchaperoned on the banks of the Gambia, and
you can only imagine the stupidity of Sumner's poor
attempts to save him by wedging his walking stick in the
animal's jaws. One of our coolies found them mid-fracas
and blasted the animal to pieces with his shotgun but,
alas, by then it was all too late. Why Sumner didn't fire
his own gun when he had the chance, no one can
understand, and it is perhaps not uncharitable to suggest
that Sumner lost his nerve or simply hadn't cared
enough to save him.

Thank God for our natives, then, who knew the
terrain backwards and cooked and carried and drove for
us and proved to have almost superhuman levels of
endurance. Each native carried a load of forty pounds
or more when our gang was on foot, and could cover

tremendous distance when not held up or halted by us. They complained bitterly if they were given light loads and the only punishment that had any effect on them was to make the ringleader walk in front with no cargo, where he would be subject to endless taunts from the others with allusions to his weakness and his mother's reaction should she see her son thus degraded!

Sumner and his cohorts could hardly have been less grateful and were insistent they would rob us or kill us in our beds in due course, and it wasn't until some time later that I discovered these bouts of hysteria were brought on by the copious smoking of opium.

In all honesty, and though it is dreadful to say it, it was a relief when he succumbed to blackwater fever, the details of which I shall spare you; suffice to say things were not looking good when last I saw him, since his kidneys seemed hours from giving in and his urine was the colour of congealed blood. Of course I was gladdened later to hear he had pulled through, yet grateful to press on without him. These complications of malaria took down most of our flock over the days and weeks and can only have spared me since I was rigorous with my doses of quinine. Disease is everywhere in the tropics, with more fevers and pox than you can imagine. At least in the cold the worst viruses perish; in the heat they flourish wildly in their millions.

In Freetown came the icing on the cake. The much-vaunted diamonds proved predictably elusive, though it seemed clear to all around us that much violence and disagreement had taken place over what little amounts of gems there had been. I knew I was in danger and that I had to leave at once, and can honestly say there is nothing about Africa that would urge me to set foot there ever again. The whole of New Guinea could be carpeted in rubies and I would gladly tell New Guinea, 'You are welcome to them.'

The voyage home was nothing less than pleasure and relief, even though conditions were cramped and thoughts of my folly plagued me in my long hours of boredom. Exhaustion came upon me and there were days when I hardly ventured forth from my cabin, but there was time for reading and for walking about the deck when I had a mood to, and it struck me on these turns about the ship that half the joy of being away is in the anticipation of arriving home. This time it was all the more satisfying. All wounds were soothed the minute we docked in Southampton by the scent of English soil and the greenest grass.

It rained hard in London yesterday, did you notice? I dashed out the moment I saw it and stood without my coat on, in the middle of Piccadilly, until I was shivering and soaked. It was a delight, the most wonderful treat. In the distance, as I turned back for shelter I saw a figure in the distance walking fast with his collar up to escape the rain and didn't recognize him until we had almost collided. There we were, face to face, and all the pain of it just as recent and as fresh as if I had never been away. What a fruitless trip this was, my dearest sister. I had almost perished to banish him yet mere days after my return there he stood. Andrew Linton, more handsome than he ever was, caught in the revolving doorway at The Ritz.

Yours,
Edith

24

'Have I ever been to tea at The *Ritz*?'

'Yes. Did Granddad ever take you?'

Nanna gave Margaret a suspicious look.

'Lyon's Corner House. That was nearby. He took me there once, does that count?'

'Is it a hotel?'

'Restaurant. Posh one. Posh for me and your granddad. Four floors, all different. The waitresses wore black and white uniforms. They called them nippies; they were ever so smart. They had an orchestra playing while you ate. You could have a four-course dinner on the top floor, as I remember, or scones and butter in the tea shop.'

'Which did Granddad buy you?'

'Scones and butter,' said Nanna, looking cross.

Nanna's crossness on missing out on a four-course dinner for scones and butter was the only blight on what was turning out, against all expectations, to be an exceptionally pleasurable Sunday. The idea had been that we would go to Nanna's in the morning and that Mum and Ray would join us for lunch. It was to be our second formal meeting, again on neutral ground, because both Margaret and I had refused to set foot in his house.

Dad drove us over and deposited us, declining to come in for a cup of tea.

'Have a cup, will you? The kettle's just boiled.'

'No thank you, Vi. I'd rather not.'

'Well, I don't see why—'

'Don't you? Really? I think you do.'

Nanna huffed and puffed and made it clear with her folded arms that she didn't appreciate the accusation.

'You won't find me taking *her* side,' Nanna said. 'I've not got a good word to say about her.'

'Roast beef for lunch, is it?' said Dad, sniffing the air. 'Very nice indeed. I hope he likes it.'

'I don't care if he likes it or not,' Nanna said. 'I'd happily serve him the soles off my shoes. The beef is for the girls and whatever I think about *him*, I'd say it was better to keep an eye on him than not.'

'I'll see you later,' Dad said to us, turning his back to Nanna. 'Both of you, remember what I said.'

What Dad had said was this: we didn't have to talk to Ray if we didn't want to. We needn't answer any of his questions. If he gave us any gifts, no matter what they were, we should refuse them politely and hand them back. On no account were we to take a walk to the beach with him, even if we were accompanied by Mum. Margaret wanted to know if it was OK to walk to the beach just with Nanna and after a pause he said he thought this was all right.

'Your dad's not shaved,' Nanna said as he walked up the path. 'His shirt looks mucky at the collar.'

He hadn't showered that morning either or eaten a shred of breakfast. I wondered if I should tell Nanna that.

'He's got it in his head that I knew all about it,' she said, 'but he's wrong. If I'd known I would have put a bloody stop to it.'

Nanna ushered us into the hallway. As she snapped the front door shut the bungalow seemed to shrink, sucking our breath out with its smallness. Despite offers of cake and the

promise of a roast beef lunch we felt full of dread for the
hours that lay ahead of us. What would Ray turn up wearing
this time? Would we have to listen to stories about his stupid
pyramids again? Would Mum do that girlish laugh and fiddle
with her beads? Would Nanna tell Mum off for not wearing
any tights under her skirt? The mood among the three of us
was bristle and gloom. Then the phone rang and changed
the whole day.

'They're not coming,' Nanna said brightly. 'Your mum's
got stomach flu. There's a film on in a minute. Johnny
Weissmuller. Who'd like a nice slice of Battenberg?'

Cheetah and Jane were lost and in danger, and it was touch
and go whether Tarzan would save them. He was making that
yodel, *Aghaghaghaghagh!* It always made me and Margaret
laugh.

'Will he get to them in time?'

'Of course he will. Of course.'

'But they might get boiled in pots.'

'Good Lord,' said Nanna. 'Look at all those nig-nogs.'

'Nanna, you *can't* say nig-nogs!'

'Why can't I?'

'Nanna, *because.*'

'I doubt I'll travel to Africa more than once,' Margaret said,
rolling her cake icing into balls. 'Once would be enough of
Africa for me.'

My sister studied the jungle scenes with interest and
muttered unusual phrases like 'tsetse fly', 'quinine' and
'dengue fever'. She seemed to know an awful lot about insects
and swamps but, given that we'd yet to venture further than
the Isle of Wight, I felt the chances of her having to turn
down a repeat visit to the tropics in the very near future were
remote.

With Jane and Cheetah moments away from being boiled

alive in pots, Tarzan swung into action. He swooped into the encampment with a wild roaring cry and a beat of his chest, and gathered them up in his arms. Back in the rainforest, in the safety of his tree house, Tarzan pulled Jane towards him and kissed her for a long time while Cheetah covered his eyes in mock embarrassment. This is what Dad needed to do, it seemed to me. He needed to sweep Mum off her feet. If only he could get around to shaving and washing his collar once in a while, he might still be in with a chance.

'Do you think he'll get her back?'

'Who?'

'Dad. Nanna, will Dad ever get Mum back?'

Nanna made a tut-tut-tut sound in the manner of a person who thought she should keep her opinions to herself but on this occasion wasn't going to.

'Many's the woman your mum's age who's dropped her drawers for a tray of chocolates and a mouth full of flattery,' Nanna said. 'It's nothing I've not seen before. If she's got any sense she'll be back before the year's out. Once *his* nonsense wears off, mark my words. Your dad's a good solid man. Granddad always said so. Your mother could have done a lot worse than married him.'

I took some comfort in Nanna's wisdom. I liked the idea of Ray's 'nonsense' and its temporary quality, as if he had merely infected Mum like a seasonal virus or a common cold.

'What can we do to speed things up?' Margaret said.

'Nothing,' Nanna said, stoically. 'Her good sense will come back when the time's right. She's deep in the sickness of it yet. It would take something dramatic to sway her now.'

Even with our stomachs full of Battenberg cake we still managed to polish off an entire roast dinner: potatoes of sublime crispiness, meat as soft as butter, vegetables mashed to pieces and inoffensive. Margaret put her vegetarianism on hold for one day only since Nanna hadn't been warned about it in advance, which seemed unfair, and roast beef was Margaret's favourite food. She asked for extra helpings and ate more than I'd seen her eat in ages. After dinner came a pudding of Bakewell tart and ice cream and we stuffed ourselves until our bellies yelled. This was the best kind of day there could be, with nothing of importance for us to care about or worry about, or do.

'Don't forget your speech, now,' said Nanna, clearing the plates. 'Your dad said you were to do it this afternoon.'

'I don't know what to say.'

'Keep it short and sweet.'

'Will you help me with it, Nan?'

'What do I know about Mohican haircuts? You were doing it for the attention, weren't you? Just say so like a grown-up and apologize, and that will be that.'

'I have to read it out aloud. In front of the school.'

'Well, then,' said Nanna, 'you'd better be sure you do a decent job.'

Margaret began to look queasy. She tugged at her hat, pushed back her chair and excused herself. The next thing I knew she was locked in the toilet, throwing up. Nanna rang Dad to come and fetch us. She said Margaret must have caught Mum's stomach flu.

25

She stood there, hardly four foot eleven inches tall, in her navy school uniform that was wide for her body, and read this. She read it with her head up the entire time, as if she were imparting a lesson of some kind, which she was.

My Mohican

by Margaret Jennifer Lester

My unusual haircut has an unusual history. The first people ever to wear a haircut like mine were a tribe of Red Indians called the Mohawk. Mohawk meant man-eater, but I haven't been able to find out if the Mohawk really did or didn't eat men. Ordinarily the Mohawk had long hair but whenever they went to war with another tribe they cut their hair the same as mine: shaved at the sides with a long strip straight down the middle. It was only the men who cut their hair like this because it was only the men who went to war. I imagine they did this to look scary to their enemies, which must have worked quite well because even nowadays people seem to be scared of people with a haircut like mine. My nanna thinks it makes me look angry all the time, and when she first saw it it made my mum cry. Today it is mostly punks or punk rockers who have my haircut and it is considered to be a rebellious haircut for people who don't like the queen.

When I go out into the street people stare at me and point, and in school I have to wear a hat. I am not wearing one now so that you can see what I am talking about, but I have to wear my hat in lessons and for sports. My head is itchy where the hair is growing back so it would be nicer to have my head out in the air. My dad says I am not allowed to shave it any more or dye the long parts pink even though I think that would make it look a whole lot better.

I have been asked to think about what I have done to my hair and say whether I think it was good or bad. Having thought about it for some time I have decided I will be both glad and sorry to see it grow back. It sometimes feels nice to upset people and so this has helped me understand what it feels like to be a punk rocker. I am also following in the footsteps of an ancient Red Indian tradition and I find this quite exciting because there are still Mohawk Indians in parts of America today and it is my plan to explore these parts of America when I am older and to ask the Mohawk if they ever did eat men. On the other hand, it will be quite nice when people stop staring at me on the high street and whispering things about me behind my back.

In conclusion, and looking at both sides of the coin, I would have to say that I have enjoyed having my unusual haircut for a while and I hope I have given an interesting explanation for it. *Nai:wen*, for listening. *Nai:wen* is Mohawk for thank you.

As she folded her paper and stood down from the plinth the assembly room was tight with silence. I wanted to clap but was afraid to be the only one and was just working up the courage to do it when the headmaster stepped forward, a look of some annoyance on his face. He coughed and said this:

'What Margaret Lester meant to say to you all is that she apologizes for what she's done. Don't you, Margaret?'

My sister issued a mute nod from the side of the stage.

'It isn't brave or clever to deform oneself and Margaret has brought her school and henceforth you, its pupils, into disrepute by doing so. Should anyone else be tempted to follow in her footsteps because of a rock group they've seen on television or read about in a magazine, my course of action will be prompt and the pupil will be suspended or even expelled.

'I'm sure we all enjoyed Margaret's little story about Red Indians, who may very well have shaved their hair into all sorts of idiotic patterns, but the last time I looked there were no Red Indians in Wicksford. There is nothing *traditional* about the Mohican in this country, nor is it a symbol of rebellion, and on this point Margaret Lester is entirely wrong. It is a symbol of ignorance and stupidity, and shows a gross disrespect for your peers.

'Now, if it's not too late I'll ask Mr Simons to come up here and say a word or two about littering and then we'll finish with a recitation of the Lord's Prayer.'

I wanted to find Margaret to congratulate her. One way or another she had got away with murder and stuck it straight to the school, and I wanted to let her know that I was proud of her. She wasn't in her form room or the toilet block or the playground and I eventually came across her by the tuck shop. She was standing in the shadows with Ian Warrington, looking shifty. I watched them for a while where they couldn't see me.

'I can have your whole lunch box?'

'Have it all.'

'I don't want the apple.'

'Just take it.'

'And your tuck money?'

'Here, put it in your pocket.'

'It's only fifty pence.'

'That's all I have.'

'Now the other thing. Don't you forget the other thing.'

My sister made a tough face.

'What if I just got you another fifty pence?'

'Won't do. No good. You'd never have got the Mohawk information on your own. I lent you my books. You agreed.'

It was the matter-of-fact way she did this next thing that shocked me. She reached up and undid the buttons of her blouse, bared her quarter-sized breasts which were hardly a summer old, and began to rub them round and round in a way that was meant to look sexy, but looked to me simply like they itched. Ian Warrington just stared at them. Impotent.

'Enough?' my sister said, after a minute or so.

'No,' Ian said, 'I want to touch them.'

He reached out and lay his podgy hands on her then, while my sister stared forward, dead-eyed.

'Do you like them?' she said.

'They're OK.'

'Do you wish they were bigger?'

'I suppose.'

When he'd finished he selected a chocolate wafer from Margaret's lunch box and unwrapped it, while she carefully rebuttoned her shirt. She was lost to the world in that moment. I wanted to save her but I didn't know how.

26

'Jessie. Can you *help* me? I think I'm dying.'

'What are you talking about?'

'I don't want to say.'

Margaret was locked in the lavatory; she'd been in there for over half an hour.

'Is Dad around?' she said, through the door.

'He's in the shed.'

'If I unlock the door, will you come in here?'

Nervously, I said that I would.

My sister was sat on the toilet with her knickers between her knees; they were stained with blood.

'What is it?' she said. 'It's dripping out of me. It started this morning. I don't know what to do.'

'Are you serious?' I said.

She looked straight at me.

'I'm not normal, am I? I'm just not normal.'

'For chuff's sake, Margaret, it's your period. Didn't Mum *tell* you about your period?'

'Jessie, it *hurts*. Am I pregnant? I think I'm going to be sick.'

My sister slumped forward, her face towards the lino, her fingers clutched tightly to the edge of the toilet bowl. I caught her shoulders just before she fainted.

★　★　★

'I have to wear these every single day?'

'Just while you have it,' Joni said. 'It's only a few days a month.'

'It's like nappies or something. It's *disgusting*.'

'You'll learn how to use tampons, they go inside you. It's really much better.'

'Inside you, where?'

'Your vagina, Margaret. Didn't anyone tell you about your vagina?'

My sister sat on Joni Lightfoot's kitchen floor holding a diagram of a see-through woman. The woman's knee was bent and her reproductive organs were on show. In her hand was a cigarette of cardboard and cotton wool that she was preparing to insert into her body.

'I'd like another aspirin.'

'I think two will be enough for the minute.'

'But it still hurts, you know. I can still feel it.'

'The cramps will go soon. I'll make you a hot-water bottle.'

Margaret clung to her piece of paper while Joni boiled water on the stove. She was dosed up on painkillers and evening primrose tea and had one of Joni Lightfoot's emergency sanitary towels stuffed down the gusset of her strongest knickers. I hadn't known where else to take her. I couldn't face Barbara Hill – who was most likely post-menopausal and lacking in suitable sanitary wear – and the shops were all closed, what with it being gone five o'clock.

Joni pressed the hot-water bottle to Margaret's tummy and the kitchen filled with the wintry scent of warm rubber. She sat down next to her and took the Tampax leaflet in her hand, ready to explain how things worked.

'This is your uterus, Margaret. And these are your fallopian tubes.'

'What's in them? What are they for?'

She went right into it then: ovaries and eggs and sexual

intercourse and cycles and the shedding of linings. It was enlightening stuff, to tell you the truth. Mum had been OK on the period part but shady on all the surrounding detail. Instead of telling me the ins and outs of sex she asked about biology lessons and if we'd started on the life cycle of the fruit fly yet. Other useless nuggets of information that Mum passed on were that Nanna called her periods 'the curse' and that when Barbara Hill had her 'monthlies' she used to tell her husband she had the decorators in. Most of the rest I'd learned from reading Harold Robbins novels and watching *The Sweeney*, and from my best friend Rebecca Witt, who thought fellatio was a character from Shakespeare and that condoms were worn on the man's balls. I didn't tell any of this to Margaret and Joni. I made them think I was up on all things vaginal, via a series of well-timed nods and 'that's right's.'

When she had done with her explaining, Joni went to the highest cupboard in the kitchen and pulled out a bottle of cooking brandy. She poured a finger-full into a tumbler and told Margaret to drink it down in one go, which she did. When she had finished, Joni reached over and smacked her hand against my sister's cheek.

'What did you do *that* for?'

'It's tradition in my family. My grandmother did it to my mother and my mother did it to me. Since your mother isn't around at the moment I thought I would do it to you.'

Margaret touched her face. She seemed bemused by the ongoing state of things: the latent ache in her belly and all the womb talk and the sex talk, and the brandy which had gone to her head.

'It's a marker,' Joni said. 'A celebration. Today you became a woman and a woman's body is a wonderful thing. I want you to love yours and to appreciate it in all of its cleverness and beauty.'

'I see,' Margaret said, holding tight to her brown paper bag full of maxi pads.

'And I like your haircut, by the way. I meant to tell you. It looks funky.'

'Does it?' Margaret said, blushing.

'Yes, it's individualistic. It wouldn't suit most women, but it looks good on you because you're so pretty.'

It was a simple trick on Joni's part but my sister positively beamed at it. She had called her a woman, which had to make things better, and described her as good-looking, which she was. All of us thought Margaret was pretty but no one – because we weren't that kind of family – had ever said it outright, to her face.

After another cup of herbal tea we went to join Jack in the living room and my sister got to talking about Red Indians, who Jack said we should call Native Americans. It turned out that Jack knew quite a lot about Native Americans, especially when it came down to what they smoked. As he carried on about peace pipes and mushrooms and hallucinogens, I wondered if I should grab Joni for a moment and run my sister's breast-rubbing, lunch-box episode past her. I would have done it, I think, if Jack hadn't started on about the where-abouts of his dinner and Joni hadn't switched on *Coronation Street*, which seemed to me to be the cue that we should leave. That was the thing about Joni and Jack. On the surface they didn't seem like the kind of people who'd watch soap operas in the evening with their dinners on their laps, but they did.

Mum made her usual phone call at eight o'clock. She rang at this time so we'd know it was her and so Dad would know not to answer it.

'Margaret started her period today,' I said. 'I had to take her down to Joni Lightfoot's.'

Nothing.

'Mum, did you *hear* me?'

'I heard you.'

'You should have *been* here. She was really upset.'

'Put her on. Let me speak to her, will you?'

'She's gone to bed; she's still got a tummy ache.'

'Jess . . . I'm so sorry. Tell her, will you?'

'You should have been *here*, though. You should have told her *yourself*.'

'You did the right thing, love. Taking her to Joni—'

'What do you know about right things? You didn't even tell her about it. She thought she was fucking *dying* on the toilet.'

'Jess, come on now, there's no nee—'

'There is, though, Mum. There actually *fucking* is.'

Dad came out to see what all the fuss was about but I tightened my lips and told him nothing. I'd kept secrets from Dad before, lots of them, but this felt different somehow. My head felt full up with the weight of things and I had the strongest urge to get my coat on and run down the street and not stop until I was quite far away from him. The place I would run to was Nanna's. I'd watch Tarzan films on the settee for the rest of my life and eat Battenberg cakes, one straight after the other, until my stomach burst.

27

9a, Cavendish Place
Fitzrovia
London
June 10th 1934

Dearest Broo,

I want to thank you for your last two letters, the second of which was succinct and entirely to the point. You are right when you say I should stay away from Andrew and correct in noting that I have been offered a trip to Luxor, but Egypt is not on my horizons for now and I would rather wait until there is another northern expedition in the offing before I make more plans to leave London. In many ways I am grateful to be put up for anything after the last fiasco but am determined to plan future trips with better thought. You will say this is all an excuse, no doubt, and that my real reason for staying is because he is here. And what if it were true? Would you have kept away from Frederick if it had worked out this way for the two of you?

Our evening at the Ritz was electric. I was meeting some friends in from Washington and Andrew promptly joined our table and charmed everyone with his stories and his lively manner. When he stood up to leave he kissed me sweetly on both cheeks, lingering a beat too long and resting his hand in the small of my back. It was the subtlest of gestures, so as not to look awkward, but when he said to me that he would call, I knew he meant to.

The frustration of it all is the hardest to take since I can never be sure when I will hear from him. He calls me some weeks and some weeks not, and I sit home and wait for his rings. They come like sirens in the dead part of the evening and I leap to them, standing to attention. When contact is rationed in this way it becomes an addiction and even his voice is enough to put powder in my veins. On come all the lights and a day that was plainness and mediocrity is lit up like the first hours of Christmas.

We talk about everything but us: the breadth of the northern landscape, the ice fields, the hunting, all our plans for future travels and trips. How clever we are in our conspiracy, Broo, with our light tone and our laughter; pretending we are the very best of friends and that friendship is entirely good enough. I don't ask about Yolande and he, for his part, never seeks to mention her. He volunteers little about family life though he sometimes talks about the baby, Lillian. She sounds like a terrific one and is, by all accounts, a joy. I like to hear about her, which is perverse, isn't it, since she is almost all of the reason why he would never leave Yolande to come for me. But there is something in the way he speaks about his daughter, a tenderness of tone, that makes me admire him still more.

How old were you when you had Edwin, Broo? Twenty-one? Twenty-two? I am twenty-six this summer and, without a hint of warning, I feel frayed about the edges and past my best. I notice women who are younger, and see them everywhere with their husbands and with their babies in prams. Last Tuesday there was a lovely one on the Marylebone Road, wearing the sweetest bootees and a white knitted bonnet. He was all smiles for his mother and she, a dowdy creature in a plain dress and overcoat, seemed immune to her own drabness and positively lifted in her spirits by its eager attempts to engage her. When she picked it up and jogged it, it laughed and she laughed as if they shared in the most glorious joke. It seems queer, doesn't it? That I had not thought of children up until now.

Lately I am reduced to the idiot wits of a schoolgirl. Some days I find myself jotting down the name Edith Linton on notes of paper and imagining Lillian were mine or that I had one just like her of my own. Of course it would be ruinous and an end to all adventures, and I can only assume the desire will pass, since there is hardly any cause to act upon it.

In any case, my dearest sister, I hope I have eased your mind a little. You have concerns, of course, but there is nothing improper for anyone to discover and so there is no point you worrying on that score. Andrew is all about honour and discretion and I have resigned myself to all our impossibilities. I apologize in advance if my infatuation appears unseemly, and confess its depths to you merely to ease the weight of it for me and because I know you would never use its ugliness against me. You are right to suggest that I am worn down this summer, and this evening I am more tired than a woman of my privilege has any right to be. Shall I come up and see you, do you think? On the bad days I feel peeled apart. Like a building taken down brick by brick.

Affectionately yours,
Edith

28

The bulldozers arrived at seven in the morning and the grind of them filled up the street. There were echoes that sounded like giant footfalls and calamitous bangs that reverberated through the thickness of walls and down into the covers of our beds. The high notes were the sound of glass shattering and of roof steels being merrily snapped into two. Here and there men's urgent voices shouted, 'Hold it', 'Hold it steady' or 'Easy, easy', 'Hold it there.'

The view from the window wasn't clear enough so we threw off our nightclothes and dressed in our jeans and our nearest T-shirts and tore out onto the street. We were some of the first ones on the scene, pressing our arms on the perimeter fence while our egg-stained neighbours peeped lazily from behind their curtains, the fabric edging this way and that. Only the early risers and commuters joined our stares and they nodded mute recognitions to one another on the pavement. They crouched at their cars, clearing dust from their windscreens, wondering about disruption and the parking restrictions and hoping the whole nasty business would be done and over with before they came home from work.

Edith's house, what was left of it, was disappearing into the ground. There was barely any house shape by the time we got there – no window shapes, no wall shapes, no doors. Everything was rubble and dust, and the bulldozers kept pushing at the leftovers, insistent and determined, for what seemed like no obvious purpose. On one side stood a crane with a giant concrete ball that would swing every now and then into the parts that were refusing to crumble. We watched it turn and swing, then turn and swing again, and could only guess how dense and heavy the damn thing was. Margaret hugged her knees in delight as the sections fell, like there was something satisfying in the pounding and the knocks.

'Has Dad left for work yet?'

'His car's just gone.'

'Shall we get ready for school or shall we stay?'

The two of us stayed for the morning until most of Edith's building had been scraped up and loaded into skips. There seemed something good about it, as if a darkness had been lifted and order restored to the street. Gone was the burnt dirt and debris and in its place all neat lines and straight edges. There was no way of telling what had been there before or of guessing about the nature of Edith's passing. The space became a fresh, new building site instead of a temporary graveyard. It was a patch of land in waiting and something different would soon go up and take its place. In the sunshine and the rising heat from the early summer's day it made the two of us feel optimistic.

'Shall we have some lunch?' I said.

'What is there?'

'Cola and crisps.'

'Good. OK.'

We made ourselves the kind of food that kids make. Fizzy drinks and chocolate bars and biscuits; raw energy and nothing of substance. There was fruit in the fruit bowls, apples and oranges, but the task was to boycott all vitamins. Margaret had extra rations that I didn't know about, a stash of goodies hidden underneath her bed: Caramac bars, Bazooka Joe bubblegum, Fruit Salads, Black Jacks and Twix. We gorged ourselves on them, elated and nauseous from the sugar rush and buoyant from the kick of missing school. When we'd finished Margaret disappeared to the toilet and I lay there in a star shape with the radio on, making plans for the rest of the day. We could walk to the park or take a bus ride to the high street or lie right where we were, not moving, not talking, just listening to the radio or our favourite records. If we went out we'd be sure to take a detour to the school; we'd go close enough to see for certain that all our friends were in there and to know, however briefly, that we weren't.

'Shhh! Shhh. Turn it down.'

Margaret came back from the bathroom looking pale and smelling of toothpaste.

'He's home. I think Dad's come home.'

'It's only one o'clock.'

'But Jessie, he is.'

The radio went off and we lay beneath the bed, keeping as still as we could and worrying about the mess we'd left downstairs. We hoped he'd think the debris was from break-fast but our heads spun with sugar and with fear, wondering what confectionery item it was that would give us away. We heard him come up the stairs with his usual huffs and puffs then he went into the bedroom and crashed around in his wardrobe as if nothing in there satisfied him. We saw his socked feet walk across the upstairs hallway, and heard him walk into the bathroom and have a wash. Back to the bedroom he went after that, and when he came out . . . new socks, new trousers, different shoes. Good ones.

'What's he doing, do you think?'

We didn't know.

★   ★   ★

All went quiet for a time after that. There was the mutter of
The Archers on the radio downstairs then the clatter of the
grill pan and the smell of cheese and overdone toast. For
almost half an hour there was nothing. Then the doorbell,
then the sound of a woman's voice. We heard him say, 'Hello,'
then, 'Please come in.'

It was a game of patience for the two of us then. How long
could we wait before this intrigue got the better of us and
we were forced down to see who it was? The voice at the
door wasn't Mum's and my stomach and my skin and my
whole head itched with the desire to find out who it was. A
teacher from school come to find out where we were? The
Avon lady with an order of Mum's?

'You'll have to go down, you know.'

'Why me?'

'Jessie, because.'

'He'll kill us. He doesn't like us bunking.'

'If you don't go, I'll have to do it.'

This wasn't the best idea. For a small person Margaret had
disproportionately clumsy and heavy feet.

I made it out from under the bed and to the top of the
staircase with no problem but the stairs themselves were
an assault course, given to endless creaks and groans even
beneath the fully fitted carpets. I took them one by one
and got halfway down in two minutes flat with only a
couple of errant squeaks. From here I could just make out
the voices; I could discern their tone but not make out
their words. The woman's voice was calm, sincere and
measured, and she seemed to be having the best of the
conversation. I felt bold enough to go for it by then, assured
of my indestructible powers. To the bottom of the stairs
and beyond. To the living room door, crouched like the
cat we'd always wanted.

'Like I said, it was good of you to call.'

'I thought I should. Though I'm sure the girls would hate me if they knew.'

'Oh no, well. They'll never know.'

'It's just that they seemed . . . Margaret especially . . . and I wondered if they had anyone to talk to.'

'Not really, no.'

'That's what I thought. And it's so important. Because it seemed to me, and I could be wrong, but it felt like they were keeping things in.'

'Right. Right. I see.'

'Has Margaret always been so skinny?'

'Skinny? Yes, well, she's always been small.'

'You ought to keep an eye on her. That's all I'd say. Young girls can be funny about their eating.'

'She is quite fussy.'

'Is she?'

'She recently became a vegetarian.'

'Well, goodness. That's probably my fault, then. Jack and I are both vegetarian.'

Just at the moment that I realized it was Joni I heard my father starting to cry.

'Hey . . . hey now, please. You mustn't blame yourself. You shouldn't, you know. It's hard for men sometimes. You're not trained in the emotional response.'

'Oh God.'

'No . . . *no*. It's good that you're crying. It's good, you see, it means that you're opening up.'

'I don't know what I did wrong, you see.'

'Well . . . you probably . . . The chances are . . . you didn't do anything.'

'I worked hard, I've been a good father.'

'Of course. Of course. No one's saying that you weren't.'

'She wanted to go on a course. I let her go on the bloody course.'

'I suppose . . . maybe . . . But when you say you *let* her . . .'

'She's a bitch . . . a *fucking*, fucking bitch.'

'Oh . . . hell. Mr Lester . . . I don't . . . Perhaps I'd better get going, then.'

'No . . . no. Please. Don't go.'

'I just came to talk about the girls.'

'You're very sweet.'

'They need looking after. However bad you feel, it's important you take care of them now.'

'You love Jack, do you?'

'Do I? Yes.'

'He's a real man, is he?'

'Mr Lester, I don't know what that is.'

'Keeps you happy, does he? In areas?'

'*Areas?*'

'Keeps you happy in the sack?'

'OK, then, that's it . . . It's time that I went. No, please don't . . . No, don't touch my hand.'

'You're really very pretty.'

'Honestly, let go. Take your hand off my knee.'

'He's younger, like you. Did you know that?'

'No . . . I don't . . . no, I didn't. It's really none of my busin—'

'How about you touch my balls, then? How about that? How about *I* get to fuck a hippy?'

Joni ran out of there, right past me. To this day I don't know if she noticed me or not. Dad came out after her and our two faces met. They were ruinous faces. Ones we'd remember all our lives.

29

Theoretically Ray's camper van was big enough to sleep seven people and this might have been true if the seven had all been dwarves. As we wedged ourselves in through the sliding door that wouldn't slide, I began to wonder how we'd ever get away from them. A week's holiday in France in the middle of a school term seemed like a gift made in heaven; a week in this camper van with our newly beaded mother and our mother's younger boyfriend would likely turn out to be a jail sentence.

Mum insisted we set off at the crack of dawn, because the crack of dawn was when all our holidays began and was the only sure way to beat the traffic. The camper pulled up at Nanna's at six in the morning but we'd been up and wide awake since close to five. Nanna had made us boiled eggs so we didn't have to drive on an empty stomach. She made us two each, which was unusual, because she was afraid that in France we might not eat a decent meal for the rest of the week. It annoyed her that Margaret stuck fast to her toast, since Nanna was fairly sure eggs were hardly more than vegetables. Margaret said this absolutely wasn't the case and that eggs were off the menu now too, on account of being aborted chicken foetuses. Nanna had had three days of 'this kind of nonsense' and you could tell she wasn't prepared to put up with it for very much longer.

The seats in Ray's camper van were lined with sheepskin, which made me feel more comfortable than I had any right to. It felt good and warm to be sitting there while Mum and Ray loaded our cases onto the roof rack and chatted about the campsite we were heading to. I was wearing my going-on-holiday clothes: a yellow A-line dress with capped sleeves and matching cardigan, and a pair of flowery sandals with cork soles. Mum wore a cheesecloth kaftan and flip-flops, and even Margaret had made the effort to pick out some-thing cool and summery, which cheered everyone up. Ray was in a different version of what turned out to be many and varied pyjama-suit combos.

The day felt rash and unsteady yet full of delicious possi-bilities. By the end of the afternoon we'd be very far away, further than we'd ever been before. Everyone we'd meet would be continental. They'd smell of garlic and frogs and wear berets on their heads, and dress in stripy tops with fisherman's jumpers knotted at their shoulders. Everything, everywhere would be unfamiliar, and the thrill of impending newness made my toes curl.

'Shall we sing a song?' Ray asked.

'Oh lovely,' Mum said. 'Good idea.'

I stared silently out of the window, clocking the start of the motorway and mentally tightening my lips. Sheepskin-lined seats were one thing but he wasn't going to win me that easily. But this was the funny thing about Ray. He wasn't quickly embarrassed like Dad, nor did he wait for anyone else to say it was OK before he decided to go ahead and do a thing. And so, for the rest of the journey, the camper van rattled to the sound of Ray's voice, which was grating and overly enthusiastic at times, but largely pleasant and tuneful.

He sang songs we didn't know by a man named Bob Dylan who we'd never heard of, and the lyrics were about all kinds of odd subjects. Surprisingly enough, Mum seemed to know exactly who he was and could mouth almost all of the words. Ray implored her to sing along but she wouldn't. I felt like she was right on the edge.

'You've *not* got rabies.'

'How do you know?'

'It didn't come anywhere near you.'

'I feel thirsty. That's a sign, isn't it?'

'You're not dribbling, though, are you? You're not shouting and foaming at the mouth.'

'There isn't any cure, you know. How about that? Once the symptoms begin to show, it's all over.'

'You're driving me mad. Just eat your bloody chips. I don't care if you've got rabies or not.'

Our first experience of French cuisine – if you exclude the rock-hard croissant we shared on the ferry deck while waving at the white cliffs of Dover – was at a roadside café outside the French port of Cherbourg. The meal had begun badly with Margaret petting a thin cat that was mooching around our table and then screaming it had scratched her, which it hadn't. On the ferry there were warning posters everywhere. Rabies was rife on the continent. Margaret had taken the threat to heart.

Roadside cafés in France were entirely different to the ones we had at home. For one thing the menu was in French and they served hot meals instead of just crisps, tea and sandwiches. It was early in the afternoon but most people were drinking wine with their chicken and their steaks and their fishes grilled with their heads on. The food smelt good and unusual. It didn't smell of dishcloths and old grease. There were candles in wine bottles on the tables, and plastic flowers in dainty glass vases. There wasn't any butter for the bread.

Ray ordered our food in French, which impressed Mum and me but not Margaret. The waiter brought chocolate milk in heavy brown bottles for me and Margaret, and a jug of red wine for Mum and Ray. The chocolate milk was especially good; it was dark and rich and strangely grown-up, and nothing like the Nesquik we drank at home. After that we ate thin chips and mussels, which looked like giant cockles and Ray said were called *moules marinière*. They were fiddly to eat. You had to dig about in the navy-blue shells with your fork and pull out the slippery globs of meat, which were sweet and chewy. Mum made us dip our bread – round and crusty instead of square and soft – into the deep pools of juice at the bottom. It tasted so creamy and delicious that I became desperate for Margaret to try some.

'Go on,' I said. 'It's out of this world. It really is out of this world.'

'I'm full,' she said, toying with her chip.

Back in the camper van I fell in and out of sleep and dreamt of foreign voices and the stink of frying fish and the incessant honking of car horns. The van seemed to bob up and down as we drove, as if the four of us were still all at sea. It was long after dark by the time we reached the campsite and there was nothing to see at first, except for tree trunks and lines of tents lit up with candlelight and torches. Some of the tents had tables outside and families sat reading books and drinking wine and playing cards. Children tore about in the grass, playing chase and collecting pine cones, while mothers called out in lazy voices for them to come in to bed. Everyone was shoeless and wore slip dresses or shorts and T-shirts and one couple were dressed in their towels. I had never been anywhere like it in my life. There were live chickens gathered in a coop by one of the caravans. In the distance someone played a guitar.

'Well,' said Ray. 'Is it how you imagined it?'

'Oh it's wonderful,' Mum said.

I don't know what time we stayed up to that first night; no one seemed to notice or ask. When we arrived late at the B&B on the Isle of Wight, Dad would tell us all to shush and we'd immediately turn the lights out and go to bed so as not to keep anybody up. No one told us to shush on the campsite and only when the torches stopped going back and forth to the shower block did Mum say we'd better call it a night. Mum and Ray would have the camper van all to themselves, while Margaret and I shared a tent. It had a ground sheet and thick pads to lie on and each of us had a sleeping bag and inflatable pillow.

I lay wide awake for a long time, listening to the sound of the outdoors: owls hooting, crickets cheeping, bonfires dying and petering out. Our new world was full of excitements and delights, stranger than the first day at school.

'Are you asleep?' I said to Margaret.

'No,' she said.

'What are you thinking about?'

'Nothing much,' she said. 'Just wondering what Dad might be up to.'

I thought about saying, He's probably trying to get into Joni Lightfoot's underpants, but I didn't. My sister didn't know anything about that or realize it was the one good reason that Dad had let Mum and Ray take us on holiday.

30

Out of the dying embers of my loyalty to Dad I tried not to make it the best holiday I'd ever had in my life, but everything conspired against me. In the morning I woke to the smell of eggs frying and bacon sizzling, cooked up on Ray's portable stove. There was fresh bread and jams to go with it and more bottles of the sweet chocolate milk that became the vacation's official drink. In the daylight you could see how unusual our surroundings were and how far we had travelled from home. We seemed lost in a clearing in the middle of a forest, enclosed by pine trees whose oval cones and scented needles carpeted the floor. It was wild, messy and sunny, full of shadows and places to hide. There were no brick houses for as far as the eye could see, no hot dog stands, no amusements, no aquarium. No red-skinned, hard-breathing, fat, gloomy men wearing plastic sandals and hats made out of handkerchiefs.

Along a pathway through the trees was a bright blue swimming pool signalled by its perfume of chlorine. Behind that stood the wooden campsite shop. It sold the chocolate milks, bread, wine and eggs that I paid for each morning with the francs Ray gave me, and unusual things like chocolate cherries and almond pie and snails in shells, and cooked pressed ducks in a can of fat. At night it dispensed whole roast chickens from a spit and baskets of *frites* to the campers who didn't want to cook. Mum had never made roast chicken like it in her life, nor had Nanna, come to that. Ray said it was because of the rosemary and garlic they used to flavour it and I wondered if this was how the frozen chicken Kievs might have tasted if the unexpected visitors had ever come and we'd got around to eating them.

We ate the chicken straight from our fingers, catching the drips of fat with our paper serviettes. Mum said we'd spend the whole of the next day at the beach, which was wide and soft and lined with dunes and umbrellas. The pleasure was almost too much to bear. My only disappointment, if you could call it that, was that I hadn't seen a single stripy top or black beret.

I annoyed Margaret with how cheerful I was and probably should have tried to hide it from her better. To pay me back for talking to Ray at breakfast and telling him that his eggs were OK she decided to make friends with a girl called Francine and ignore me for the bulk of the holiday. Francine's dad was English but her mother was French and so Margaret soon learnt the ways of French girls and lorded her expertise over me. The duck in a can was called *confit*, the snails in shells were *escargots*. Every day was full of comments that started with Francine says this and Francine says that and Francine's mother says the other.

'Francine thinks Mum is overweight. Don't you think Mum is getting fat?'

Mum sat on her beach towel with her toes in the sand, reading a book about being scared of flying. She looked calm and pink and happy. She had on a one-piece swimming costume decorated with plastic flowers at the hip. Mum didn't wear a swimming costume much. There wasn't a lot of sun bathing to be done in the Isle of Wight since the sun hardly shone and the beach was rough and stony instead of golden and soft. I hadn't looked at her properly for a long while but, staring at her then, I had to concede she looked a little lumpy around the middle. It probably had to do with her being in love, an opinion I declined to share with Margaret.

'I think she looks fine. She looks pretty, as a matter of fact.'

'You think those earrings suit her?'

'What's wrong with them?'

'Francine says you wouldn't catch a French woman dead wearing earrings like that.'

The earrings were wooden like her strings of beads – which seemed to be multiplying and appearing in endless different colour combinations – but I liked them and told Margaret as much.

'You wouldn't understand,' my sister said, haughtily. 'You don't know anything about fashion or style.'

For her part Margaret had taken to wearing a baggy shirt over her swimming costume, and she never took it off because she never went into the sea even though it was warmer and cleaner than any we'd ever swum in, with no tampons or turds to be seen. I could spend hours in it, on my back, in the shallows, letting the waves wash right over me. I could swim all the way to the rocks and straight back again without getting out of breath because the tide was so generous and gentle.

As often as I could I told Margaret what she was missing, but I never managed to coax her in past her knees. She hardly sunbathed either and missed out on that hot, pinched feeling you get after long hours in the sunshine. She sat in the shade with Francine and gossiped about actresses and pop stars and who was thin and pretty and who wasn't. She never once shone from the coating of sun oil on her skin or smelt tropical and intoxicating like Ambre Solaire. I supposed it all had to do with her wanting to be fashionable and stylish. But it didn't.

★   ★   ★

It wasn't that I grew to like Ray over the course of the week, it's more like he stopped annoying me quite so much. We came to some agreement or other in which I stopped ribbing him about his outfits and his hippydom in general and he stopped asking me so many questions about my feelings.

'It's unnatural,' I told him once, when we set off for another round of spit-roast chicken, 'for someone to ask you what you think about things all the time.'

'I'm interested, that's all.'

'No, you're not. You're blind nosy.'

'Your mum likes it when I ask how she's feeling.'

'I don't need to know about that.'

'No,' Ray said, in an understanding way that was typical of the way he tried to aggravate me.

'What about Margaret?' he said, as we moved up the queue. 'How is she getting along?'

'She doesn't like you, that's all. She's punishing everyone. Except really she's punishing herself.'

'How so?'

I sighed because it was obvious and sometimes Ray seemed unbelievably thick for someone who had a degree in psychology.

'Because it's nice here,' I said. 'It's amazing, in fact. I've never been anywhere like it in my life. No one looks at you funny or cares about your business, and I don't feel like we're freaks in the least. I like it how everyone runs around in the evening until it's late and there's guitar music playing and no stupid television, and the beach is just incredible, and sleeping outdoors makes you wake up hungry.'

'It does?'

'It does. And the thing is, I'll probably move to France one day and open a campsite of my own, and the point is it's Margaret who's always on about travelling to strange places and foreign parts but she's here now and she's not getting the best of it and I keep telling her she's missing out but she doesn't take any notice and if you ask me she'll be sorry by the time we get back home. It's really very simple,' I said, catching my breath. 'Nanna would say she's cutting her nose off to spite her face.'

'Because of me and your mum?'

He was slow to catch on, what can I tell you?

At the front of the chicken queue Ray picked out a large one with crispy skin, and a lady called Odette wrapped it in a layer of special paper that stopped it from burning your hands. I noticed that it was almost all men in the queue, men with one or other of their children. It seemed strange to me that at home it was the women who bought the chickens and cooked the chickens, but out here on the campsite it was the men who queued up to buy them. I wondered if this was something to do with the macho quality of the spit roast or the fact that we were in France; or perhaps it had to do with how pretty Odette was and how many buttons she undid on her blouse.

'I'm glad you're enjoying yourself,' Ray said, as we walked back to the tent. 'I was nervous about it, you know.'

I wanted to say, So you should have been, but instead I said, 'That's OK.'

'Your mum too, of course. She's so happy that you came. I've never seen her quite this happy.'

I wanted to say, That's because she's with us, her family, that union that you ruined, and if you had any shred of decency you'd sod off and give her back to us. But I didn't. Instead I said, 'Well . . . that's good.'

Ray looked awkward then, in that peculiar way he had of changing from confident to shrewish in a heartbeat. It was like sometimes you didn't notice his spectacles and sometimes you did.

'I imagine you're worried about the future.'

'I hadn't thought about it,' I said, which was true, at least for that last week.

'Things will sort themselves out, you know. Between your mum and your dad. Six months from now, a year maybe. In cases like these the adults sometimes turn out to be good friends.'

'Oh no,' I said immediately. 'That's not going to happen. Dad could never be friends with a man who wears pyjamas in the daytime.'

Ray smiled until I didn't notice his stupid spectacles quite so much.

When we got back to camp we were still in good spirits and Margaret caught my eye and gave me a look that was all daggers and almost put me off my chicken. We'd come here to pull them apart, Mum and Ray, hadn't we? That's how I'd sold it to Margaret. And here I was behaving like I'd gone for a stroll in the park with a friend, bringing back the dinner that she couldn't eat with a smile on my face. She ate twice as many chips as anyone else did that night, one after the other, and three slices of almond pie that up until now she hadn't liked. After that she went to the shower block alone, with her sponge bag, even though I offered to go with her. Mum lay back on the grass with her book after that and Ray patted her tummy gently from time to time. They'd been careful about not kissing or hugging or doing anything else disgusting in front of the two of us but this level of affection I could just about stand if I didn't look either one of them in the eye. I imagined the tummy patting had to do with him teasing her about how much she had eaten but it would later turn out to be something different.

31

Going home was difficult. Taking down the tent made me cry. I hid one of its wooden pegs in my wash bag as a keepsake even though this would cause problems for Ray the next time he came to put it up. When our time was over I waited on the front seat of the camper van with Mum while Ray went off to fetch Margaret, who was saying her third set of goodbyes to Francine. Mum said I had the look of a condemned man about me and that I made the same noises as Dad's huffs and puffs.

'It won't be so bad,' she said, taking off her string of wooden beads and lowering them over my head. 'Things are on the up now, aren't they? You and Ray got on OK and Margaret will come round soon enough.'

I tried to speak but found I couldn't.

'I've been meaning to say,' she said, setting the necklace on my shoulders, 'that when we get back to England, when things are sorted out, I want you and Margaret to live with me.'

I lowered my head. I took my time studying the beads.

'I mean, if that's what you'd like,' she said, cupping my chin. 'I wasn't always sure how things would turn out . . . for me and Ray . . . but I didn't plan on leaving you . . . no, not for a second. I'd always planned to take you both with me.'

Something about her saying this made me cross. I wanted to say, Come on, then, why didn't you? What are you waiting for? Let's go.

Instead of this I said, 'And so . . . but what about Dad?'

Mum nodded. She tried to look like she had it all worked out.

'Well, you'd live with him too, I expect. For some of the time. I know he would like that. Once he finds a new place, there'll be a room for the both of you. And now you know how things are . . . perhaps you'll come to Ray's house at weekends. If you want to . . . until things are settled.'

It seemed logical, of course, given the week we'd had, but I didn't see how things could be the same when we got back to England. Out here things weren't real; they were dream-like and sunny and simple, with no school, no headmasters, no period pain; no Dad, no Joni, no Nanna. By the end of the day we'd be back in the beige house, on the plain, tree-less street, wearing our hard shoes in the rain. Our situation would be a situation again. Things that seemed acceptable would cease to be acceptable.

'Are you worried about your dad? Is that it?'

'I do . . . but I just . . .'

'He'll come around, you know,' Mum said, clearing the hair from my eyes. 'I know he was a bit up and down before we came away on holiday but I'm sure the break has done him a lot of good.'

'I'm not . . . so sure.'

'It's OK, you know, that you came. He doesn't expect you to take sides.'

I'm sure she believed this but I knew very well it wasn't true. If Dad had been the one to run off with someone young, Mum would have taken our loyalty for granted. In Dad's mind there was a wrong and a right to all this. Going to France with Ray might mean we would never be forgiven.

In truth it would mean that *I* would never be forgiven, since Margaret had successfully managed to keep her guard up.

'What about . . .'

'Jess, I don't think you need to think about that any more.'

'But . . . I do.'

'Listen,' she said, taking her time to choose her words, 'your sister's just coming so let's not go into it all again. When people are hurting, they do things that are quite out of character. You've been such a grown-up girl about everything up to now. Will you try to forgive your dad this time? For me?'

Margaret climbed into the camper van. She had watery eyes and wore a red and yellow friendship bracelet knotted around her wrist. I scrambled from the front seat to the back seat to join her, quietly promising Mum that I would.

The journey home set our lives into rewind and seemed like the unravelling of pleasure. There was no singing or lunch stops at roadside cafés and the nearer we got to Dover the paler my skin became and the colder and stiffer I felt. Our country was bathed in its gloom. It greeted us with its drizzle and its tarmac and its weather forecasts, and even the pine cones that I'd stuffed in my pockets seemed to have lost their medicinal, sunshine smell. Mum and Ray dropped us off at Nanna's and I politely shook Ray's hand and said thanks. Margaret didn't bother to say goodbye to him and Nanna didn't bother to ask us how the holiday had been. She saw the looks on our faces and called us sourpusses and said she had known it would be like that all along.

Dad had made a huge effort. There were jam sandwiches laid out on the table when we got home the next day and a glass jug filled up with orange squash. Everything was tidy and polished on account of him having taken on a cleaner called Pam who came in and 'did' two weekday mornings and would even take care of the washing and the ironing. He had dressed nicely and shaved and was trying hard to be cheerful and not to be snippy about the holiday or camping, or France in general.

'You had good weather, I heard. I kept my eye on the weather. They have the French forecast in the papers.'

Margaret rolled her eyes as if this was unsophisticated behaviour.

'Things were quite different to the Isle of Wight, I imagine? Took some getting used to, I'd expect?'

Margaret drank her juice down in elaborate gulps and then some surprising stuff came out. She said the jam in the sandwiches was nothing like French jam and that French jam was fruitier and more sweet. She was sick of squash actually and wondered if Dad had any chocolate milk in the fridge, but made it clear that Nesquik wouldn't do. Jessie had eaten chicken with garlic every night and why didn't Dad like things like garlic? Even though Margaret hadn't tasted it herself she had thought that it smelt very good. She rubbed it right into him for the rest of the evening: the sea we had swum in, the languages we had heard, the late nights, the camp fires, the music. She didn't go so far as to mention Ray and his singing or his ability with a portable stove, but I felt she was a heartbeat away from doing it.

'Well, I'm glad you enjoyed yourselves,' said Dad, clearing away the half-eaten sandwiches. 'That's what's important. That's the main thing.'

In bed that night, as she rustled with her secret papers under her covers, I asked Margaret why she'd been so rough on Dad.

'I liked Joni,' is what she said. 'I thought she was nice and that we might have been friends.'

'You *know* about what happened?'

'I was right behind you on the stairs, I'm not an idiot. I know a whole ton of stuff that you don't know about.'

I felt a little blindsided by her then and didn't know what I was meant to do or say. In the end I repeated what Mum had said, that when a person was hurting as much as Dad was it could make them behave entirely out of character.

32

Dearest Broo,

One evening late last week Andrew Linton called around and behaved in a way that was entirely out of character. It is fair to say things had been brewing for some time and you were right to think our involvement must come to a head.

We had been running into one another more and more often lately, since summer brings forth its rash of parties and events. Dispiritingly, this increase in our contact did nothing to mend our frustration and I'd go so far as to say it was becoming unbearable to see him. I found it a strain to remain sanguine in company and to pretend that seeing him with Yolande in tow, which she very often was, didn't hurt me.

As awkward as it was, we developed a routine of sorts for these occasions. At some point or other in the evening I would excuse myself from the main room of the party and find a smaller, secluded place where I

would wait for Andrew to join me. In these minutes
we would catch the mood of one another and engage in
some looks, a touch if we felt brave, a carefully judged
yet loaded conversation. To begin with I cherished these
excitements and sought them out, but weeks of them left
me feeling quite worn out. The anxiety of it all was such
that I felt I was being dangled from a cliff by a string
which might be cut in two at a moment's notice. Yolande
might call to him from the next room or a mutual friend
might join us without warning and when they did I
would resent them, even the ones I had affection and
regard for. The remainder of the evening would be spent
in stares and smiles, and an awkward regimen of
punishment or reward depending on which of us had
been chiefly responsible for curtailing our conversations.

Enough was enough and so I decided to put an end
to it one evening at Teddy Hallam's, when the brush of
Andrew's hand along my forearm caused me some
annoyance instead of the usual excitement. He
demanded to know what was wrong and so I told him. I
had grown weary of our furtive assignations, I said, and
since there was no obvious resolution to be had I had
decided it was preferable to give them up. His look was
all charm then, and close to a dare, and it suggested I
would never keep it up. As you well know it is a foolish
man who sets me a challenge, and as much as I adored
him and his look at that moment, I resolved to keep my
distance from him.

From that night on I took to ignoring him in public
and made a point of seeking out other people whom I
liked and with whom I had failed to keep in proper
contact. I would notice him disappear into the usual
anterooms and hallways but even after minutes I would
not follow him. On your advice I curtailed our telephone

calls by making sure I was out when he rang, since I
didn't believe I had the strength not to answer had I
been at home. It was quite the hardest task I have ever
set myself, Broo. I would rather have walked over ice
flows.

It was a Tuesday night when it happened, which
seems so innocuous, doesn't it? I had been for a meal
with Teddy at Claridge's and had hardly been home
thirty seconds when the pounding began at the door. It
was Andrew and he was drunk and the first thing he
told me was Yolande had gone up to her mother's. I
said, 'Well done, Yolande,' and this sarcasm wasn't
received at all well but I invited him in nevertheless. I
keep gin on the sideboard for cocktails and he immediately availed himself of a generous glass even though it
was clear he had taken quite enough.

What was going on, he wanted to know. Why was I
dining with Teddy? Why didn't I answer the phone? Why
had I ignored him on the last two occasions we had
met? I reminded him of my decision and he brooded on
it then, and looked pitifully close to tears. Wasn't it
punishment enough for him to be living with a woman
who bored him? A woman without class or education
who sold her affections to him with the connivance of a
prostitute? Wasn't it enough that she kept herself availed
of his whereabouts at all times of the day and the
evening and smothered him like a baby's nanny? Over
the months I have made clear to you my feelings about
Yolande but even I felt uncomfortable to hear her
described in this way. And so, since I was feeling
resilient from a social evening and fine supper, I told
him so. The walls came down then and out it poured.
How dare I take the role of Yolande's defender? He had
never come across such duplicity in his life. After all we

had been up to, over so many months, how dare I lecture *him* about his morals? At that point I made the not unobvious point that we had, in fact, been up to all but nothing.

It is hard to know if it was this statement that caused it all or my insistence that I would have to call Teddy if he didn't calm down immediately and leave. Yolande had made it difficult, didn't I see that? Did I imagine that he hadn't longed to see me? Hadn't our separation caused him pain? These were words I might ordinarily have longed to hear but he stood up, full of spite, and began to shake them directly into me. Did I think he lacked the courage, he wanted to know, to properly consummate our affair? If there was nothing going on between the two of us, he said, then it was terrifically easy to remedy.

This next part is difficult to write and I have gone over it a hundred times or more, wondering if perhaps I deserved it all. It's uncanny the speed with which his idea gained momentum until there seemed no chance at all of his backing down. He strode around the apartment for some seconds working up to everything that was coming. He is tall and slim, as you know, but there was a metamorphosis about him in those moments in which he took on the appearance of a bull. He had his hands clasped at my shoulders and his face pressed on to mine, and then his fingers at the buttons of my blouse. I couldn't open my mouth to speak since his mouth was pressed to mine so tightly and so hard, and the mixture of sensations, the smell of alcohol, the push of his fingers, the impact of his hefty body, left me reeling and quite off my guard.

When finally he pulled his lips away, my bones came back at once and I shouted at him to leave me and to stop. 'This is what you want, Edith, isn't it?' he said. 'You would have in the cave, if I had asked you?' I felt confusion then, since there was truth in his words and there is no way to pretend that I had not longed for him physically. 'Not like this,' is all I said to him, over and over. 'Not *this* way. Don't make it be like this.'

I should have screamed louder, you would say that I should have, and yet I choked then and found that I couldn't. My shouts became silence and I stared at some small point on the ceiling as he went about it all and while he finished. I imagined myself somewhere else in the world as his hands compressed my skin and his hips left their bruises on my hips.

There were small tears in my blouse that I noticed in the morning and not a shred of tenderness in it all to remember or to act as some comfort. It was fast and furious and meant to wear me down, and was the logical conclusion of all our punishments. He left while I was sleeping and so I must have managed to close my eyes at some late point. I bathed for a long time that morning but failed to dress or even to brush my hair. I'm not entirely inexperienced, Broo, and so it is not about that, but the humiliation of it all is quite something. It is my own fault, I am sure, which makes it so very much worse. How pathetic to imagine he loved me.

He phoned me some days later, though I didn't count how many, and in any case our conversation was mercifully brief. He was unable to call sooner since Lillian had been taken ill with a cold that had settled on her lungs. Yolande had nursed her round the clock until she rallied and I could not imagine how frightening it all had been. There was no mention of us, or what had happened, nor a stroke of the old softness in his voice. Though I hardly cared by then, I knew our bubble had been burst and that all his curiosities about me had been dealt with. It was entirely the end of things, and as if to make this plain he drove it home by telling me, with all sincerity, that Yolande was a wonderful wife and mother. I felt bereft then, empty and quite hollow, aware in an instant I was mourning something greater still than him.

And so another voyage and journey beckon. Another race to the back of beyond. I wish I had the strength and courage to remain here in London since the running makes it all seem so much worse. But today I find I long to feel the heat of the Egyptian sun on my skin, and the surprise of this is close to encouraging. You were right, my dearest darling, about everything, and I shall listen to you always in future. But all is done with now and I can think of no better treatment than to vanish from it all for a time. If only the leaving could be quicker. I feel seasick already and am yet to set foot aboard the wretched boat.

Always yours,
Edith

33

Margaret was cock-a-hoop. It was six and a half weeks since she'd had her first period and since then not a cramp nor a single drop of blood. I told her that periods could be irregular to begin with but my sister had it in her mind that she'd never get another for as long as she lived. It was almost enough, but not quite, to make her try a spoonful or two of Dad's scrambled egg.

Dad had taken to cooking in the mornings. It was all part of his new popularity drive and a direct response to Margaret letting slip, on purpose, that Ray cooked for us each morning on the campsite. His first impulse on hearing about a man who could cook was to write Ray off as a fairy, but Margaret said it was a modern thing for a man to be able to do, so Dad had taken to going to bed with Delia Smith. There were half a dozen recipes in his repertoire now: various eggs, pork chops, lamb chops, nut roast, apple baked with currants, baked peppers stuffed with rice and a decent shepherd's pie. No one knew why he bothered with the baked apple. None of us liked it, least of all him.

'Still no eggs, Margaret?'

'No eggs, Dad. Just toast.'

'Butter?'

'Yes, please. Lots.'

Margaret drank two glasses of water while she waited for her toast and gulped them down quickly one after another.

'You're thirsty?'

'Yes.'

'One glass wasn't enough for you?'

'No. And anyway Francine says lots of water is good for you. French women know about these things. It flushes you out.'

I squirmed in my chair, partly on hearing the scrappy French girl's fancy name and partly because it seemed to me that Margaret was talking a lot like Nanna these days. She'd be drinking syrup of figs and discussing her number twos before you knew it.

'Pamela is in today,' said Dad, scraping soft eggs and streaky bacon onto my plate. 'So everything will be tidy and ironed when you get home from school.'

Dad referred to Pam the cleaner as Pamela and his extra familiarity annoyed me. But the eggs he'd made were good and it seemed to me that an ironed school uniform was marginally preferable to a creased one.

Margaret was struggling with her toast. She'd loaded it up with too much butter and the bread was so fresh and warm it looked like she'd coated it in sauce.

'Oops,' she said. 'Too much.' She squeezed the toast lightly, like it was a cloth she was wringing out, until most of the butter had drizzled into a fatty pool on her plate. She picked at it then, tearing the mangled slice into pieces and carefully removing all the crusts. At the end of her meal there was still some left over but it was scrunched into damp balls in the butter. I'd seen her open and close her mouth and chew several times but it was difficult to know if anything had actually gone down. Dad gave us Sandwich Spread sandwiches for our packed lunch that day with Penguin chocolate biscuits on the side. Margaret said, 'Ooh, Penguins,' but I had an uncomfortable flashback just then and worried she'd give her biscuit to Ian Warrington.

At school I was becoming something interesting. Hardly any of my school friends went on holiday during term time and if they did it was hardly ever as far away as France. A few of my classmates had been to Spain and one had even been on a cruise. Darren Low – who had been kept down a year for repeatedly failing his exams – had once been all the way to Disney World. We nodded to one another knowingly as I bragged about Odette and the chicken and swimming pool, and the general ambience of the campsite. We were paid-up members of the jet set, the two of us, even though I had yet to set foot on a plane.

It seemed to me that the back row of the classroom, where I'd decided to take my post-holiday seat, was markedly more interesting than the middle. The strange mix of miscreants and troublemakers that Rebecca and I studiously avoided had turned out to be mostly all right. They were a tough bunch, who you had to work on, but my parents' divorce, my sister's weird haircut and my recent penis episode with the head-master meant they accepted me into their clique a little faster. In the back row I wasn't the only pupil with problems, which made me feel less of an outcast. Sara from the council flats had never met her dad. Bradley – who had a habit of putting his face unnervingly close to yours when he spoke to you – reckoned his dad had two completely different families. Lisa had no problems at home that she could think of but still stole lunch money off the girls in the first year and so it seemed to me she must be naturally mean-spirited. Hailey's mother was dead. Gavin's dad was still going bankrupt.

'Did you have sex on holiday?'

'Sod off, Gavin.'

'So you did?'

'You're still a prat, then?'

'Uh? Yeah.'

This sophisticated exchange with Gavin got me to thinking. It seemed to me that Mum was right and that problems at home were an excuse for behaving out of character and generally badly. Dad had done it, as had Mum and Margaret, but I had kept control of myself. I wanted to do a bad thing and it irked me as I made my way home from school, through the underpass and up Lordship Avenue and past the building site that was Edith's old house, that the best bad thing I could think of at that moment was having sex in the park with Gavin Hillier.

Pam the cleaner was busy with a feather duster. She cleaned and tidied in a completely different way to Mum. She never got dirty herself or raised a sweat and if you'd been feeling uncharitable, which I was at that moment, you'd say she mostly just stirred the dirt around.

'You missed a bit,' I told her.

'Did I? Where?'

I wanted to say, All over the place, but instead I said, 'There, behind the telly.'

She started on the vacuuming then, and the Hoover whined and hummed because its bag was full to bursting, but Pam was too lazy to bend down and change it for another one.

'He's a good man, your dad,' she said, as she missed out the corners of the carpets. 'Such a shame. Such a shame. And bringing up you two girls on his own, now. That can't be easy, I shouldn't think.'

Pam had hair that flicked up at the edges, blonde and rigid with hairspray. I imagined that on her best days she thought she looked like Farrah Fawcett-Majors. It wasn't that she was unattractive, she was pretty in a cheap sort of way, but to me she looked brittle and worn out. She was young to be a cleaner, since I imagined most cleaners would be old. It was a job you did because things had gone wrong in your life and I wondered what had gone wrong for Pam so early.

'My two girls are four and eight, so I know how hard it is,' she said, expertly rolling a cigarette. 'I've brought them up on my own, but that's easier because I'm their mother.'

'What about their dad?'

'He left when the second one was born. Couldn't stomach it.'

I didn't ask her what he couldn't stomach and instead I asked her how old she was, since this suddenly seemed important even though it was cheeky to ask.

'Twenty-seven,' Pam said. 'How old are you?'

'Almost fifteen.'

'Nice age for a girl.'

'Is it?'

'Yes. Everything still to look forward to.'

'My mum's not left us, you know,' I said then, because I felt it needed explaining. 'We're going to go and live with her soon. And sometimes with my dad. When things are all sorted out.'

'The divorce, you mean?'

'That's it.'

'Might get messy. It did for me and Kenny. At one point he said he was taking the kids even though it was the kids that drove him off me in the first place. He was a nasty man, was Kenny. Had a right nasty streak about him.'

I wondered if he'd hit her but I didn't want to say that, so instead I asked, 'Nasty how?'

'He didn't like me wearing perfume. Have you ever heard the like of that? A man who doesn't like his wife in perfume.'

It was hard to know where Pam the cleaner was going with this but then a plan hit me and I ran with it.

'Dad told me he thought your perfume was very nice.'

'Did he?'

'He said it reminded him of gardens.'

'It's musk.'

'Is it?'

'So it's not very floral.'

'Well, I wouldn't know about that. But anyway, he definitely said it suited you.'

Pam brightened at my made-up compliment. She whistled happily while she didn't clean the crumbs from inside the toaster and merely polished its edges. I had done a bad thing, though I wasn't sure who to, and it didn't feel as good as I'd expected. Knowing my luck she'd mention the musk mistake to Dad and he would end up propositioning her and marrying her. I wasn't at all sure that I fancied sharing a house part-time with Pam the cleaner and her two girls. I wondered if they all bleached their hair like that, until it was raw at the roots.

I balled up a piece of the homework I was doing and aimed it at the waste-paper bin. If I got it in first time then we wouldn't have to go and live with Pam the cleaner. If I missed then we certainly would. There was a lot riding on this throw and as the paper left my hand I closed my eyes. Perfect shot. Perfect landing. Relief. Because I was perverse like that I decided to go over and pick it out again and risk my life's future to the best of three. There was something else scrunched up at the bottom of the bin, an envelope of thick, creamy paper. I smoothed it out, wondering where its insides had gone, and saw that the masthead on the envelope read Arthur, Chase and Pelmont. I didn't know any kind of business that had three names in a row, other than undertakers and solicitors.

34

Dad didn't care for his older brother – our Uncle John – all that much so it was a surprise to see him and our Aunty Agata in the hallway at 10 a.m. on a Saturday morning. I was still in my pyjamas and usually I'd have been eating beans on toast on the settee and watching *Swap Shop* with Margaret, but my antennae said something weird was going on.

As usual, Aunty Agata had brought a bag of strange biscuits. These were made with cinnamon and poppy seeds and were thin and square and too crisp to eat without grating your tongue and almost buckling your teeth. The best bit about them was the sugar on top, and if you licked at it for long enough the whole thing became moist and just about edible.

Agata was Polish and Uncle John had met her when he was in the army and stationed briefly in Warsaw. Uncle John had only been in the army for three years before getting discharged on health grounds and taking up a career as a car salesman in Northampton, where he had lived with Agata and his two children – our cousins Lucas and Jane – ever since. He had never travelled abroad again, even to visit Agata's family, or done anything vaguely noteworthy or interesting save getting fat and joining the campaign for real ale. Nevertheless he flaunted his exoticism over Dad, who he seemed to regard as browbeaten and worryingly liberal, verging on left wing.

'How's life in the public sector?'

'Fine, how's life at the garage?'

'We're just driving a new Rover.'

'So I see.'

'It's got a radio and cassette deck built in.'

'Has it now?'

'No radio in the Cortina yet?'

'Not the last time I looked.'

'I keep telling you to come up. Why don't you come up? I could do you a deal.'

Agata invaded our kitchen, opening cupboards and drawers and setting out her hard biscuits on one of Mum's large oval plates with the pictures of vegetables around the edge. Margaret and I were loitering.

'How are you, sweethearts?'

'We're fine,' Margaret said. 'Why wouldn't we be?'

'So don't worry about anything. After tea I will make you some soup.'

'Will there be beetroot in it?' I said.

'You're staying for *lunch*?' Margaret said.

'John has important things to talk about with your father. John knows a lot about the law.'

I wanted to ask if this had anything to do with the VAT man nearly putting John in prison two years ago, but I didn't because it was a family secret.

'How is your mother?' said Agata, which seemed to me to be a loaded question.

'She's fine.'

'Her health is OK?'

'Why wouldn't it be?'

'So that's good,' said Agata, playing nice.

'And this man?' she said, raising her brow. 'You've met him, I understand? On your holidays?'

'I didn't like him, if that's what you're getting at,' I said. 'We're not being disloyal to Dad.'

Margaret gave me a look. 'Well, *I'm* not, anyway,' she said.

The set-up seemed to be that Margaret, Agata and I would sit in the living room breaking our teeth on the biscuits and watching Saturday-morning television while Dad and Uncle John took care of the serious stuff in the dining room. She was aware of our curiosity and frustration at staying put, and employed any number of devices to keep us sat where we were so we couldn't act as spies for our mother. We got to hear all about Lucas's achievements on the cello and more than we'd ever wanted to know about Jane's activities at the pony gymkhana. She went on and on about music lessons and horses' hooves and grooming and kit, and seemed to have an endless appetite for speaking about our cousins' out-of-school activities and her part in them, which seemed to me to consist of little more than driving them back and forth to various playing fields and church halls and shelling out shed-loads of money. Our out-of-school activities were confined to the park and the garden in summer, and our bedroom and the porch in winter. For this reason Aunt Agata pitied us and perhaps she was right. It wouldn't have killed Dad to drive us to the occasional after-school activity every once in a while. For my own part I'd always fancied taking up trampolining.

Half an hour into it I found my loophole and broke her guard by telling her I had to use the toilet and take a bath. I had a bath on Sundays usually so this was a bit of a red herring but Agata was fastidiously tidy and clean and I hoped this excuse would appeal to her and buy me more time. Margaret was wise to me on account of the bathing lie, but her face said she was prepared to give me back-up so long as I found out what was going on.

I dressed, brushed my teeth, combed my hair and splashed cold water on my face in five minutes flat. I calculated, at best, that I had another fifteen in the bag and could hear Margaret beginning on the history of the Mohawk Indians in a bid to keep Agata in her place. Dad and Uncle John were in the thick of it. They hadn't any reason to keep their voices down.

'It's a nasty business, that's all I can say.'

'I thought Joy would be fair.'

I heard Uncle John laugh.

'You think he's put her up to it?'

'What do *you* think?'

'It was only—'

'An indiscretion, you don't have to tell me. You think I've been faithful to Agata all this time?'

'Haven't you?'

'Come on, David. Be serious.'

'She's trying to say that it went on before.'

'It didn't?'

'No.'

'Then it's easy. This girl will just say so.'

'It's not . . . she . . . I made—'

'A fool of yourself.'

'Yes. Thank you.'

'It's a smokescreen. That's all it is. Let the bitch take it to court. This woman, what is she? Some tart from up the street. Who's going to believe you laid a finger on her?'

'I *didn't*.'

'Call Joy's bluff then.'

'I don't. . . .'

'Call her *bluff*.'

'What if . . .'

'Or lie down and let her shit all over you. Let her say you're a lousy father. Trying to fuck some woman who didn't want it while your kids were upstairs in the house.'

'That *isn't* how it was.'

'No? Doesn't matter. She'll twist it every which way to make it seem so. She'll get what she wants. And he'll get it too. His boots under your door, you prepared for that?'

'I can't believe it. I can't.'

'Christ, David . . . it's no time to feel sorry for yourself. Stand up and *fight*. Do you think I'd let Agata walk out on me? Into the sunset with the house and the kids after *screwing* around on me with someone else?'

'No. I don't.'

'I'd throttle her, that's what. I'd *throttle* her.'

'You never liked her, did you?'

'Agata?'

'Joy.'

'David, for fuck's sake. The woman can't even cook.'

Dad and Uncle John were silent for a time. My hands shook. I wanted to leave.

'Who told her about it?'

'Jess.'

'Jess? Perfect. Stupid, stupid little girl.'

I waited for my dad to defend me. But he didn't.

Agata made thin soup with beetroot and was the only one to finish her whole bowl. On the table I could see the letter from Mum's lawyers, plump with its threats and allegations, and I stared at it in the hope that it would burn.

'What's wrong with you?'

'Nothing,' I said.

'Finish your food.'

'Why don't you make Margaret finish her food?'

'I don't like beetroot.'

'It's bloody vegetarian. It's *good* for you.'

Uncle John sighed as if everything was getting out of hand and only he could be the one to truly handle it.

'Listen,' he said, addressing Margaret and me, and wiping his chin with a napkin. 'It's not easy for you two with your mum gone, and it's not my place to say it but I'm going to say it anyway.'

'John . . .'

'No. It's got to be said. Do either of you realize what she's done? She's been a whore. Do you know what that is?'

'*John.*'

'She's slept with another man. Had sex with him. That makes her less than nothing in our eyes, mine and your aunt's, and now she wants to take the house away from your dad. Everything he's worked for. Not her, see? *Him.* Did you know that your mother was a thief?'

'*Enough!*'

'Fine, *fine*. But they stopped being kids when *she* walked out the door. So they need to make their minds up, the two of them. Work out whose side they want to be on. And Jess, do you hear me? Some things you *don't* tell your mother.'

I had never seen my father like it. He would have punched his brother, I'm almost sure, if a part of him hadn't thought that Mum would find out and use it against him. He forced them out of the house with his words, all of Uncle John's hefty bulk. Their coats and shoes went on in a cloud and Agata looked frightened and said, 'Don't worry, my sweethearts.'

When they had gone the silence was everywhere and I stared hard at Dad for some seconds before I crumbled and ran to my room. 'I'm sorry,' I said. 'I didn't mean to do it. I'm so sorry.'

He followed me up there with Margaret. He perched on the dressing table while I lay face down on the bed and sobbed until my ribs hurt and my throat hurt. He didn't say anything, not for a long time, then this:

'Don't worry, Jess. It's OK, I promise. I've never liked beetroot soup either.'

35

Margaret whirled like a dervish. She called it dancing but it wasn't really, it was more like a compulsion to keep moving until she was wasted and out of breath. These episodes took place two or three times a day but lately they'd been happening more and more. If she kept going for a long time, twenty minutes or so, she'd note it down in her log book with a comment like: 'Twenty minutes this lunchtime. Long one! Good!' Otherwise she might say, 'Five minutes, useless or fair.'

Ray's garden was good for dancing. It was loose and overgrown, filled with plants and vines and cracked paving stones, littered with muddy pots and bicycle parts. Margaret used these obstacles like theatre props, nipping behind a set of bricks here, twirling with a broom handle there. You'd think she was Gene Kelly in *Singin' in the Rain*, except it wasn't raining and Margaret was an eccentric mover at best, not a good one.

At the back of Ray's garden was a shed that looked like it might blow over in a good gust of wind. It was nothing like Dad's shed at our house. Dad's shed was solid and green with a new pitched roof and was full of tools he didn't know how to use. Ray's shed was brown and had holes in its boards. It was filled up with rubbish.

'Why do you keep all this stuff?'

'I might need it one day.'

'What is this?'

'A kite.'

'But it's broken.'

'Nonsense, it's just a bit tangled. That will fly lovely, mark my words.'

I wasn't in the mood to mark Ray's words since I'd only come to visit him and Mum on sufferance. I liked them both much less since the Joni issue had come up in the divorce papers and it was touch and go whether I would ever forgive Mum for betraying me and mentioning it.

She came out to join us, all smiles. She carried a metal tray on which she'd balanced a bottle of lemonade, a packet of KitKats and a set of cups and glasses that didn't match. Nothing in Ray's house matched, not even his socks. It was a small terraced place, more like a cottage – two up, two down – without a driveway or even a porch to speak of. The windows were square and leaded and it was cramped and dark inside, even though every wall had been painted white in an attempt to make it feel bigger. Each room smelt of dusty books and stale patchouli and there wasn't a wall without a poster or a painting pinned to it. The posters were mostly about nuclear war, pyramids and Che Guevara, and the paintings were ones that Ray had done himself. A few of them looked like nothing at all. A few of them resembled people and were quite good.

At the top of Ray's staircase was a bathroom without a lock and set back from the garden was the tiny kitchen. It had a grey lino floor and wooden cupboards without doors that were filled with curry powders and wholewheat pasta and odd condiments. There were records lying everywhere: on chairs, on tables, on the carpet, on the stairs and peeping out from the bottom of the sofa. Some were naked and scratched, without their sleeves or even their protective dust covers.

The feeling you got when you walked into Ray's house was that no one cared too much about things. If you dropped something toxic on the carpet that might stain it, Ray would be unlikely to shout. The next day you'd have trouble picking out the stain anyway, since his carpets were navy blue and peppered with marks and bald spots already. In a strange way I sort of liked it. His house wasn't trying to impress anyone. There was a Russian balalaika in the hallway. Ray was teaching my mother how to play it.

'Margaret, will you come and sit down now?'

'Five minutes. Just give me five minutes.'

'What is she *doing*?'

'Expressing herself,' Ray said, approvingly.

The three of us ate KitKats and drank lemonade in the sunshine while we watched my sister express herself.

'I don't know where she gets her puff,' Mum said, sounding a lot like Nanna.

'She's a kid,' Ray said. 'Kids are full of puff.'

Mum eased into the Dad conversation gently and I kept my opinions to myself until I couldn't keep them in any longer.

'He totally *hates* me. And it's your fault.'

'He doesn't hate you, Jess.'

'He does. And I wish I'd never told you. I shan't tell you about anything, ever again.'

'Well, that won't help anyone.'

'It'll help Dad, so there.'

'You don't know what he's like.'

'What does *that* mean?'

'He was going to make things difficult.'

'No. You're wrong. Because that's *you*.'

Ray took his glasses off, spat on the lenses and rubbed them. His face looked naked and pasty.

'Jessie, your mother has worked every bit as hard as your

dad. She may not have gone out to an office every day, but she's made a good home for you all and been a good wife and mother for many years.'

'So?'

'So, your dad doesn't want to share any of what he was with your mother. He doesn't think she's entitled. He's playing a tough game and your mother had to get a little bit tough back with him. That's all.'

Mum sipped her lemonade from a cup with a chip in it. She looked unhappy about it.

'I put you in an impossible position, Jess. I didn't mean to . . . I didn't think . . . it would all come out so quickl—'

'Rah, rah **rah, *rah*!**'

'What's she doing now?'

'Singing.'

'With her fingers in her ears?'

'How can you *say* that? It was bound to all come out. We'd probably have been called up to be eyewitnesses or something.'

Ray refitted his glasses to his head.

'Is that how you feel, Jessie? That it's fair for your mother to be left with nothing?'

'*You've* got a house. Why can't Mum just share yours and leave Dad with ours and be done with it?'

'Well, this is *my* house. And I'm happy to share it and everything in it with your mother, and you and Margaret if it came to that. But think about it: doesn't your mother deserve half of what she helped your father build?'

I wanted to say, Not on your Nelly, given that she had screwed around on him and swapped him for wholewheat spaghetti and balalaika lessons.

But instead of that I said, 'I think I'd like to have another KitKat, please.'

★   ★   ★

Margaret didn't have an opinion on the house question. She said it didn't bother her one way or the other so long as she didn't ever have to sleep in bunk beds.

'What's wrong with bunk beds?'

'I don't like them.'

'Which bit of them?'

'The top and the bottom.'

'It seems unfair, though, doesn't it?' I said, now that I'd taken the time to think about it.

'What does?' said Ray, who liked to make us think that he worshipped at the altar of fairness.

'If Dad only gets half then Mum will end up with more.'

'How so?'

'She gets to share all yours as well. You could sell your house and add that to Mum's money and that way you'd have a nicer place to live than Dad.'

'She's smart, this one. I like her,' Ray said, in a way that made me detest him.

'Well, that doesn't seem right, then,' said Margaret, licking the chocolate coating off her KitKat. 'Because Dad didn't do anything wrong.'

Mum looked at her broken cup. I thought she might cry. Ray took the cup away and held her hand.

'Girls, your mother is feeling vulnerable today. It's difficult for her too. You should know that.'

Margaret blinked. Uncompromising.

'We just want to get things sorted out, that's all,' Mum said. 'Have things settled with the minimum of fuss.'

Ray put his arm around Mum's shoulders and I couldn't tell if the physical stiffness was with him or with her, but there was clearly an awkwardness about it. Here in his house – where she'd chosen to be – the two of them just didn't knit. His skinny frame resting against her full one; his narrow, bespectacled face pressed beside her round, clear and open one. She wore clothes that day that had patterns on them and my mother wasn't generally one for patterns. She had made the effort to look hipper and younger and more modern but there was something about her hairstyle and the way she held herself – her sharp angles on Ray's slouchy deckchair – that made her look like she was a relation of Ray's rather than his lover. Ray wore plastic sandals. Mum wore her leather flats with silver buckles. Whatever it was that had worked so well on holiday seemed unbalanced and out of kilter here. She seemed at odds with her hippyish outfit and looked bloated around the waist and about her middle. She seemed flushed too, somehow, too pink for the weak English sunshine, as if she had a permanent embarrassment about her. As the clouds came over and the air began to chill and make us pull our bodies inward, Mum let a tear fall down her cheek.

'It's so different,' she said. 'Everything here is so different.'

'But in a good way. It's different in a good way.'

Mum shook her head, no.

'I miss my girls. I miss my girls.'

'Of course you miss the girls. But they're here now, aren't they? Soon enough they can be here every day.'

'I'm not changing schools, if that's what you're thinking.'

'*Margaret.*'

'No, Mum. No way.'

Mum sniffed then and let another tear or two go but Ray said she wasn't to worry because feeling emotional was entirely normal in the first few months, especially given everything that had happened.

'I just want . . .'

'You're outside your comfort zone, Joy. Change is difficult, isn't it? Moving your life forward takes courage. We've talked about it, haven't we? Rocking the status quo, it's the hardest challenge we face.'

He had his face close to hers. He talked to her like she was his pupil.

'I don't know . . . I just . . . any more.'

'This is wonderful, Joy. It's an inspiring time. Think how happy we're going to be as a family.'

My fingers went cold, then my heart.

'First few months of what?' I said, rising up off my chair. 'First few effing months of *what*?'

'Your mother is going to have a baby,' Ray said, quietly and just like that.

Margaret was whirling like a dervish. She had her fingers in her ears. 'Rah, rah, *rah*,' she began to sing.

36

9a Cavendish Place
Fitzrovia
London
September 15th 1934

Dearest Broo,

The dress, since you ask, was a lovely one, cut from
shot silk in the deepest midnight blue, sewn by
Mummy's dressmaker from an Italian design by
Schiaparelli. Esther is a genius with cloth, an artist
even, and in any case what she managed to do for me
that evening was close to magic. The clever part was in
the cape she made, which in ordinary circumstances I
might have removed at the door but was able to keep
on wearing with no questions since it was cold, un-
seasonably so, in the hall, and some women with bare
arms were visibly shivering. The cape was made of
wool yet was fine enough and almost translucent, and
wrapped around my shoulders there was a fold that
dropped as far as my hip. I looked capable and elegant
and, I hope, a little pretty, and you'll be pleased to
know all was a success since no one asked a single
awkward question.

It was a charming affair and so exciting to be honoured in such a way. Did you listen to the broadcast on the wireless? I rather fluffed my acceptance, I thought, but it was more out of a sense of feeling overwhelmed than down to nerves or being unprepared. When they said my name and I stood up from my chair there was such generous applause that I felt touched by it. The first female fellow of the Royal Geographic to receive the Cuthbert Peek Award: an achievement indeed! I dedicated it, in part, to Hanson and the others who had been with me in Greenland but could not ask them to collect it with me, as had once been my intention, since this whole Luxor trip was named as being such a big part of it.

On Egypt I had to profess a certain amount of luck was involved, but I suppose luck is always a part of it. To come across another tomb like that, in a place crawling with archaeologists on their hands and their knees, is a blessing indeed and perhaps had to do with us not being archaeologists and looking in unexpected ways. One hopes that the find will prove to be as significant as everyone imagines, not unlike those of Tutankhamen, and indeed the fuss of it so far has been something to behold. And yet I couldn't help but think, as they handed me the prize, that they would have snatched it back at once had they known about my keeping the ruby bracelet. It is a small piece, made for a child, a prince no doubt, or a king. But it is delicate and so perfectly beautiful, Broo, that I decided when first I lay eyes on it that it mustn't sit alone in the dark any longer or spend its life on duty on some dusty museum shelf. As you know, I don't believe in curses and am happy in my heart that this bracelet was meant to be worn and to be loved by the living.

Of course, Andrew was present at the dinner and there was some satisfaction to be had in knowing he had been up for this too. I was good in not looking for him or for Yolande and if it seemed like our paths might collide at any point he was the one to switch direction and make his way to join another conversation. Yolande found me later to offer her congratulations which seemed decent and genuine enough. It is impossible to gauge what she knows and what she doesn't but, as was always the case with Yolande, her first instinct is to do the polite thing. At some moment while we were talking I longed to tell her the whole of it. At another, when the fire kicked off in my belly, I vowed to tell the whole of it to him.

The sickness in my stomach becomes most active after dinner and is lately quite debilitating, as if the tide itself ebbed and flowed in my belly. Nothing is digestible these days and the comfort of eating and of fullness is replaced with ordeal and acids. There was champagne to drink, but the sipping of it only made things worse, which is a shame since I could have done with its relaxing properties. As the evening wore on I was approached by so many strangers that I felt sure one would guess my situation. I tried to be patient with all who wanted to speak with me but there were times when I felt put upon and prickly.

The men and women who shook my hand seemed mostly happy for me and I felt envy and resentment from only a very small few. Some men who were older couldn't hide their resentment and some women who had kept their hats and gloves on felt I had overstepped the mark. There were mentions of the debacle in Africa that were meant to wound me but on the whole it was an atmosphere of great support. I should have been happy then, shouldn't I? Yet I couldn't help but wonder how their opinions of me might change if they new the truth. I am lucky, I suppose. Another week or so and there could have been no hiding it. I remember you just after this stage with Edwin, that day up at Monmouth in the snow when you held your waist and said you had popped. It was a delight to you, as I remember. It won't be in the least so for me.

I made a point of getting home just after midnight since it is preferable in these things not to be among the first or the last to leave. Teddy was my escort through all of it and made a wonderful one, appearing at my side when I needed him, corroborating stories and anecdotes and disappearing when he thought I could manage quite easily on my own. Should I marry him, do you think? How simple it would be. The thing is I think he just might do it. Take me in, with all my inconsistencies, to have me as his wife, and raise the child as his own. I haven't the time to find another man, Broo, so this would be my very last chance. Of course, I don't love him in that way, and so I suspect that is that, after all. I haven't the patience, I don't think – nor the strength, nor the frailty – to lock myself inside a loveless marriage.

There are opportunities appearing for me this season that I could only have imagined up to now. Offers of trips to Persia and the East Indies and a welcome return to Greenland, which has lately become my dream. I have had to put each of them on hold and hope that my reputation will see me through the six months plus of absence. It seems incomprehensible to some that I should drop off the map at such a moment. I should grab these chances with both hands while I can, and indeed when I began to make excuses for not doing so I couldn't help but think them lamentable. The story is this: I am off to the south coast to begin work on my memoirs and to study my recent diaries while they are fresh; I will return with a set of papers to publish by the spring and confirm my newest expedition before next autumn. Maybe I should have claimed something more pressing or glamorous, an illness, perhaps, or some weakness in the lungs, to explain these long months of confinement.

How will it be, Broo, can you say? I have moments when I long for it all to be over and know without a doubt that I want his bastard gone, and could not bear to see it, nor even to touch it. On other days I feel quite the reverse, and find this the more shocking still. At these times I am weak and if you said so for a minute I would rush up to stay with you and have the wretched baby there and be done with it. I can hardly be said to have played the good role up to now, and since we have money and privilege how much more difficult would it be? On the whole I do not think it would reflect badly on Frederick or even on you, as you suggested in your letter of the ninth. It is not as if you would be harbouring a criminal, after all. Just a silly woman. Just a sister.

Do not think me ungrateful, my dearest, you have done wonders in finding the right place. But I need to be sure that you are being true and honest when you say it is the good thing to do. It is a burden, I know, since without Mother and Father to lean on I am putting all the pressure on you. Just say the word and I'll forget all about it and be with you on the very next train. Everyone can know and dash the lot of them. What use is reputation to anyone? One cannot grow old on adventures alone.

Do write soonest, my dearest darling. The circles in my head are never ending.

Yours,
Edith

37

It was well into August but Margaret wanted Dad to put the heating on. Barbara Hill thought this was strange.

'It's a warm day.'

'I can't help that.'

'I didn't say you ought to help it.'

'Well, it doesn't feel that warm to *me*.'

My sister was dressed in flared jeans and a jumper and had her *Star Wars* T-shirt on underneath that: Princess Leia with a lightsaber in her hands and a transfer of R2-D2 on the back. Barbara had on a tea dress patterned with pansies that fell to her ankles, the sort an older woman might wear to a village fete.

'It's due close to Christmas, I hear?'

'Well, yes. That's what she told the girls.'

'Another one at her age. Has she thought this through, do you think? Has she thought what it will do to the three of you?'

'It came as quite a shock. Because I hadn't . . . but that's how it is.'

'Of course, of course. A shock in a year *full* of shocks.'

I'm not entirely sure at what point it was that Dad started to entertain Barbara Hill. A subtle shift in situations had taken place one way or another and it seemed to me she was now firmly in my father's camp. Something of the fun had gone out of it for Barbara and it had suddenly become much more serious. Mum had ceased to be the interesting and long-suffering party and had mutated into something more brazen.

'I'm shivering, Dad. Don't you care?'

'It's not like he can even support them both, can he? He doesn't earn much, from what I've heard.'

'Joy has her typing. She can always go back to that.'

'But for how long, though? She'll not have the time once the baby comes.'

'That's not my problem.'

'It isn't.'

'So, then.'

'Can I put it on, or what? The thermostat's right down at zero.'

'Margaret, for God's sake. It's *sunny*. It's hot. Why don't you go and run around outside?'

Barbara raised her eyebrows to show her support and to let Dad know she knew how young girls could be.

'My Julie was just like that,' she said, smoothing down the folds of her pansies. 'I expect,' she said, dropping her voice to a whisper, 'It's . . . *hormones*.'

'Sorry?'

'*Hormones*,' Barbara Hill said emphatically, in a voice that was suddenly much too loud.

'You're *Mum*'s friend, aren't you?' I said to her, right then. 'Why don't you go and drink tea at Mum's house?'

'Well,' Barbara said with irritation, 'she hasn't asked me for a while. But, truth be told, I was never all that keen on his herbal muck.'

She turned to Dad for approval but he didn't give it. Barbara annoyed him. He was too polite to say so.

'I'm going upstairs, then,' said Margaret

'Don't draw the curtains.'

'I can if I like.'

'It makes the house look like a morgue.'

'The light's too bright up there. It hurts my eyes.'

'Wear some dark glasses.'

'Dark glasses, are you *mad*?'

'Why is that mad? It's quite sensible.'

My sister went off to do whatever it was she did up there. Barbara Hill stared out of the window.

'I love what you've done with the garden, David.'

'I haven't done anything.'

'But still.'

In those first weeks after Mum's announcement Margaret and I went our separate ways. She craved her own company, the company of dark rooms and library books and secrets, while I craved people and pavements and the outdoors. I had made a new family of sorts: Sara Crowley, Lisa Wright, Hailey James, Darren Low, Bradley Bird and my old enemy, Gavin Hillier. When school finished for the summer one of them could always be found at the playground, moping by the roundabout or the swings; or sat outside the Wimpy Bar by the Odeon cinema; or smoking roll-ups in the green wooden bus shelter. Though no one had said it out loud, it was taken as read this private members' youth club would sustain us until the new term began.

Hailey James was always there before the rest of us. She was taller and louder and better-looking than almost every other girl. Her skirts were more flared, her hair was thicker and more flicked up at the ends. She was older and wiser and more experienced and often carried a Tizer bottle contaminated with a decent slug or two of vodka. She'd had sex with at least two boys to my knowledge, which made her a cross between queen bee and class slag.

'Darren will be here soon.'

'Shall we have a séance again?'

'It was good the last time.'

'No, it wasn't. It was crap.'

'The glass moved. I was shitting it.'

'Rubbish. It didn't. Gavin pushed it.'

Darren, the class hunk, arrived on cue in his zipped-up, tight leather jacket. He didn't look hot or flustered like the rest of us; he never did. He didn't say much. He didn't have to. I loved him. He loved Hailey. His jeans were done up with a safety pin.

'Whatcha.'

'Whatcha.'

'We were saying . . . about doing a séance.'

'No one brought the cards, though.'

'We could chalk up the letters on the ground.'

'I can't be bothered.'

'No, neither can I.'

Sara Crowley went home for lunch just after one, which left Hailey, me and Darren on our own. I kicked about for a bit and smoked their cigarettes but felt plain and like a spare part. I was wearing the same denim shorts and T-shirt that I'd worn the day before but had drawn black eyeliner on my lids to make the difference. Margaret said it made me look like I was developing an eye infection.

Hailey had on one of her perfect maxi denim skirts. I'd scoured every shopping rail in town and searched hard through Mum's catalogues but I'd never found a skirt to equal Hailey's. I wondered if she made them herself or went to a whole new town to buy them. This one was almost at her ankles and had a yellow broderie anglaise trim. It might have looked prissy on some girls but on her it looked glamorous and sexy. She had lipstick on too. It was orange. She had high-stacked sandals and a proper cleavage.

Gavin turned up then, which eased the awkwardness for

me and there was some talk of going to the pictures. We had money between us to buy a single ticket and the trick was for the person who had paid to let the others in through the fire exit once the film had started. The Odeon was showing *Close Encounters*. Hailey and Darren had already seen it.

'You two could go.'

'You want to?'

'We haven't got enough for the ticket.'

'We'll lend you.'

They lent us the extra fifty pence it cost for the single ticket so we would sod off and leave them both alone. They were probably heading to the park. They were probably going to have sex.

Gavin took an age to let me in through the fire exit. He had to work up the guts to sneak out past the usher, and by the time I got in there and got comfy in my seat Richard Dreyfuss was already going mad. I watched him mould his mashed potatoes into the shape of a mountain, and imagined Dad at home doing something similar: carving his chicken pie into the shape of a hippy, a hippy with glasses and a baby. I thought he might like to do this and that it might help. In a weird way I thought it helped Richard Dreyfuss.

Gavin and I snogged during the boring parts. We didn't fancy each other especially – not in the way I fancied Darren or the way I imagined Gavin fancied Hailey – but I concluded he was OK at kissing since I didn't have a lot to compare him to. He didn't try to do anything funny like touch my breasts or undo the button on my shorts and in the darkness of the cinema, with the space ship landing and the aliens coming, it struck me Gavin Hillier was mostly talk. I wondered if he had an erection and if I was expected to touch it. Hailey said you were meant to rub it up and down with your hand but I had no idea how hard I was meant to do it or for how

long or how I would know when to stop, so I didn't. When
the film finished and the lights came up Gavin made a point
of saying we weren't boyfriend and girlfriend. This annoyed
me. I didn't want to be Gavin Hillier's girlfriend. I wondered
if he'd have asked me to be his girlfriend if I'd rubbed his
erection.

Hailey and Darren were back from the park and had been
joined by some of the others.

'Look what Darren got me,' Hailey said.

She had something round and red in her hand. It looked
like something Joni Lightfoot might cook up from her
cupboard, something she might add to one of her stews.

'Look, see. It moves.'

The red thing pulsed on cue.

'It's a Mexican jumping bean. That's what it is. It has a
tiny worm inside and if you hold it in your hand you can
feel it moving.'

We took it in turns to hold the precious jumping bean and
it didn't so much jump as push and spasm in the heat of
your palm. Hailey was delighted with it nevertheless and told
us several times it was imported and incredibly rare. I realized as I took the bean from Darren that it was Hailey's
reward for having sex with him. Her envy-making skirt had
fresh mud stains at the hem and her hair was flatter than it
had been two hours ago despite her lacquering it solid with
hairspray. Darren seemed high on having sex. He smiled at
the day and at the world. He looked like he owned Hailey
James and her jumping bean and I wondered if they'd done
it in the toilets or out in the open air. I wondered if they'd
remembered to use a rubber Johnny.

'Where were you?'

'Cinema.'

'What did you see?'

'Close Encounters.'

'You want to see what I've got?'

'Show me if you want to. I don't care otherwise.'

Margaret held out her hand. I knew what it was right away.

'It's a Mexican jumping bean,' she said.

'I know what it is.'

'How come? Have you seen one already?'

'I've seen one today, as a matter of fact.'

'Oh. Because . . . they're pretty rare.'

'Where did you get it?'

'Gift.'

'From who?'

'No one in particular.'

'Fuck's sake, don't say Ian Warrington?'

My sister shut her eyes.

'What did you have to *do* for it, Margaret?'

'Nothing. Not anything. Shut *up.*'

Dad yelled up and called us down for dinner. I had the
sickest feeling it was likely more than snogging.

38

Pam the cleaner's duties were expanding. Along with polishing and ironing and dusting around the house she had taken it upon herself to bring us the occasional baked dessert. It was hard to mind too much about this since they were usually pavlovas, discs of soft meringue piled high with whipped cream and topped off with generous helpings of tinned fruit cocktail. Sometimes she'd pour too much of the fruit cock-tail juice on top, which made the cream runny and deflated the meringue, but all in all we looked forward to her arriving with a cake tin and a roll of tin foil under her arm.

Ours wasn't the only house that Pam cleaned on our street. She did bits and pieces for Barbara Hill, which is how Dad found her, and also 'did' for the Dunns and the Rosens. This made her a useful source of gossip as well as number one know-it-all and busybody.

'Your dad has a good standing in this street,' she said, as she slapped dust from our curtains and watched it settle back onto the sofa. 'So he needn't worry on that account. He's not to be embarrassed. You tell him.'

'Dad is embarrassed? About what?'

'Well, I don't know.'

'Mum?'

'That's right. But I don't like to say.'

'My mother's having a new baby with her hippy.'

'I know that.'

'Is that what's embarrassing?'

Pam went to fetch the Hoover. She whistled 'I Feel Pretty', from *West Side Story*.

'What are they saying about her?'

'Oh . . . I couldn't. It's your mum.'

'Come on.'

Pam sighed and dipped her head to one side. She ran her tongue along her teeth as if there was much to consider.

'All this women's lib stuff,' she began. 'It's getting out of hand, that's what I'd say. They're not all cut from the same cloth, you know. Not all of them are idle, useless bastards.'

'Mothers?'

'*Men.*'

'Oh.'

'Women want it easy now, see. But it isn't always easy and a good wife has to face up to that. Of course it's lonely. And it's boring. At times I could have screamed my head off between the two of them, but where would it have got me? Nowhere. Yelling on the streets with their placards. Who's got time for that? You have to muddle through it, thick and thin.'

'Is that what you did?'

'Yes. And proud of it. I couldn't just swan off like she did, could I?'

I didn't know if she could have or she couldn't.

'Equality, yes. I'm all for that, up to a point. But women are better at some things than men, and that's a fact and we just ought to face it.'

'Better at what?'

'Bringing up the children, for one thing. Kenny would have been all at sea. He'd have sent my girls to school without their shoes on.'

'I've got my shoes on.'

'Yes, but you're older.'

'So, Mum trusts us.'

'You still need her, though, don't you? Look at Margaret.'

'What about her?'

'All I'm saying – all everyone is saying . . . well, the ones that I talk to – is that a woman's place is with her children. So if you really want to know I'd say it's selfish what your mother has done. It's all a bit stiff. There it is. I've said it. I'll shut up.'

First Jack, then Barbara, now Pam the cleaner and, by implication, the Rosens and the Dunns. I tried not to care. But I did.

'I don't think Mum . . . She wasn't happy with my dad any more.'

'Why ever not? What did he do to her?'

I tried to remember about the kitchen cupboards and the Isle of Wight but felt I might get it all the wrong way round.

'She was probably brainwashed,' I said, out of desperation.

'Yes,' Pam said. 'Highly likely.'

It struck me then, as she went about her business, that Pam the cleaner was a jolly good advert for women's lib herself. She was working to support a family. She was bringing up her kids on her own. I ran this argument past her. She didn't care for it.

'Oh no, that's quite wrong,' she said, correcting me. 'I'd be glad to stay at home if I could. You wouldn't find me out at work unless I had to be. It wasn't me that wanted the divorce.'

'But he didn't like you wearing perfume.'

'That's not the half of it.'

'Isn't it?'

'Too right, it's not.'

'So you're better off, then?'

'Without him? Oh well . . . but if the right man came along, I'd marry again in seconds flat.'

She recommenced her whistling, content she'd settled our disagreement. She whistled the same way she did when she was beating the curtains; the same way she did when she picked up Dad's envelope of money, rubbed its sharp corners between her fingers and folded it into the pocket of her nylon housecoat. I wondered if Pam didn't enjoy her cleaning work just a little bit. If not the scrubbing itself, then the envelopes and the intrigue and the luxury of being in and out of our neighbours' houses and interfering in their personal business.

'Why are you always whistling that same tune?'

'I like it. It distracts me. We do it in my amateur dramatics.'

Even up in my bedroom the smell of her lingered long after she'd packed away her dusters and gone home. Her musky perfume had grown stronger and louder over the weeks and I guessed this was because Dad had failed to pass comment on it in the way she'd expected him to. She was spraying it on in larger and darker doses in the hope he'd give her a compliment. Even all that musk couldn't hide the true smell of her: beeswax and Dettol and BO.

'Don't forget the pavlova in the fridge, tell your dad.'

'Yeah. I won't.'

'It's a thank you in advance, tell him. He said he'd help me pick out a new car in the week.'

'Did he?'

'The big end's gone on mine.'

'What's that?'

'How should I know? Ask your dad.'

'Dad didn't like my mum driving.'

'Didn't he?'

'No.'

'Well, goodbye.'

I got through almost half the pavlova before Margaret found me eating it and Dad came home from work.

'Pam made you this. For the car thing.'

'There's not much left, is there? You won't want dinner.'

'It wasn't that nice, not really.'

'I can see that.'

He went upstairs to wash and to change his work clothes.

'What's that song he's whistling?' Margaret said.

'"Maria",' I said.

'What is it from?'

'West Side Story.'

39

Dearest Broo,

The house smells of newly boiled cabbage, even on
the days when no cabbage is being cooked and
instead they are preparing another of the infernal milk
puddings we are obliged to eat for the health of our
babies. Tapioca is the worst since it has the unappe-
tizing consistency of pond slime but avoiding it
attracts the wrath of Mrs Ellory, our matron, who is
virulently opposed to an unemptied plate. Also on the
menu is liver, and lots of it, for the iron, and endless
steamed fish, junkets and custards. We eat as if we are
invalids yet do not feel like invalids in the least. Only
last weekend I took a good day's walk along the coast
as far as Shoreham and returned home bristling with
energy. Of course, I was made an example of and
roundly told off over supper. We are not encouraged
to wander out on our own even at this early stage, or

to be gone for more than four hours at a time without leaving strict instruction as to our whereabouts.

If we think it sensible to disregard this advice we are reminded of a woman called Angelica who left the nursing home without saying where she was going and was forced to give birth to her baby in the train station! For the moment I find these lectures curious and amusing (there is something almost admirable in the way matron keeps her starched white cap and collar on during meal times) but how long this will remain the case I can only guess. Perhaps a train station might prove to be a happier place to give birth than this; I have always found the porters to be most helpful.

The rooms themselves are clean and pleasant enough, though the overriding colour scheme is a mouldy green. The view from the windows is down to the sea, which makes things better, and the lawns are a nice place to sit and read when the sun shines, which it hardly ever has this rotten summer. The most difficult thing, of course, is the mood. We are all of us outcasts here, though no one speaks of it, and though we talk incessantly about our little aches and pains and of our weight and our water retention there is precious little talk about the obvious. For me and others like me it is easy to pretend that the labour will never happen since it is all still some long months away. We look fattened and rounded and fit still, and in the right smocked blouse and neatly buttoned overcoat could be mistaken for simply being overweight.

Not so the ships in full sail. They amble around these grounds with their flushed faces, distended forms and duck waddles, and protrusions the size of

inflated beach balls. It is a shock to see them gathered
together as if one had come upon a colony of aliens.
They slump on their chairs, all blue-veined, bow-
legged and heavy, and knit and sew and write letters,
and seem to talk less among themselves even than us
newcomers. They never venture into town as we do
and I have not yet worked out if this is because they
lack the energy or because their situation is so obvious
they do not want to invite the judgement of the locals.
Whatever the case, we new ones barely mix with the
long-termers even though I have tried. They stick with
one another, glued by the bonds of passing months,
and regard us as if we know nothing and have everything to learn, yet are patently unwilling to teach us.
They are impatient with our moments of levity and
frown on any loudness or laughter. I wonder if we
half-dozen that have arrived in quick succession will
end up drained and dowdy like them. My dearest, I
can only hope not.

Yours,
Edith

> Northwood Nursing Home
> 15 Wykeham Street,
> Worthing
> West Sussex
> November 20th 1934

Dearest Broo,

Despite my very best efforts, the characters in this
house refuse to blossom. Reservation overcomes these
women and regardless of their pot bellies, that grow
fuller and rounder with every hour, they still make all
pretences to normality. The larger we grow the more

perverse it seems to keep up this steady state of denial. Yesterday in the library, while I was reading, the baby kicked so hard from its hiding place beneath my ribs that the book I was holding almost fell to the floor. 'Goodness,' one of them said, 'that was a quite a go,' and then went directly back to her newspaper. We walk around in a haze of formality, both aware and unaware of who each other are. I know where each of these women comes from and what their fathers do, but of their hopes and their fears and their views about things I know next to nothing.

Alice and Evelyn are the exception and without their friendship these last two months I would likely have gone mad or absconded. Alice is from a family of dairy farmers and it is simply not in her nature to say anything other than what is on her mind at a given moment. She is used to the muck and blood of farm work; this is a girl of mud and boots. Nevertheless she has the looks of a Harlow or a Hepburn – from the neck up at least! – and I have sworn to take her with me to America when all this is over so she might pursue her dreams of becoming an actress. This – and some shoddy mistake with a much older boy – is the reason for her being here, since her family are the most supportive I have yet to hear about. Her father and mother were content for her to keep the child – marriage, husband or not. Alice refused on the grounds she is only nineteen and is not done with dreaming just yet. I respect her for it, if I am honest.

Evelyn's background is quite different again since her father is a county court judge. He disapproves of her situation so completely that he is packing her off to stay with an aunt in Brize Norton for a further six months beyond the birth. He says it will take that amount of time at least until she looks the way she did before it all began and he can stand to lay eyes on her.

I can only imagine, from their reluctance to talk, that the situation for some of the women here must be very much worse. While it is against my better nature not to pry I have learnt to respect their secrets and to be more circumspect with delivering up my own. The fight has gone out of me lately and I have found it easier as the weeks pass to sit back and rest and keep the peace. New girls appear every month or so but I have ceased to make the effort of welcoming them in, or of countering the early mood of coldness that circulates in this place. And so we sit up most evenings playing rounds of bridge and gin rummy. We content ourselves with our talks of aches and pains and tapioca, and for the most part we avoid the rotten truth of it. We are all of us in limbo, bound together in our pretending and by our hiding.

Thank God for my map books and periodicals, Broo. I would be entirely lost here without them. At night I write up my travels and study Burma, Alaska and the waters around Taipei, while the kicks jump and struggle in my belly and my mind kills its questions stone dead. What enormous distraction it gives to me. Any state furthest from confinement. Any place furthest away from here.

Best,
Edith

Northwood Nursing Home
15 Wykeham Street,
Worthing
West Sussex
December 1st 1934

Dearest Broo

Last morning Phyllis, a long-termer here, was carried off
from her room in some awful pain. She is still early,
some weeks at least, and all about the home was a
dreadful panic. It is unusual to see such commotion
surrounding an exit, though common for girls to leave
here with some speed. We often go to bed in the evening
and wake to find another of our number gone. For some
reason the worst of it tends to begin at night, or
perhaps, as Evelyn suggests, this is when matron judges
it most convenient to remove us. The dreadful thing is
that once a girl is gone, it tends to be the end of things
and one never gets to hear how it went or what
happened, or even if they gave birth to a boy or to a
girl. In Phyllis's case, since we were all of us worried
about her, I made it my business to trek up to the little
hospital the following day to find out how she was.

My dearest, how I wish that I had not . . .

40

Dad came home with Tupperware boxes containing food Pam the cleaner had made. This time she'd prepared a series of savoury courses and I wondered about this sudden change in tempo and about its significance in general. There were baked tomatoes stuffed with peas for Margaret, and a prawn and avocado cocktail followed by veal escalopes in a mushroom cream for me and Dad. The mayonnaise on the prawns tasted strange and Dad said this was because it had a splash of cognac in it but I wasn't to worry because it was only there for flavour and wouldn't make me drunk or do me harm. On the whole, I wasn't worried about getting drunk, I was worried about how bad it all tasted. The prawns were soft and fishy and collapsed to a mealy powder as I chewed them, and the mushroom cream was sweet as well as savoury, like sugar mixed with scrapings from a forest floor. Margaret's pea concoction looked more reasonable and I thought long and hard that Wednesday evening about the benefits of becoming a vegetarian.

'Veal is bad karma,' said Margaret sanctimoniously, tucking into her peas. 'They keep the baby calves in crates so tiny they can't even stand up or stretch out.'

'Margaret, I'm sure that's not true.'

'It is too true. That's how come the meat is so pale. The

animals have no muscles because they never get to move or turn around.'

'We all need meat, Margaret. It's good for us. Humans are designed to eat it, for the protein.'

'There's protein in vegetables.'

'Not the right kind.'

'It's exactly the same.'

'I don't think so.'

'It *is*, Dad. They told us all about it in Home Economics.'

'What about this mushroom sauce, hey, Jess? Very nice, I'd say. Quite unusual.'

'It tastes like dessert.'

'They starve them of vitamins too.'

'It's nice. Nice and sweet.'

'It tastes weird with the meat.'

'And they leave them in the dark all the time.'

'I think it goes together very well.'

'They take them away from their mothers, did you know that?'

'Stop it, Margaret. No, they don't.'

'And they keep them so thirsty they lick their own piss up off the floor of their crates.'

'*Stop* it. This instant. We're eating. We're having a nice bloody meal.'

'It's not nice, though, *is* it? It's cruel.'

Dad wrenched his chair back and slammed down his own knife and fork. We were still for those seconds, watching him, wondering which way he would go.

'You've made your choice, Margaret,' he said, finally and calmly. 'We've all been very supportive. But if you don't shut up right now and stop ruining this for all of us, we'll eat liver the rest of the year, you included.'

Margaret stared down at her plate. She toyed with her tomato skins, neatly peeled.

'Liver is good for you, actually,' she said, quietly. 'When you're pregnant, for instance, for the iron. But there's iron in vegetables like spinach. So you can still be a vegetarian and be pregnant.'

Since Pam had failed to come up with anything remotely appetizing to finish off the meal, like gateau or pavlova, Dad said we could all leave the table.

'Jess, you wash up. Margaret, you dry. Put the plates away and tidy when you've finished.'

I studied my father's face for lasting signs of anger but couldn't pick anything out, save a familiar tightness to his lips. Something about his day out choosing used motorcars with Pam had made him unusually stoic. He cleared his throat contentedly as he scraped our leftovers into the swing bin and stacked the dirty Tupperware by the sink. I had expected, what with Margaret bringing up the P word and indirectly invoking Mum, that he would go directly to the drinks cabinet and pour himself a scotch like he did most evenings after dinner. He did something more unusual instead. He went to the dining room, where we kept the table and chair set that we never ate at and the hi-fi system no one ever listened to, and chose himself a record from the sideboard. He spent the rest of the evening alone with his feet up, studying the album cover and humming along to *Band on the Run* by Paul McCartney and Wings.

The two of us left Dad to his humming and took to the streets. The evenings were bright at this time of the year, humid and easy and long. I was happy to be out there in the warmth, away from the sitting room, its squareness and its gloom, and its too-soft armchairs that held you captive in front of the TV, a prisoner to sitcoms and quizzes.

We walked forwards then backwards down the centre of

the road, which seemed like a wild adventure after the strains and complications of dinner. We bent back the wing mirrors on our neighbours' well-scrubbed cars, the ones whose bonnets we had clambered on last summer. I wondered if our footprints were up there somewhere, still, and if Margaret was in any mood for climbing.

Halfway down the road we changed tactics again and switched our full strides to fairy steps, creeping along the kerb edge – heel to toe, heel to toe – as if pretending to walk the tightrope. Our street was exactly four hundred and twelve fairy steps long, at least it had been the last time we'd measured it. Margaret had probably been six or seven years old, me no more than eleven. It seemed that our feet had grown much larger since then, or perhaps the street had shrunk over time. After only one hundred and seven short steps we were already halfway down it and outside Edith's.

'Look, the foundations are set,' I said.

'Yep,' Margaret said, 'so they are.'

'They did a good job with all that concrete.'

'It's nice and smooth, isn't it? I might like to go and lie down on it.'

We lay on the new bed of concrete, our arms stretched out making crosses, our eyes fixed on the rose-coloured sky. The concrete was cool beneath my back and I took off my shoes and socks so I could feel it better. I wondered why other people in our street didn't come and lie down here like this in the evenings, since it felt so peculiarly good. Margaret knew the secret of some things; I felt happier and safer and more completely hidden than I had done since we'd come back from holiday.

'The roof will go up next, I suppose,' I said.

'Let's just enjoy it until then,' said Margaret.

I would have lain there all evening, until the sun went down and the sky turned pitch-black, if Margaret hadn't started on about her Mexican jumping bean. I would have pushed my soles harder and deeper into the floor, looking for dents and scratchy bits to rub my toes against. A line of clouds passed above my head like a strip of film, hiding faces and animals and monsters in their midst, carved from their white puffs and pillows. I felt like I'd gone to the cinema again, except this time there was no one I had to kiss. My slate was wiped clean, all upsets done and dusted with the burning and rebuilding of this old house and its opening up to the sweet late summer air.

'Do you want to have a go with my jumping bean?' she said. 'It's all over the place in this heat.'

She held it out in front of me and just the sight of it made me cross and caused a roof to appear on Edith's house. I was back indoors suddenly, and the forms I remembered from the clouds were Ian Warrington and Ray, and my mother's great big belly so fat and distended and round that her skin might burst apart at any moment. Inside her would be maggots, like a dream I'd had where Nanna didn't cry at her funeral. No one cried, not even Ray. Not the neighbours. Not Dad. Only Margaret and me, and Pam the cleaner.

'Put that thing away, can't you?'

'Keep your hair on, why don't you?'

'I don't like it. It gives me the creeps.'

'You don't like who gave it to me, that's what.'

'Same thing, isn't it?'

'It's not.'

'I don't like what you had to do for it, that's all.'

'I didn't do anything I didn't want to.'

I thought she might elaborate but she didn't and I remember feeling jealous of her then. Margaret seemed content not to tell me things. Her secrets about Ian. Her thoughts about Mum and Dad. The baby, and Ray, and it all.

'I kissed Gavin Hillier,' I said, suddenly.

'I bet he was rubbish.'

'He was all right.'

'Are you going out with him now?'

'Don't be stupid.'

'Because I wondered if you were. You're never around.'

'I'm around all the time.'

'No . . . no, you're not. You're not lately.'

I calmed down a little after that. The roof that I'd made pulled apart again, and the sky and the sunshine flooded back. I didn't want to hit my sister quite so much.

'Your new hair's growing in,' I said.

'Is it?' Margaret said, looking chuffed.

'It's better since you cut off the Mohican. You don't look like a punk any more. You look like someone getting over cancer.'

Surprisingly, Margaret seemed to like this.

When our spines began to ache we sat up from the concrete and positioned ourselves outside on Edith's lawn. Her garden was long and untidy, still strewn with debris from the fire. I kicked at a charred slab of wood and Margaret found an old piece of plastic that she wrapped and unwrapped from her fingers.

'Where will Mum have it, do you think?'

'The baby? In a hospital, I suppose.'

'Could anything go wrong?'

'Like what, for instance?'

'I don't know, Jessie . . . it's just . . .'

She lay down her plastic.

'Things don't go wrong, do they?' I said. 'Not any more. It's a piece of cake having a baby nowadays.'

'It wasn't always, I don't think. Not when Edith was young.'

'Well, no, but nothing was. It was all wars and corsets back then.'

'Ray will look after her,' she said, nodding, after a while. 'Make sure she eats lots of iron.'

When we stood up to leave Margaret said, 'Wait a minute, I don't want to keep this any more.'

She reached into her front jeans pocket and dug out the Mexican jumping bean. She threw it as far and as hard as she could, so it hit the far fence with a tap and bounced back into the piles of charred debris: buried and lost for good and ever.

'Stupid thing,' she said firmly. 'Stupid worm.'

We counted four hundred and twelve fairy steps back. To the end of our street and then home.

41

Dad took the morning off work in order to take Margaret to the doctor's.

'What's wrong with her?'

'Nothing.'

'Polio,' Margaret said.

'Don't be so stupid,' said Dad.

'Well, it could be.'

'No, it couldn't. Eat your toast.'

'It's burnt.'

'No, it isn't.'

'But it *is*. Just look at this bit.'

The two of them were gone for an hour or more and came back with looks on their faces that made me think Margaret might have polio, after all.

'What's she got?'

'Sit down, Jessie.'

'What is it? Is it *bad*?'

Dad set down his jacket and carrier bag and Margaret slunk off to her bedroom, shutting its door behind her with a well-timed clack. He began several times before he managed to get it out and I knew it was serious because he sat down when he spoke to me when usually he preferred to stand up.

'Your sister has anorexia nervosa. Do you know what that means?'

It turned out I didn't, which Dad found irritating. I thought it meant Margaret was nervous.

Anorexia wasn't a disease as such, it wasn't a thing you could catch. There weren't anorexia germs floating around in the air or hiding underneath toilet seats waiting to infect you. Dad said it was an illness that started in the head, and I took this to mean that Dad thought Margaret was mental.

'Your sister doesn't want to eat, you see. Eating is a problem for Margaret at the moment. She thinks she's very fat, though that's clearly not the case because Dr Gordon says she's seriously underweight.'

Our GP, Dr Gordon was a strange one. Mum said he was a hypochondriac and that this was an unfortunate thing for a doctor to be. When Nanna had her fibroids, for instance, he near as damn it told her it was tumours and that she only had a matter of months to live, even though all she needed was a metal ring stuffed up her fanny and, a few months later, a hysterectomy. It was the same thing with Barbara Hill's waterworks. Dr Gordon had said the whole lot would have to come out but it turned out she only needed penicillin.

'What does Dr Gordon know?' I said. 'He's an idiot. You ought to take her to see someone else before he puts her in the lunatic asylum.'

'In this case,' said Dad, 'I'm sorry to say, I think he might have it right.'

'But I don't think—'

'So you see what this means?'

'But I'm not—'

'It's *our* job, Jessie. It's up to us. We have to see that Margaret puts on weight. We must sit with her at every single meal, even breakfast, and not let her down from the table until she's finished every single last bite.'

I chewed this over in my head. On the one hand I wanted to help my sister put on weight, on the other it seemed like a lot of effort.

'But why, though?' I said. 'Why is she mental?'

'No, no, *no*. No, she's not.'

'She is. You said it's in her head.'

'Well, it is.'

'So how did it get there?'

'How should I know?'

'Well, somebody *ought* to.'

Dad said, 'Jesus Christ on a bike.'

He took a breath then, and shut his eyes for a second, which seemed to be his way of saying he wasn't sure how much more of this he could take. When he came up for air he had his eyes open wide and had moved off on to a different tack.

'We have Pamela to thank, of course.'

'Do we?'

'Yes. If it wasn't for her noticing—'

'*I* noticed.'

'No, you didn't.'

'Yes, I did. Every single day she gives her packed lunch away to Ian Warrington.'

'You saw this?'

'Yes.'

'For heaven's sake, Jessie. Hell. Now then, for *heaven*'s sake.'

He tried not to be angry but instead of finding my lunch-box observation useful it suddenly seemed to Dad that Margaret's new madness was entirely down to me. I ought to have said something. I ought to have done something. I was her big sister and this role came with serious responsibilities, didn't I know that? How could it be that Dad had been made to wait in the dark all these weeks and hear about it second-hand from an outsider? I'd been going to the park too much lately this summer, so that would certainly have to stop. I'd neglected Margaret and been selfish to boot, and it was about time someone set me straight.

We batted it back and forth for a while until Dad got upset about my shouting and said it really wasn't anybody's fault, except perhaps Mum's, given what she had done to him and to us and the entire family. All we could do now was be supportive to one another and try to help Margaret stop thinking she was ugly and fat. With this end in mind it was agreed Dad would take the rest of the day off from work and that the three of us would go to visit Nanna.

Nanna put a plate of cheesecake in front of Margaret and held out a fork for her to eat it with. The cheesecake was flavoured with lemon and had a digestive biscuit base a good inch thick. We were silent. We stared at her. We toyed with the lemon peel pieces on the top that looked like crystallized worms. Margaret sat with it, hopeless. I had no idea why the sight of a slice of cheesecake could make a person want to cry.

'Stop staring at me.'

'We're not.'

'Yes you are.'

We pretended to look away and Nanna began a conversation about the weather and how hot it had been lately. She'd barely been able to sit out in the afternoons but, even so, it was nothing like as bad as last summer. What a summer *that* had been, like the devil himself had made it; who could forget the summer of '76? She prattled on about hose-pipe bans and lawns that looked like deserts and about the Baker twins from the council estate across the road who spent their days fighting with water pistols, even though water pistols had been banned. They were bad kids, wicked kids, rotten through and through, and as proof of their rottenness Nanna prophesied they would both end up in borstal before the year was out. It wasn't their fault, of course, it never was. In cases such as this, it was always the fault of the parents.

I thought about the Baker twins' mother going to visit them in borstal and snuck a look at my sister eating cheesecake. Ordinarily I might have been so engrossed in my own slice that my sister's method with a fork would hardly have bothered me. I noticed that she ate with peculiar care, like a prisoner checking for poison. There wasn't a crumb that wasn't poked about or picked at before it was lifted to her mouth. I realized she did this with most of her meals and it occurred to me that if you broke a plate of food into enough tiny pieces it began to look like you'd eaten some when you hadn't.

This time she had to eat all of it. The soft doughy clots of dismembered cream cheese, the mouse-dropping piles of digestive crust. She suffered the cheese parts like they were candle wax, solid and oily, and impossible to clear from her tongue and teeth. The biscuit bottom caught in her throat at each attempt and she coughed and rasped at every swallow. She took half an hour about it, which seemed an impossible length of time to spend on a sweet, while tears fell from her cheeks to her lap. I wanted to take that awful cheesecake away. It seemed to me like it was hurting her.

'*See*,' Dad said. 'Now that wasn't so hard, was it? And I'll bet it was delicious, now, wasn't it? See what you've been missing all this time? See how stupid you've been?'

'I'll give you the rest to take home in a bag,' Nanna said. 'You'll have another slice with your dinner.'

Margaret stared at the window.

'Can I go outside and play now?'

'Yes, you can. Yes, you *can*. But only because I'm pleased with you. Only because you were good and finished.'

Margaret went to the toilet immediately and then danced for an hour in the garden. It turned out Dr Gordon was limited in his grasp of the symptoms of anorexia nervosa and knew nothing about the being sick part of it, or the million other devious and ingenious ways in which Margaret could continue to make herself ill and pathetically thin. Getting her better was never going to be as easy as a trip to the doctor and Nanna's plastic bags filled with cheesecake.

42

Margaret sat cross-legged in Ray's garden, crouched beneath one of his pyramids. The structure was open to the elements, a skeleton frame of metal rods and aluminium tubing: robot bones. Ray sat beside her like a wizard – moon shapes sewn onto his jacket and his trousers, a book of spells open on his lap – while Mum and I watched from the kitchen window. When he had finished speaking, Ray took his sandals off and lay his small hands on Margaret's shoulders, rubbing them up and down like he was pummelling dough, which she didn't seem to care about or mind. Mum said it was all to do with relaxing and taking in the energy but on the specifics of which energy and from where, she couldn't be drawn. That day she seemed a long way away from herself. She wore a pair of towelling trousers in a buttercup-yellow colour that reached up over her belly and settled in an elasticated bunch at the spot where her waist had once been. She looked tired and puffed and unhappy, her old body lost in its inches-thick overcoat of fat. It seemed to me like the baby was stealing her and that there wasn't much left of her to steal.

Ray abandoned Margaret and came inside. He'd left her to her chanting, he said. She had chosen her mantra and was learning to meditate, which would surely help to gather her thoughts and soothe the confusions in her mind. Margaret ought to sit out there for an hour at least – Ray seemed to think this was the minimum time required for my sister to get her head together – and after that he would talk to her 'properly'. It was hard to gauge what talking to her properly might mean but when he said this to Mum she seemed relieved. 'Oh,' she said, 'that's good,' and sat down at the fold-out table with a book called *Birth and Re-birthing* and a packet of cream crackers to eat.

Mum ate seven cream crackers with butter and jam, and then two tubs of mandarin yoghurt. She washed it down with tea and finished her meal with a bourbon biscuit. Ray ate nothing and read from a dog-eared paperback by Richard Bach about a seagull named Jonathan, which he claimed was entirely relevant to understanding Margaret's condition. No one spoke to me or asked my opinion about things and I realized I preferred Dad's technique, his blaming me and the row about Ian Warrington, to this odd quiescence and silence. I wasn't offered anything to eat, not even a biscuit, but this wasn't because Mum and Ray didn't want me to have one, it was because Ray was of the attitude that when a person was in his house they should help themselves to what they wanted without asking. This was all very well in the case of cream crackers but I felt thirsty for something other than water from the tap, and in the quietness of it all, which seemed almost prayer-like, I felt awkward about going to the fridge.

'Can I have some squash?'

'We don't have squash, Jessie. We have real juice.'

'Can I have some of that, then?'

'I've told you, haven't I? What's mine is yours. You don't have to ask.'

All that was Ray's turned out to be a plastic jug with an inch of sticky liquid in it, squeezed from a sorry orange some days earlier. It was thick and warm and unpleasant and I was grateful there wasn't much of it.

'It's been an hour now,' I said, 'more or less.'

Ray kept his nose in his book as if my time-keeping was an annoyance to him. He might have looked at his watch to check, but he didn't own one.

'Take her out some crackers,' Mum said.

'No,' Ray said. 'Let her be. She'll eat when she's hungry.'

Considering how little my sister was eating I presumed she must be hungry all the time. Ray said the problem with Margaret was that hunger was a feeling she enjoyed. She wasn't properly hungry, like I might be after a long night's sleep or a morning without elevenses, because her stomach was filled up by its emptiness. Not eating was exciting for Margaret and every time she succeeded in giving away another meal or pretending she had eaten one when she hadn't, her brain received a little kick, like drugs, like an electrical boost. To Ray's way of thinking, and to experts on the matter whose books he'd consulted, her problem wasn't to do with food at all, nor was it particularly to do with feeling ugly or fat. Margaret's problem had to do with control. Her world had lost its patterns and so Margaret was putting those patterns back. She'd concocted her own set of rules and regulations since she felt her life ought to have some but didn't. The problem being that Margaret's rules were far too strict and too tough.

Ray's theory seemed plausible to me and I tried to overlook the slow, smug way he expressed it. He knew a lot about stuff, about the workings of people's minds and the way their heads got crowded and out of sorts. In the matter of Margaret's illness he was knowledgeable enough; in his manner of addressing it he was clumsy, perverted and next to useless.

Mum wiped tears of fury from Margaret's eyes. Her knuckles were raw where she'd hit them on the table and embedded cracker crumbs into the scratches.

'Don't let him *touch* me. I'm telling you now. Mum, just don't . . . or I'll *kill* him.'

There was a knife on the breadboard, innocent beside its brown loaf, that Margaret had marked out as her weapon. She wouldn't have got to it, Mum had her arms pinned, but the idea that she wanted to scared me shitless.

'What did he do to you?'

'Nothing,' Ray answered, unperturbed. 'Margaret,' he said to her, 'let's try to calm down now, shall we—'

'*You* calm down, you bloody sex freak. What's it got to do with *you* . . . my . . . *periods*. They ought to put you in prison. They ought to put you *away*.'

'I was only asking—'

'Why would you, though . . . but why *would* you?'

She was shouting, hoarse with the strain of it, her eyes rocking slowly in their sockets as if she couldn't focus on the room or on us, because her head was so stuffed full of rage.

'He tried to *touch* me—'

'No, Margaret, I didn't. You shouldn't say that because . . . it's not right.'

'He did. He *bloody* tried to touch me.'

'Why are you saying these things?' Mum said then, and to begin with I couldn't work out if she was asking this of Margaret or of Ray.

'We're trying to help you. Don't you understand that? Ray's only trying to help.'

'He isn't . . . that *isn't* . . . No, because I *don't* think he is.'

Margaret breathed sharply like she might just pass out and I thought she was having hysterics. I waited for Mum to leap into action, to hug her very tightly or splash cold water on her face but instead of stretching her arms out or going to the tap she said, 'Ray, I don't . . . What should we do?'

I hated that she asked him. I really hated it.

'Just leave her be,' Ray said easily. 'She'll come to her senses in a minute. Sit *down*, Joy. Just sit down.'

Mum looked heartbroken but she did it, obeying Ray's quiet order.

'I wasn't touching you, Margaret,' he said, starting on my sister. 'So don't you say I did, it's wrong to say that. And the reason I asked you about your periods is because they've stopped for you, haven't they? Aren't I right?'

'What's it to *you*? It's none of your . . . it isn't *your* business.'

Margaret seemed exhausted with the fight of it by then and lay down on the sofa and cried. Mum stood up to go to her but Ray sent her back and said her crying like this was a good thing and that it represented some kind of a breakthrough. As my sister cried into his rough raffia cushions Ray cut himself some bread with the knife Margaret wanted, and talked about her like she wasn't there. Puberty had settled in early for Margaret and that was most of her problem. Anorexics stayed thin because it stopped them menstruating and staved off physical changes in their bodies. Margaret, it seemed to Ray, was scared of becoming an adult. I wondered, just then, who could blame her.

I didn't know if Ray had touched up my sister or not but I did know one thing for sure. You wouldn't catch Dad, or any man in our family – even Uncle David – using words like 'menstruation' or expressions like 'physical changes' in front of an eleven-year-old girl. I wondered why none of them could see the plain, simple fact of it – that Margaret was dying of embarrassment. Dad was quite right, as it turned out. Being an older sister came with certain responsibilities and, even though Ray warned me not to, I sat down next to Margaret and promised her an outing to Edith's house that very night and a nice lie-down on the cold concrete. All my sister needed at that moment, it seemed to me, was to know someone good was on her side.

43

. . . To begin with, I had a frightful time just getting in and only made it past the door after threatening to scream blue murder if they didn't open it up at once and let me in. If they had told me Phyllis was tired or sleeping I would likely have gone away, I should think, and that would have been that, but the head nurse – a stout and most unpleasant little woman – aroused my suspicions right away. What did I want with Phyllis? How well did I know her? What were the rumours I had heard? By this point I was all for making a ghastly fuss and was pouring out all manner of threats to the point where it is a wonder they didn't offer to sedate me. But my hackles were up, as much as my curiosity, and I felt in my bones this was not a time to be fobbed off by minions.

When finally I arrived at her bedside the look of her was quite something. She was in a frightful state in both body and spirits and though we hadn't developed a friendship of any depth she seemed pitiably happy to see me. Her feet and ankles protruded bare from her bedclothes and were swollen up like balloons. Her hair was matted and all over the place, her body so bruised and so sore she could hardly sit up well or speak easily.

'Shall I fetch you a brush?' I asked her, and though she didn't answer I fetched it for her anyway from her nightstand, knowing full well she had not the will nor the energy to use it. As I sat down beside her and ran it past her knots and tangles she wilted on her pillow and began to cry. I ceased with my brushing then and held her, and Broo, she felt so brittle and so hard in my arms, as if no one in her life had properly held her. I kissed her poor forehead and stroked her arms then, since that was what Mummy always did when we felt out of sorts. It took a half-hour of this before she spoke readily and told me the whole dreadful story. I can barely stand to recount it.

It was all so enormously painful, the only consolation being that the labour, perhaps to do with the baby being so small and so early, was mercifully fast. Even so she was surrounded by instruments of all kinds and suffered some bleeding which may well have killed her had it gone on for very much longer and which has left her frightfully weak. She is sewn up like a cushion and has suffered the indignity of enemas before and since, but her physical position is hardly the very worst of it.

Her pain is all to do with the baby and her version of things, which she believes so completely I feel compelled to write it down to you now. Though every other person would contradict her, she is quite certain that her baby was born alive. She swears she heard him cry and that his cries were quite something and entirely different to her own which were still brewing from her when he came out.

Needless to say, when he was born all Phyllis wanted was to hold him but Matron Ellory herself had been called in to watch over things and it was she who bent down and took him from her. Phyllis says she saw his face quite clearly and that it was a perfect and beautiful one: pink and firm and less troubled than it had any right to be given the circumstances of his birth. His eyes were wide open and a glorious blue colour, and he looked up at his mother with such love and such longing that she felt her heart snap and her arms reach out in earnest to protect him.

When Ellory wrenched him from her – to help him, she said – he looked for his mother again and thrust out his tiny fists as if to say he would fight for her always. His eyes were so full of hurt as they carried him off that she immediately threw off the covers from her bed and tried to drag herself up and go to him. Of course, she hadn't the strength and couldn't manage it, and though they told her she collapsed she doesn't remember doing so, and can only remember the smell of the cloth and the chloroform which even now sits bitterly in her throat and in her nostrils.

When she came to she was in another room entirely, with clean sheets, fresh nightgown and a nurse reading magazines at the foot of her bed. Immediately she stirred, the nurse went for Ellory who broke the news to her with little softness. Her poor baby had been stillborn, and though it was natural for Phyllis to imagine she had heard him cry it simply couldn't have been the case since his poor lungs weren't nearly strong enough; the implication was, Phyllis thought, that she ought to have done a better job in hanging on to him those last few weeks.

The dear girl broke down at this point, and it was as much as I could do then to keep sober. She wept for her poor baby and clawed at her bedsheets and at her mattress as if he might yet emerge pink and perfect

from the covers if only she could rake them off in time.
Her guilt was the hardest thing to stand, she said, since
they had made a pact together and she had broken it.
Each night after dinner, though she is naturally reticent
and had felt dreadfully awkward about it at first, she
had spoken aloud to him as he grew inside her belly
and he had returned her coos and whispers with his
kicks. She had comforted and carried him and longed
for him in secret all these months, and promised to be
with him no matter what. They had stolen him from
her, no doubt about it, the only thing on earth she had
ever loved.

When I asked what on earth she could mean she said
there was not a shred of doubt in her mind that her
baby was still alive and perfectly well. His early arrival
meant she hadn't completed all the papers, and though
they had tried to get her to do so in the midst of all the
panic she had refused and told anyone that would listen
that she had changed her mind entirely, and had sworn
to keep the baby and to name him Eli since she was
certain she was carrying a boy.

The braveness of this woman is hard to measure,
Broo. She would have taken him home with her had he
survived, I have no doubt, even though her parents are
devout Baptists and would surely have done worse than
disown her. She begged me to search the hospital for
him since she swears she hears Eli's cries at night and
in the morning when she wakes, and I fear she will hear
them now and for all her life. Of course I found
nothing, but when I asked Sister if I might see the
body, which seemed reasonable, she accused me of
madness. I asked if Phyllis might not be allowed to see
him, to settle things and give her mind some rest, but
this suggestion was met with great distaste and did I

not realize a sight of such a kind could entirely destroy a woman.

I relented then, since perhaps they were right and what Phyllis needs most now is to begin the process of forgetting. I cannot imagine for a second they would have lied to her about the baby or had her parents complete the adoption papers as she believes. It would be too cruel and too awful, Broo wouldn't it, and illegal too, I should think? I can only believe they are doing, in their awkward way, what they think is best. And yet, my dear sister, there is something uneasy in the cold, hard bones of this institution. A less generous person might find it dishonest.

In any case, since it was all I could do, I returned to visit Phyllis every day until she left, and brought her gin and cigarettes and smoked them with her some afternoons. When her day came to go I waved her off like a broken pot, with all her cracks on show, a shadow of herself. Her parents had come to fetch her and they were stiff as boards the pair of them and didn't touch her once, not even her hand, which made me long for the affections of our own mother and father, and though I ran to the car to kiss her cheek through the window as they drove away I was certain it could never be enough.

What months these have been, Broo. What vivid changes. The longest and the furthest of all my journeys. I had wondered so often why the girls spoke so little to one another towards the end but I understand it all now, quite completely. The nearer it gets the more they are plagued by their doubts and confusions and can hardly stand to share them, yet find nothing else to speak of since this is entirely all there is.

I have to confess that I lied to them all, even to Alice

and to Evelyn, since I didn't care to upset everyone and told them only that the birth, for Phyllis, had been a difficult one. The truth would surely have hurt them and dented their resolve, precisely in the way it has done mine.

More soonest and when I can.

Your sister,
Edith

44

Mum didn't buy us new clothes often. It was hard to judge when they'd appear and unlikely they'd be bought when we wanted or needed them most. We went entire winters in coats that were too small for us and shoes that were too tight, wearing jumpers that rode up over our middles, with sleeves that ended closer to our elbows than to our wrists. Later, out of the blue and when the sun was shining, Mum would come home from a trip to the high street laden down with jackets, boots and cardigans that she'd snatched up in a dash around the sales. We spent at least one season of each year in the wrong type of clothes. In summer we might have drawers full of new cords and woollens, and in winter a surfeit of flowery dresses. I wondered why Mum never thought to buy larger sizes in the sales so that Margaret and I might catch up by the following year and grow into them. Perhaps Dad would be better at this kind of planning. In any case, that early September Saturday was the first time in his life he'd taken either one of us shopping.

'You girls hurry and run to C&A now. I'll catch you both up in a minute.'

I hated how he always made us do this. The moment he'd parked – with the engine still running – he'd have us rush out of the car and run directly to wherever it was we were

going – the cinema, a burger bar, the pier – while he scrabbled in his pockets for change. It all had to do with Dad
maximizing the time he could achieve on the parking meter.
He even did it when there were friends of ours in the car,
and in that case we'd have to tell them it was some kind of
a game so as not to make them think Dad was tight. Which
he was. Us running to C&A and him catching us up could
only have bought him an extra five minutes at most, yet this
kind of money-saving device was something Dad appreciated very much.

He arrived shortly after us, his eyes on his watch, puffing
and lightly out of breath. He seemed annoyed that we hadn't
made our way up to the children's department on our own
and saved him an extra thirty seconds. He was silent on the
escalator, refusing to hold Margaret's hand, even though he
knew she was nervous of moving stairways.

'Right, then, OK. Frocks, I should think. A frock and a
skirt each. And how are we doing for socks and underpants?'

We were mortified by the way he said underpants, with a
cough of embarrassment in his voice, yet grateful he hadn't
said knickers. That was left to Pam the cleaner, who arrived
five minutes later, to Dad's great relief, with a checklist of
purchases in her handbag that read: vests, plimsolls, knickers,
bras, blouses, school uniform. She looked different out of her
pink nylon housecoat. She wore high-waisted jeans and a
flowery blouse with a good long collar, and without the greasy
film she usually wore across her forehead she looked softer
and sweeter and prettier.

'Margaret, this way now. We're going for bras. It's about
time someone sorted you for a bra.'

There was no hint of embarrassment from Pam in this
duty, as if she'd happily have devoted the whole of her weekend
to Margaret and her newly emerging chest. It's not that my
sister's boobs were very much bigger than they had been at

the start of the summer or even really needed a bra yet, but Pam seemed to think it would make Margaret feel better about things and more grown-up.

'What about these with the flowers?' Pam said, merrily. 'My Susan has one just like this. Training bras, they call them. You could get a white one but they look so plain and stuffy, don't you think?'

'I like the yellow one.'

'Good. I do too. What do you think, Jessie? You like the yellow?'

The yellow one seemed all right. We bought two of them, 32AA, and a set of four matching knickers which Margaret seemed unpredictably thrilled by.

'It's nice. A nice set. First set of matching undies. Quite the young lady in those.'

Pam went to the checkout and paid for the clothes with money from her own purse, which I thought was strange. I guessed Dad must have given her the money in advance, so this whole outing must have been pre-arranged.

'Why are you buying us our clothes?' I asked her, crossly.

'Somebody's got to,' she said.

'We could have done it just as well with our dad.'

'Well, I don't think that's true now, though, is it?' she said. 'He's embarrassed about girls' things. Soppy sod.'

She said this softly, with affection, and it bothered me. She let Margaret carry the plastic bag, with her new underwear purchases wrapped up in white tissue paper.

'Now then. What about school things? You'll need a couple of new grey pinafores to go back with, I should think.'

We walked around the department store, picking up school clothes and home clothes and later a packet of spring onion-flavour crisps for each of us, and everyone assumed Pam was our mother. One of the shop assistants even said as much. 'Oh,' she said, 'that blouse is a perfect fit on your little girl.'

Pam rolled her eyes and as we walked to the till she coughed sharply and said, 'Silly Moo,' which made me smile. Mum was always polite to shop assistants, as if they were the doctor or the tax man or somebody important that she ought to be nice to. Pam was only polite to people that she liked and in every other case, including shop assistants, she refused to give the benefit of the doubt. 'Snobby little cows,' she said later, as we walked around the clothes rails in the ladies' section. 'Think they're quite something when all they do is hang out clothes and sweep up dusty floors, the same as me.' I came close to pointing out that Pam rarely hung up clothes and didn't do much sweeping come to that, but when she said we could go for burgers at the Wimpy Bar, where Dad would be joining us, I changed my mind and thought better of it.

Pam ordered the mixed grill with a fried egg on top. I ordered a cheeseburger and Margaret said she'd have a plate of chips. We ate casually and happily, Pam scoffing down her gammon slice and runny egg, and me dripping red sauce down my chin because Pam said it was OK to ignore the knife and fork and eat with my hands if I wanted to, which Mum would never have allowed. Even Margaret ate all of her chips without arguing and I think this is because Pam didn't look at her once or seem to care if my sister finished her chips or not. When Margaret had finished Pam didn't say well done or anything like that, she just said, 'I'm having a banana split for afters. Who wants one?' She asked the waitress for three.

We were halfway through our splits when Dad turned up, and I think Margaret might have polished hers off completely if Dad hadn't made such a fuss and started exclaiming about how clever she'd been with the empty chip plate and the half-finished sundae. You could see her mind going over it as he spoke; she mentally put down her sundae spoon, the tightness returning to her throat.

'You're late,' Pam said. 'You missed out on a nice mixed grill. Shall I order one up for you now?'

I noticed Dad shift in his seat and felt the full strain of his awkwardness, which made me wriggle on my chair along with him. Dad didn't like to eat in restaurants if he could possibly help it, not when there was good food to eat at home. He'd planned this as a treat for Pam and us and had timed his arrival to miss out on paying for an extra plate. He tried not to look at his watch but couldn't help it and smiled a stiff smile while he thought about the ticking parking meter.

'Oh well, it'd take too long now, I'd expect.'

'Nonsense. That stuff's all pre-cooked. All they have to do is heat it up.'

Dad looked unhappy. He didn't want to seem like a skinflint or someone who didn't know how to enjoy himself, and yet the harder he tried to appear casual the more uptight he looked and the looser Pam looked, and the younger and more jaunty her bleached hair and Farrah Fawcett flicks seemed to be.

'There's still some shepherd's pie left in the fridge. That'll suit me fine. Just fine.'

'If you're sure, then?'

'Oh yes. Don't worry about me. Not at all.'

Pam looked disppointed and Dad compromised by ordering himself a banana split which I knew he would hate because he was a savoury kind of person and wasn't all that good with cream and fruit and glacé cherries and the handling of a long and dainty metal spoon.

'Umm,' he said, enthusiastically, when it came and he had to eat it. 'Very good, this. Very good indeed.'

On the way home – Pam riding with us in the car – Dad went on and on about how good that banana split had been, to the point where I felt uncomfortable for him. I noticed that he drove extra carefully that day and that he didn't shout 'Pillock!' at anyone, even when they hooted at him at the traffic lights or cut him up on the flyover. I didn't appreciate his tiptoes behaviour and I wondered why it was that Dad altered his character in front of his prospective girlfriend, since I had to presume that's what Pam was. Pam made no concessions to anyone. I had no doubt in my mind that had Dad turned up to the restaurant any earlier she would have scoffed down her gammon steak just as hungrily and still wiped up the spilt egg yolk with her bread.

'See you, then,' Pam said, as she climbed out of the car, and tossed her white handbag over her shoulder.

'See you,' I said, not returning her gaze, secretly glad to see the back of her.

Margaret waved and waved. She didn't seem to mind that Dad was walking Pam up her pathway and past her front gate.

45

It was late in the evening, half past nine and close to bedtime, when Margaret said we had to go to Mum's. Dad said she could phone her, but no, Margaret said, a phone call wouldn't do and she absolutely had to see her this very minute. If Margaret had been happier and non-anorexic he would have packed her off to bed with no question, but as it was there was something in her eyes and in her pale, gentle face with all its pleadings that made Dad put his shoes on and bundle the two of us down the drive and into the car. Margaret gave no explanation but just tapped on her knees with the tips of her fingers, light strokes over and over as we went, as if she might be counting the yards until we got there.

It surprised me that Dad knew where Mum lived. He had the address, of course, but it wasn't a part of town he might have been expected to know the ins and outs of or to have visited before, and yet he drove directly to Ray's house without a map or a single wrong turn or hesitation. When he switched off the engine and parked – a few houses away, so as not to be seen – he took up a peculiar position in his chair; he was not slumped, exactly, or upright, just low down and crumpled around the edges.

'How long do you need?'

'I can't say.'

'Try.'

'Ten minutes. An hour.'

Dad sighed since there was no discernible correlation between these two estimates, and resigned himself to sitting there all night.

'You can say you took a taxi.'

'She won't believe that.'

'Well, don't say I'm still out here. And take Jessie with you.'

We hadn't called to warn of our arrival since Margaret seemed to think this might alter things and it was important to surprise Mum and to find her just exactly as she was. I couldn't guess what was going on in my sister's head but could sense it was a pinch away from frantic. Perhaps it had to do with her birthday, which was a week away and had never been spent apart from Mum. I wondered if the buying of bras and the hanging out with Pam had unhinged her temporarily and perhaps all she needed that evening was the reassurance that our mother still existed and would definitely be there, inside that tiny house, when Ray came to open the door. I half expected Mum to answer and for Margaret to say, 'Well, that's OK, then,' and to turn around and get straight back into the car.

Ray came to the door in his usual get-up, looking shifty, as if he might have been expecting the police.

'What's up?' he said, doubtfully.

'Nothing,' Margaret said. 'Where's our mum?'

Mum was in the sitting room watching television, with a packet of peanut brittle on her lap. There were leftovers on the dinner table and a half-finished glass of lager perched in front of Ray's uncomfortable wooden dining chair. Apart from the beer, which Dad never touched, it was a scene you might have found back at our house. It was plain and domestic, banal instead of cosy, and I wondered whether the afternoons of balalaika playing and silent book reading might not be over and done with.

Mum stood up quickly, fatter and rounder than ever, rocking ever so slightly with her newly displaced sense of gravity.

'What is it? What's the matter, has something happened?'

Margaret stalled for a moment, deciding, then ran directly to her, locking her arms around Mum's middle.

'Hey, now hey? What's all this?'

Margaret cried silently and when she'd calmed down and caught her breath, Mum gathered her up and kissed her and took her to sit beside her on the settee. She stroked her head gently, her arms and then her neck, and threw a consoling look to me. She didn't once bother to glance over at Ray, which both pleased and surprised me.

Margaret kept her face tight and safe in Mum's lap until she found her voice, and when she finally did it was a strong one.

'I'd like to feel him, please. If it *is* a him. I should be able to by now, I think, and I'd very much like to.'

Mum seemed taken aback, her face a mix of surprise and delight.

'I didn't think you . . . but of course . . . but he might not be moving, or she. If you lay your hand here . . . this is the place you can feel it most often.'

Margaret lay her hands on the side of Mum's belly, just below her ribcage, and waited. After five minutes of nothing Mum rearranged her bulk and pulled up her jersey so Margaret could lay her hands on bare skin.

'Oh!' she said, finally. 'There he is, there he *is*!'

'Did you feel it?'

'I felt it. It's strange . . . it . . . it's nice.'

Margaret exclaimed two or three more times as the kicks and turns pushed softly at her fingers.

'Can he hear me?' Margaret asked.

'Well, I don't know,' Mum said. 'Perhaps he can.'

'I hope it *is* a he. I really do hope so. A brother would be especially nice.'

'Do you want to try, Jess?' Mum said, beckoning me over. 'The baby's quite active this evening.'

'No thanks,' I said. 'I'd rather not.'

The more delighted Margaret seemed to be the more sour my expression became until I could hardly contain my irritation at her for dragging us over here for this. Mum's belly might just as well have concealed Father Christmas or an alien, or too much cherry pie for all I was bothered. I didn't like the baby or care about it much or feel connected to it in the least. I imagined it swirling around inside her, a scrawny scrap of a thing, naked and bloody, a pair of Ray's wire-rimmed spectacles pinned to its oversized head. It was the physical manifestation of Mum and of Ray and their relationship, which seemed increasingly sick and wrong-headed to me the more I thought about it. If it wasn't for this baby there might not be a Pam and my mother would likely forget all about things and come home to Dad. Why Margaret seemed to like it and wanted to feel its kicks was beyond me.

'Are you going to tell me what this is all about?' Mum said, gently, when Margaret was satisfied.

'I was worried about the baby. That's all.'

'The baby's just fine. The doctor says we're both fine.'

'Are you sure?'

'Yes, I'm sure.'

'The baby's not going to die?'

'Goodness . . . *no*. Not at all. Not at all. Why would you say such a thing?'

'Because they do sometimes. I heard that they do.'

Margaret refused to elaborate on her dead-baby worries even though Mum tried hard to coax her, and so we sat eating lumps of peanut brittle – Mum and me making hard glassy crunches with our teeth – until Margaret said she felt better and was ready to go.

'Wait,' Mum said. 'I have something for your birthday. It's only one of the things, you can have the other on the day.'

'I'm going to *see* you?'

'Of course you are, didn't your dad tell you? Ray and I are taking you to the zoo.'

I stared at Ray, and Margaret did too. For those brief few seconds we were united in our loathing and I wondered if deep in her psyche Margaret still held murderous thoughts about the bread knife.

'Zoos are cruel,' said Margaret, looking directly at Ray.

'Well, it doesn't have to be a zoo, then. Perhaps we'll drive to the safari park, those are better for the animals, aren't they?'

Mum took Margaret upstairs to unwrap her birthday package. It was soft and square and tied with a bow inside a sheet of sparkly metallic paper. Mum was wonderful at wrapping things up; she could probably have made a living doing it. Inside the package were layers of yellow tissue concealing two bra and knicker sets, neatly folded. Broderie anglaise. White.

'Oh,' Margaret said.

'You don't like them? No . . . I suppose . . . it's not really much of a present, not really. Open the other, then, why not? No point in saving things, is there? I can get something else for you . . . for Saturday.'

Mum scrabbled about under the bed and brought out a second package that was obviously a book. Margaret unwrapped it carefully, her thin, pale face exploding into a smile when she saw what it was.

'An *atlas.*'

'Yes. And it's all in colour and it has facts and figures on every country in the world . . . the North Pole and all that.'

'I love it,' Margaret said and kissed her. 'I love it very, very much.'

Margaret didn't thank Ray for her knicker sets or her hard-backed atlas even though the card was signed from both Mum and him. She didn't say goodbye to him either and later, on the journey home, she scrubbed out Ray's name from her birthday card with a pencil and placed it in the centre of her brand-new atlas next to a relief map of Egypt.

As we neared the end of Ray's turning I looked back and glimpsed Mum at the curtain, still standing there, still watching. She had an unfathomable look about her as if she might have stood in that very same spot on another night, or several nights, and watched Dad's car pull away.

46

Northwood Nursing Home
15 Wykeham Street
Worthing
West Sussex
January 19th 1935

Dearest Broo,

Your last letter, which arrived this morning, was quite
unusual, I must say, and even though I have read and
reread it a dozen times I still cannot be certain it came
directly from you and was not dictated by another and
merely set down in your hand. The language has the
lawyer's tone about it, don't you think? The feel of
Frederick at one of his lunches. In any case, I searched
hard for my sister in the words but could not entirely
find her.

Since you write to me in points, I will reply to you in
points and deal with them expressly and one by one.

To begin with, I have not made plans to leave here, as
you suggest, nor any firm decision on the adoption. I
wrote only to gauge your opinion on these matters and
had hoped you would respond to my concerns with

kindness instead of panic, since they are quite obviously the hardest I have ever faced.

You ask if I was aware of Frederick's intention to enter politics this year and I can honestly say that I was not. In any case, your implication that by keeping the baby I would damage his reputation was deeply hurtful. You write as if it is my express intention to damage Frederick's career – and also you – when this could not be further from the truth, since all I have ever wanted is your happiness.

You say I am to think of the child and to imagine its poor life without a father and that it would be deeply selfish of me to keep it. It would be better off without me, free from the dreadful slur of its illegitimacy. You are at great pains to emphasize that my own life and travels would be over and done with since the Royal Geographic and all its attendant friends and organizations would surely turn their backs on me at once. You present these summations as facts, threats even, and I wonder why you continually make mention of our inheritance and remind me that its funds are under your discretion, as the elder sister.

Is it your intention to withhold my share of the monies if I keep the baby? I wish you would have the courage to say so, since alluding to it makes life unclear and you must be perfectly well aware that I could not entertain bringing up a child alone if my means to support it were taken from me.

But enough of all this. Enough of writing to you via Frederick! I am worn out and cross this evening and this bickering can do us no good. I shall sleep on your letter, if sleep is at all possible, and continue my replies in the morning.

★   ★   ★

Today the dawn rose early, full of birdsong, and with a light so rosy and golden I felt for a moment as if I were back in Italy and were happy. It is so dreadfully quiet here at night, Broo. The darkness brings forth its blanket of isolation more potent than all my hours in the Arctic storms.

Let me be honest, dearest sister. I understand that my misgivings about the adoption will have come out of the blue and must have been a shock to you, but these doubts came upon me with a suddenness and a force I could not have expected and am finding near impossible to bear. In truth I have been entirely at a loss since poor Phyllis went and am depending on you for some resolution.

I have always considered myself a capable person, and a decisive one, but all problems up to now, most especially on my travels, have been practical ones and there was either a solution or there was not. Plainly the case is quite different here. Everything is grey and not the least of it is black and white, and whatever I decide from one hour to the next seems inexplicably wrong. I twist this way and that, until my head and my heart are tied in the most complex of knots and I am unable to think any further since I have not the effort nor the talent to untangle them.

What has become of me, Broo? Something queer happened not so very long after I crossed the threshold of this dreadful place. Perhaps it is the endless milk puddings and the forced hours of exercise, the walks in grim circles round the grounds. Dinners come on time here, to the second, every day, as do all the breakfasts and our lunch. I have become a woman of routines and regulations, reliant on someone else's markers to indicate the passing of the days. Christmas and new year passes without good signal or any flourish; it is as if the world moves on quite merrily without us.

At every opportunity we are encouraged not to feel or to worry or to think and I am ashamed to say I have grown quite used to it all and become compliant in both body and in soul. I have abandoned my books for the fripperies of magazines and have barely read a newspaper or spoken to a living soul outside these walls for many weeks. The telephones are barely ever working, as I have told you, and in my dark times I think this is intentional and that the wires outside this house are perfectly fine. Letters are so pitiably slow to arrive. By the time I receive a reply to one question it is likely my mind will be focused somewhere else entirely.

This ongoing problem with my blood pressure, which lately confines me to sitting still for hours on end, cannot be helping but in any case I feel my resilience slipping with each passing day. One evening this last week, while I was still able, I walked to the cliff edge and screamed out to the waves for Edith to return and for whoever had taken her from me to let her back. What have they turned me into, Broo? I cannot believe I would have felt like this only two short months ago, and some nights look at pictures of myself, sturdy and strong in the tropics or in the desert, and see in them a quite different person.

Please understand when I ask you for help. There is nobody left for me but you. I feel her kick just now – since I am duly convinced she is a she – and it is a vivid kick and a strong one, and full of hope. I begin to see her face and her hands and her mouth and to sense her own thoughts and her imaginings. How can I do this thing, Broo? Where will she go to? Who will her

people be? They could be anyone. *Anyone.* And no
matter if they were a king and queen, they would not
be me and how will they know how to love her? You
say they will be a good pair, a couple in need of affection and eager to give it, but it is not her job to ease
their pain, is it? Why should she be born to such a
pressure?

You suggest I cast my mind back to the way she came
about and I wonder what you meant by this exactly? Do
you imagine I will see Andrew in her face, that I will
despise her for what he did to me? I cannot think that
this would be the case since – I am sure of this already
– she will be entirely her complete and own person. Is it
possible to fall in love with a face you have never seen?
A body you have never touched, a voice you have yet to
hear?

Write to me soonest and without Frederick standing
at your shoulder. Do not abandon me now, Broo. I
need you as I have needed you always. Since we were
women. Since we two were only girls. Go this evening
and sit with the boys as they sleep. Take your pen to
me directly after that. Think not of convention and
society and politics, but only of the truth. If you can
tell me honestly, with all your heart, that my course
here is the right one then I will listen and trust you
and swallow it all, and not look back for a moment.
But if you have doubts then, I beg of you, have the
courage to share them with me. I shall not listen to
lectures on pity or morals or respond to any more of
your lawyer's speak.

You have been there, Broo, and I have not and I shall
know if you are writing from your bones. You have held
both your sons in your arms in the very moments after
they were born from you. If you tell me you could do

this thing, knowing what you know, experiencing what you have, then I will find the strength to do it and believe you.

Yours in best faith,
Your sister,
Edith

47

The thing I hadn't expected about feeling fed up with things was that other people are not at all sympathetic. On the whole, people don't like to be around people who are fed up unless they are fed up themselves. I suppose this is the reason that Margaret hung around with Ian Warrington so much – a darker soul it was hard to imagine – and I hung around with Gavin Hillier and his crowd. Otherwise, it was all too much pretending. You had to pretend things were funny when they weren't or important when they didn't seem to be. You couldn't just be your own low self for a couple of hours, not without some smart alec asking what the matter was without really wanting to know. You weren't expected to go into details of your fed-up-ness, you were meant to snap out of it right away. I could do this most days – I could make the brave face – but, even in those times when I made the effort, something indefinable, like the way I held my pencil or the height of my socks, always gave me away.

Kids from the happy homes seemed smug and simple to me, and I seemed complicated to them. In my bitter moments, unsuited to a girl of my age, I wanted to wreck their steadiness: their laughter, their easiness, their luck. But I didn't know how. So I went about wrecking myself.

'It doesn't hurt, you know.'

'That's what you say.'

'It's only glue.'

'That doesn't make sense.'

'Why doesn't it?'

'Because it doesn't mean anything. You could say war is only war, or a nuclear bomb is only a nuclear bomb. That doesn't mean they're not dangerous.'

Gavin shook his head. He didn't get it. He held his hand tight around the bag.

'How much do I take?' I said.

'Put it over your mouth and nose and take a good old sniff. It'll make you feel dizzy, but it's supposed to.'

I leant over and peered into the bag. At the bottom was a pool of gloopy solvent, thin and white, stolen from the arts and crafts block.

Gavin Hillier and I were sharing our lunch hour. The two of us loitered like petty thieves behind the sports hall, hidden by the rusty fire grilles on the slammed-shut doors. The shutters were down and it was dark inside, closed up for three months of refurbishment that was meant to have been finished during the summer holidays. A miserable winter of outdoor sports lay ahead: hockey and rounders and cross-country runs; short skirts and white, frozen legs.

The winter before, when the sports hall had been in use, I'd troop in most lunchtimes, with my old friends, to practise dance moves in my leotard and plimsolls. We'd worked out a good routine to the *Starsky and Hutch* theme tune and were perfecting it for the end-of-year review. There was plenty of kicking and crouching at the start and then we'd all line up with our arms in the air, our heads swaying in opposite directions. The whole thing climaxed with the seven of us forming a sort of human pyramid with Rebecca at the top barking orders and smiling, while we tried not to wobble her on our shoulders.

'What's the matter, Jess? Are you chicken?' Gavin said.

'No. I'm not chicken. Hand it over.'

I didn't take much of a sniff of it – I was never all that brave in such things – but I made a big amount of noise, mostly through my teeth, to make Gavin think I'd inhaled more than I had. Even so, the fumes left me reeling; I was breathless and unsteady like someone had punched me in the chest, and I immediately knew I would be sick. I slunk down on my knees and the stuff was spilling – sour and bitter – from my mouth before I'd had time to prepare for it. My head stayed exactly where I had left it – floating in the clouds, feet above me.

'Oh yeah. I forgot. Ha, ha, ha . . . it sometimes makes you puke up. Good, though, is it? Is it good?'

It was hard to say if it was or if it wasn't, or even if I felt happy or sad, when my whole world was so full of whiz. The ground moved quickly beneath my knees like a conveyor belt and I heaved hard again but nothing more came out and I began to cry.

'Why are you crying? Fuck's *sake*. You're not going to tell on me, are you?'

He sounded so scared that I felt he might kick my head in. I wondered if Gavin had even sniffed glue himself, or if I wasn't just part of his experiment. I ought to have told a teacher. Or someone. The pity was I couldn't tell his dad. His dad had just been banged up for fraud.

'Gavin, I think—'

'Just shut up.'

'I was only—'

'I *don't* want to hear it. Don't say nothing about this. Don't even *think* it.'

I concentrated hard and struggled with my jelly legs, willing my body to stand upright. I wiped the vomit from my lips and their edges felt sore and swollen where the glue residue and stomach acid had met. My head ached and my eyes blinked over and over, as if the fumes were still there, swimming round in them. All I was thinking about was this: I wished I'd practised my dance moves to the *Starsky and Hutch* theme tune more diligently; I wished my girlfriends hadn't turned their back on me on account of my unappealing fed-up-ness and cast me out of their dance troupe without so much as a farewell tube of lip gloss. More than anything in the world I wanted to be back inside that worn-out sports hall in a winter lunch hour, the rain pouring thin and cold outside its windows, my leotard stretched tight across my shoulders, Rebecca Witt heaved high upon my back.

'What's wrong with you?'
  'Nothing.'
  'Your eyes are red. Your mouth looks puckered at the edges.'
  'I had cheese and onion crisps for lunch.'
  'Oh.'
Margaret walked a half-pace behind me going home. She did this all the time, it drove me crazy.
  'First day back, then?'
  'First day back.'
  'It's worse than it ever was. Worse than before the holidays, I'd say.'
  I lengthened my stride and my sister struggled hard to keep up with me. It was difficult for her to talk from her half-pace behind my shoulders, to break her day's news and to share her worries.
  'My class were all whispering about me,' she said. 'From the moment I walked in this morning. At break time they said I was a bastard. But it's not . . . that's not fair. It's not right.'
  'That's nothing,' I said. 'That's as mild as you like. They can call you whatever they want.'

'I don't mean it's not right as in the right thing to say,' she said. 'I mean, it's not strictly *correct*.'

I hitched my rucksack further up my back. She tried my patience sometimes, she really did.

'Because bastards are illegitimate. And we're not illegitimate, are we?'

'No.'

Margaret advanced a quarter-step.

'Mum is a stinking slag bag. Her baby will be born out of wedlock, so *it* will definitely be a bastard. And she's a whore. That's what she is. She should be ashamed of herself.'

'For fuck's sake, Margaret. Who told you *that*?'

'You're not supposed to swear.'

'What about *you*? I didn't just call Mum a slag bag.'

'It's not me. It *isn't*. If you'd even *bother* to listen . . . I'm only trying to tell you what *they* said.'

Off she marched then, a good pace ahead of me, her head held erect on her bony shoulders. Acting like the argument was my fault, as usual. Stealing the moral high ground.

48

On the morning of our proposed birthday visit to the safari park the sky threatened murderous storms. The sun was in hiding, lost to a mound of black clouds; everything was shrouded in a permanent dusk like on those short days you get before Christmas.

'I didn't want to go anyway.'

'It's better than the zoo. The animals get to run around.'

'No. I don't think so. It won't be any good in the rain.'

'But we've worked out the route. Ray has already bought a map.'

'If it's OK with you, I'd just as soon go into town for a birthday lunch.'

Ray winced and Mum sank from her shoulders. Lunch was problematic. Food of any kind was problematic. Already the day was growing tense.

'Well, what would you like to eat? Burgers?'

'No.'

'Fish and chips?'

'No.'

'Ice cream? Cake?'

My sister put her hands in her pockets.

'I think . . . I might like pizza. If that's all right?'

'*Wonderful.* Brilliant. Pizzaland it is, then. Pizzaland.'

Mum seemed so happy to have found a resolution that she gabbled non-stop all the way. We took a bus to the high street because you could never find a parking space, and it was fun on the bus, the bus was fun. Mum bought the tickets and ushered us onto the cramped double-decker but no one offered her a seat even though she was puffed out and wider than the aisle. 'I'm fine, I'm fine,' she kept saying. 'Don't mind about me.' And no one did.

At the depot in town the bus emptied out and Ray helped Mum through the sharp-elbowed crowd. Margaret practised her half-pace-behind-us-all routine, walking slowly with her head down, morose in her birthday dress and raincoat.

'Twelve years old. Oh my goodness. Nearly a teenager, all grown up. It only seems like yesterday the two of you were in nappies. And they didn't have disposables in those days. Well, they had them but they were far too expensive. Your dad wouldn't let me buy them, which was all very well, but it wasn't him that ever had to wash them. I had to wash the lot of them. All that washing and it never seemed to end. You liked peas, Margaret, pureed peas. Never known a baby that liked to eat peas quite so much. And bananas, of course, and rosehip syrup. You drank bottles and bottles of the stuff. It's bad for your teeth, we found that out later, but Nanna carried on giving it to you regardless. I worried that your gums would rot and all your teeth would fall out, I really did. But they were fine, you had good teeth, good and strong. Not so much as a filling, not until you were eight and only then because you chipped an incisor on a peppermint. Your dad gave you that peppermint. And I said it was too hard for you. Rubbish, he said, it's not too hard. Serve him right when the dentist's bill came, that's what I said. Let him put his hand in his pocket for once. Nanna wanted to come today, by the way, did I say that already? She sent you a birthday present anyway and I have it in my bag here, and I'll give it to you when we all get inside. Her legs aren't so good this week. Her ankles are swollen up, just like mine. Water retention, I suppose. I'm worried about her. Perhaps I should take her to the doctor.'

Ray cast us both a weary look and even though Margaret and I had no time for him, we took a moment to acknowledge it and to work out its likely translation. She's like this, your mother, at the moment, it said. Can't shut her up. Not for a second.

'We're here. Here we *are*. I'd forgotten how far down the high road it was. I could eat an entire plateful and a baked potato too, come to that. Ray, you go in first. See if they have a table. For four of us. A table for *four*.'

She shouted this at him as he sloped through the door, as if he might have forgotten how many we were. You could see her wondering if she'd sent the right person and if she shouldn't have gone in herself. Her inclination at such moments was to send the man of the family but Ray wasn't family and, in his red pyjama bottoms, he looked quite unlike a real man.

'Do you think it's OK?' she said, rubbing at her round belly. 'They're looking at him funny. Are they looking at him funny, do you think?'

The storm broke just as we were waiting there for Ray, and even though we dashed inside quickly the rain still managed to wet our hair and coats. We sat at a table by the door looking pale and bedraggled, our hands filled with outsized plastic menus.

'Well,' said Mum, gamely, drying her neck with a paper napkin, 'isn't this lovely? What a treat.'

The meal itself went better than expected. Mum ate an entire pizza and a baked potato on the side – just like she'd threatened to – and I had a margherita with green peppers, onions and extra cheese. Ray and Margaret stuck to the salad bar, which was especially good value because you could take as much as you liked and go back as many times as you wished. Ray chose a florid concoction of pulses, beetroot, bean sprouts, salad greens and radishes. Margaret ate mostly raisins and diet coleslaw.

Nobody commented on Margaret's choice of food, and things were left mostly like that. Margaret unwrapped Nanna's present, a pair of hand-knitted gloves in a bad orange colour, and just as she was trying them on the waiters arrived with a sponge cake studded with candles and sparklers, ready to sing her 'Happy Birthday'.

'Who told them?'

'I did, when I went to the loo.'

Mum smiled at me to say thank you, and bit her lip because she hadn't thought to organize it for Margaret herself. Ray nodded and pushed back his spectacles, amused by the novelty and eager to clap along with the waiters, who sang in deep, clear voices – mock-Italian – not quite hiding the fact they did this type of thing twenty times a week.

'Oh,' Margaret said, when they'd finished and she'd blown out her candles. 'That was fun. Thank you, Jess. Thanks a lot.'

'You're welcome,' I said. 'It can sort of be your present. Because . . . I didn't. So anyway. Happy birthday.'

By the time we were done with lunch there was enough mess on the table, streamers and whipped cream and mayonnaise and cake bits, to look like we'd had a good time. There had been no talk of babies or divorces or anorexia or Pam and Dad, and you'd almost think the four of us were a normal family.

'Well, I never. I thought it was you. I *said* so, didn't I? That's definitely Joy.'

'Oh,' said my mother, standing up.

'No, no. Don't get up.'

My mother still stood there. To attention.

'We had the prawn cocktail. Did you try it? Or are you meant to lay off prawns? In your condition?'

'I didn't . . . Well, I'm probably not supposed . . .'

'Who's this with you now? Is this him?'

'This is Ray,' Mum said, looking awkward.

'Congratulations, then . . . *Ray.*'

Ray said thank you.

Gloria Hillier was all of a piece. Her hair was solid and set and her face was layered in make-up – oranges, browns and powder blues. She stood with a woman I didn't recognize but they both had the same rich look about them, rueful and snobbish and kept.

'How is David *coping*?' she whispered.

'David is fine.'

'Well, that's good, then. Isn't that good?'

'And Laurence?'

'Oh, Laurence, believe me, is fine. It's only three months, not much longer than a holiday. Says he's never eaten better in his life!'

She laughed as if it were nothing, her eyes staring straight down her nose at us. A face full of pity, if only she'd known what pity was.

'Your birthday, is it, sweetheart?' she said, turning to Margaret. 'Aw, now . . . how lovely. This will all seem strange to you, I expect.'

Margaret coughed on a raisin and said, 'Not really.'

'And you're big, Joy, aren't you? Very big.'

'I'm gone eight months now.'

'And you're definitely keeping it, I hear?'

'What do you mean?'

'Me? Oh nothing. You're terribly brave . . . but *some* people might say—'

'We don't care what people say,' Ray interrupted.

Gloria forced a smile as if to say that was obvious, and glanced at her shoes to show the embarrassment she thought he and my mother ought to be displaying. Her brown-painted fingernails click-clacked accusingly against one another and a long gold box-chain swung heavily in the crease of her bosoms. I wanted to reach up and grab it and strangle her snobbery with it.

'Hold on just one minute,' I said. 'My mum might be having a bastard baby with a hippy . . . but at least *her* husband's not gone to *prison*. And you can say it's only three months if you like but that's just a lie because Gavin says it might be a year. And it's no good you flashing your jewellery because we know you're going bankrupt and will have to live in a caravan, and if my mum has a boy at least he won't turn out to be a . . . See, your son is a drug pusher, did you know that? He makes girls sniff glue in the *bloody* playground. And they didn't want to do it. They didn't, so there. They didn't even bloody want to *do* it!'

The manageress arrived with our bill after that. Ray paid it in cash without bothering to check how much it was. My voice was sore later. I hadn't realized how loud I'd been shouting.

49

In retrospect, I think going to hospital that afternoon was Mum's way of trying to take care of us. She always swore it was the pineapple on her pizza that brought the labour on, but I couldn't help thinking it was me. It had to be my outburst, I was sure of it, and the stark revelations about the glue. One daughter in trouble she could cope with, two daughters in trouble she could not. In Mum's mind there was nothing else for it. She would bring on those contractions – two weeks early, if she had to – and gather us all together: Margaret and me, and Nanna with her legs, and her brand-new, about-to-be-born baby, safe from harm in a well-scrubbed hospital corridor.

We travelled by taxi from a spot fifty yards from the restaurant, not too long after the second twinge came.

'This is it,' Mum said, at once. 'I think it's coming.'

'Are you sure, Joy?' Ray said. 'Because it might just be wind. You ate quite a lot . . . with that potato.'

Mum glared like she might thump him and, dense as he was, he seemed to take the hint then, and thrust out his tunic sleeve to hail a taxi.

'She won't have it in here, mate, will she?' the cab driver said.

Ray said, 'She might do. She might do unless you bleedin'
hurry up.'

I'd not seen Ray panic before, not even on that day with
Margaret and the pyramid and the knife. He seemed shaky
and out of his depth: a cluster of awkward habits instead of
a man, all sighs and bitten nails and absent comforts. At the
hospital gates, when he realized he didn't have enough cash
left in his pocket for the fare and would have to ask Margaret
to pay it from her birthday money, he looked close to the
edge of a nervous breakdown. He flapped about, counting
out the notes from her cards, while Margaret held him steadily
with her most evil eye. The taxi driver waited for his tip.
Mum said Ray ought to call Nanna.

Nanna turned up promptly with slippers and night clothes
for Mum, a pair of grubby pressure stockings rolled haphaz-
ardly along her swollen legs. She came laden with supplies,
as if the hospital were an air-raid shelter and we were facing
a night of bombing in the blitz. She wore sturdy shoes and
her best navy overcoat and carried biscuits, cakes, toffees and
sandwiches, loose in a plastic carrier bag, enough to feed the
five thousand. She handed Mum a tin of fruit travel sweets
to suck, which seemed perverse since Mum was hardly likely
to be going anywhere.

'These will keep your strength up,' she said to Mum, in a
way that sounded like a chastisement.

'God, let it be quick,' Mum said, red and breathing quickly
on her seat.

'Unlikely,' said Nanna, gloomily. 'The third one can often
be a beast.'

In all of the fuss and the excitement I hadn't noticed we
were being looked at. Other women, with lumbering bodies
and varicose veins that pointed like wonky arrows from their
ankles to their thighs, cast suspicious frowns across the five

of us, as if we were creatures from the zoo. At one point
Nanna's carrier bag fell to the floor with a thud and she
reached down and swore, 'Damn and blast it,' as a hard-
boiled egg escaped its paper serviette and smashed. She
picked up the spilt bits of egg white and shell with her finger-
tips.

Margaret had taken off her raincoat and baggy jumper,
exposing her insufficient body. Revealed beneath her clothes
were the sharp bones of her shoulders, giving way to the
beginnings of her ribs. They jutted through the thin, flowery
fabric of her dress, giving stems to the blossoms that didn't
have any. Perhaps it was the hard fluorescent lighting. Perhaps
it was the juxtaposition with the pregnant women sitting by
us who were grossly inflated and round. Whatever tipped
things over, it was suddenly apparent that what was left of
Margaret was stretched like tissue paper across her frame
with barely enough flesh left to support it.

I tried not to stare at her myself and became conscious
that my hair had dried madly from the rain and was attracting
its own level of attention. I pressed my hand over the ulcer
on my lip, the one that had sprung up from the sting of
Gavin's glue and was beginning to turn dark and crusty.

And then there was Ray, whose strange garb and demeanour
always attracted long looks. I wondered if perhaps that's why
he wore those dumb clothes, to appear in some way different
or exceptional. And yet the more I got to know him the less
exceptional and different he turned out to be. His outfits
were always variations on the same pair of outsized pyjamas,
as safe in their own way as the nurse's white uniform or the
doctor's. Nanna sucked hard on a toffee. Oblivious to the
dirt on her pressure bandages. Oblivious to the sticky clip-
clop of her dentures.

In the outside world, beyond the confines of the hospital,
Mum would have been the odd one out. But inside, on that

night, she looked by far and away the most normal of the five of us. The hospital gown they had dressed her in was the same as other women's hospital gowns. The trolley that she lay on while she waited for a room was squeaky and high like all the rest. The sounds that she made were loud like the other women's and made me think of an injured animal. Nobody batted an eyelid at her cries. All of the women were in pain.

Even in the midst of this madness came forms and charts and papers that needed to be filled in. They wanted to be sure they had all things quite right and to find out who everyone was. Margaret, me and Nanna they were happy with. Ray was more problematic.

'So you're not *Mr* Lester?' said a woman who must have been a midwife.

'No. No, I'm not. I'm Mr Parry.'

'But *you're* the baby's father.'

'Yes, I am.'

The mothers in labour with their husbands by their sides were a mixture of interest and judgement; they were grateful to have a moment of face-twitching to take their minds off their own contractions. The single girls thought it was a hoot – an older woman in a spot of bother, just like them. Margaret tapped her fingers on the base of her plastic chair and stared back. Then she stood up from her seat and went directly to Mum's trolley and lay a protective arm, thin and pale, across the width of Mum's angry belly.

I don't remember how long it was before they moved Mum into her own room. Beds were tightly rationed and you only got your own when you were close. Mum was getting closer, you could tell. You could tell because her waters suddenly broke.

'Oh no, what's all that?'

'Christ, here we go. It's only my waters, Margaret. Don't you worry.'

'I'll take them both home.'

'No, Mum, I want them both *here*.'

'What good will it do them? This muck and this nonsense.'

'They're staying, you understand me? I want them with me.'

'Should there be so much blood?'

'Of course there should be *blood*. For God's sake, why wouldn't there be blood?'

'This is my first experience of childbirth, Joy. I'm not to know all the ins and out—'

'I told you, *didn't* I? Didn't you read any of the bloody *books*?'

'Now, try to calm down. You're getting yourself into a state.'

'*You* calm down. Oh, you've calmed down fairly well already, haven't you? What were you doing in the toilet, Ray? Rolling yourself another bloody *joint*? Oh, for fuck's sake, for fuck's *sake* . . . I need to get something for the pain. Where's the bloody midwife? Where's she gone?'

'Went to fetch a bedpan,' said Nanna, through her toffee. 'Don't swear now, dear. Not if you can help it.'

'*Mum.*'

'What?'

'Take the girls outside.'

'I said that, didn't I? You should have listened to me in the first place.'

'Not too far away . . . *please*. Girls, why don't the two of you wait outside?'

Nanna stood up then, pulled a hankie from her pocket and wiped it ever so gently across Mum's cheeks. Something kicked in, something warm and maternal, even her rough, old fingers seemed to soften.

'It'll be all right now, pet,' she murmured, sweetly, to her daughter. 'Mark my words now if it won't. We'll be right outside the door if you need us. We're not going anywhere, are we, girls?'

I said no straight away, because I'd never seen my mother in so much pain. I wondered if the baby might be killing her, because suffering of that cruelty could not be normal. I wasn't going anywhere. Not until it was all over. Not until that bastard was good and out.

The last things I heard were Ray saying, 'Do you want to practise your meditation techniques?' and my mum saying 'I want the injection, you hippy *fucker*!' The nurse barged in with the bedpan just then and I distinctly heard her say, 'No, that's not good.'

Somewhere in among all that I sensed Margaret go quiet and when I turned round to look at her she'd fallen to the floor in a faint. When the doctor picked her up he looked at me and then at Nanna and said, 'Jesus, poor little mite, she's skin and bone. Get her on a drip, she's dehydrated. Her pulse is all over the place.'

I went with my sister and Nanna, rushing along with Margaret on a trolley of her own, the corridor singing with Mum's terrible barks and screams.

50

Northwood Nursing Home
15 Wykeham Street
Worthing
West Sussex

February 9th 1935

Dear sister,

Three weeks gone already and still no word from you,
just that strange conversation with your housekeeper late
last evening when she swore you were in France and not
contactable, while I am utterly convinced that you were
there. Can it be possible that you would leave now, when
I so desperately and dearly need to speak with you? I
waited hours for a line and it was late, yet I am certain I
heard Frederick, or the boys, or some other person
issuing instruction directly to her. Where in France, I
asked her, and then was sure I heard someone whisper
Nantes. What is their address? Which telephone number
may I use? How must I reach my sister in an emergency? No information was forthcoming yet the idea you
might leave Norfolk without giving every manner of
foreign contact to your staff is entirely unthinkable.

This morning, after more hours of waiting, I managed a line to Frederick's offices. They were similarly unhelpful and obtuse. Congratulations, Broo. You have turned all your world into liars.

Is it Frederick's instruction that you not talk to me or answer my letters? Does he imagine leaving me stranded with no comfort or support will put paid to the worst of my plans? It is quite the gamble, I should warn you, and in all my years of knowing Frederick I have never found him to be much of a risk taker. Wasn't I always given to do the opposite of other people's wishes: to wear red when Mummy wanted me dressed in blue; to leap up when Daddy needed me to be quiet? How unlike our mother you are in all of this. How empty and so like a coward. Do you think she would be ashamed of *me*? I am quite certain she would be ashamed of you.

If you care in the least, my physical comfort is fast deteriorating. My legs are all pains now and filled up with water, one day the texture of tight balloon skins, one day the texture of sinking dough. I sleep in fits and starts, called hourly to the lavatory, and even in the minutes in between it is bitterly hard to get comfortable. The stress is in my hip joints, which the doctor says are worn from all my walking, and my blood pressure seems to rise daily to dangerous levels, and so they may be obliged to bring it on. A week or so more and I am considered safe and ready, and so you can see there is hardly any more time.

You will be pleased to know that Alice and Evelyn, whose limited counsel I am forced to keep, are on your side and there are moments when I wonder if you have not travelled here in secret and paid them to offer up your own opinions. Alice squats beside me through the long afternoons, her own body a notebook of complaints. We look at pictures in the fashion magazines and sometimes at our envelopes of photographs. We marvel at our once-slender frames and pick out dresses we might wear when our bodies are diminished and returned to normal. In truth, I have little interest in her gabbling but it usefully wastes the hours and Alice's enthusiasm for a life beyond all this is a tonic, since I have lately come to believe this limbo will never end. If I begin to raise my doubts she will happily say I am quite mad. What kind of hindrance is a baby, she wants to know. What pressure. What weight. What dreadful shackle.

Evelyn's insights are kinder – since she is older and entirely the more thoughtful of the two – but she is less keen on dialogue these days than on issuing forth her sermons and her warnings. My life will come undone if I choose to keep this baby. I ought never to underestimate its cost. She swears that in the beginning they are unfortunate and unlovely creatures, barely more likeable than cats. Even so, I am to do my very best not to hold it for very long or to spend too much time alone with it after the birth, since its hope will be to put me underneath its spell. She swears she will not look hers in the eye, since its brand of black magic happens all too quickly. Lord knows where she gathers all this nonsense. I can only imagine she receives it directly from her mother. When I ask her if she means it, she crosses her heart directly but then her pale features turn away. I know she hides the pain of it buried in her heart, so deep it is beyond me to unfurl it.

And yet she is true about one thing. The attachment comes quickly and intensely, since I surely feel its stranglehold already. We are one, the two of us, a single creature. We wake and sleep and think and breathe together, and share the last days of our confinement with equal fortitude. I long for her with every scrap of patience I have left in my spreading bones and know she waits with all her love for me. I reach to stroke the imprint of her toes with my swollen fingers. I begin to feel the push of her tiny head. I imagine my life with and without her, as one would life with or without one's own heart.

Last night I dreamt of Phyllis. I saw her standing alone at the car with her empty arms wide open and no one good to love her or to hold her. Could we make it alone, Broo? Must the two of us make it on our own?

Find it in your heart to answer, if you can.

Edith

51

Margaret lay there pale and sedated, a scrap of a thing, beneath her thin, grey-white hospital covers. I wanted the nurses to wake her up so I could tell her everything was OK. Mum was fine and the baby was fine, and the midwife's outburst of worry hadn't been directed at Mum at all, but at Ray, who'd fainted like a blood-shy girl at the sight of a pair of forceps and cracked his skull open on the metal bedstead. But the doctors weren't about to wake Margaret up just yet, and there was talk of inserting a plastic tube through her nose and down her tired throat to feed her, since it seemed clear to the doctors she had grown incapable of feeding herself. Dad, who they'd called on right away, seemed to think this was ridiculous and the argument raged back and forth with what seemed like little care for my sister who lay still with her creased eyelids flickering.

And so it was that evening that the hospital came to contain the whole of my immediate family, its impostors and its most recent newcomer.

'Do you want to go and see your mother?' Dad asked me. 'Pamela and I will stay here with Margaret.'

'Are you sure?'

'Of course we're sure.'

'What if she wakes up?'

'We'll be here.'

'But . . .'

'Go,' Pam said. 'See your mum.'

Of course, Mum didn't know what had happened to Margaret
and I was under strict instruction not to tell her.

'Not a word, now,' Nanna hissed through her dentures as
I went inside. 'If you worry her it'll only stop her milk.'

What this meant exactly, I could hardly guess, but I was
cheered by the sight of Mum sitting upright in her bed, pink-
cheeked and healthy with a wide smile spread across her face.
In her arms – one arm really, since the package was so small
and deceptively insignificant – lay a stranger, a newly sleeping
baby.

'It's a girl,' is the first thing Mum said to me. 'Another
sister. Do you think Margaret will mind?'

I went closer to look at it, to peer in through its layers of
crisp white covers. It was all blanket and bonnet, and peeping
out from the top was a face as pale and creamy as Palmolive
soap suds. Its lips were bright red and its eyelids were quiet,
and its tiny chest rose gently up and down.

'Look at her fingers,' Mum said to me.

I looked at them. I touched them. I felt awkward and clumsy
and wary of their perfection, and pulled away, worried I might
hurt them.

'It's OK,' Mum said. 'She won't break.'

'She's pretty.'

'Isn't she? She has blue eyes just like Margaret's. And
Nanna's turned-up nose and your full mouth.'

There was no talk of Ray. No talk of what bit of the baby
was just like Ray.

'Did it hurt a lot?' I said.

'Oh, it wasn't all that bad. It was all over so quickly in the
end. You were two days coming and Margaret, almost as long.

Four hours,' she said, sighing and shifting her bottom carefully. 'Well, it hardly seems like anything, not really.'

On closer inspection, it looked like those four hours might have been something after all. There were still streaks of blood here and there on Mum's covers and I worried that Mum's cheeks were red with effort and exhaustion not robustness. Her hair was matted from where she had been sweating and it had dried in a thick and gummy clump. She winced as she moved up the bed, and her covers fell to her waist exposing the shapeless form of her empty belly, which swilled from side to side, loose like the skin on an aging custard.

'It was good of Margaret to go home with Nanna. I know she was desperate to stay.'

'You didn't mind?'

'It could have stretched on a long time. I'm just glad they went back together.'

'Well, Nanna was . . . getting tired. And . . . she didn't want to go home on her own.'

'I'll have them come first thing in the morning. The nurse is bringing me the phone in. You don't think it's too late to call them, do you?'

I wondered about this error in communications. But the nurse couldn't know that my mum was trying to phone her daughter who was flat out in a ward one floor below her.

'Well, it might be, I mean . . .'

'It's only nine, after all. Nanna will still be up watching the news.'

I longed for this to be true. For Nanna to be at home in her bungalow watching the news, with Margaret curled up next to her on the sofa. Nanna would be moaning about the state of things and sipping from her usual mug of Ovaltine, and Margaret would be reading about polio or the desert or the rainforest, or some such, in one of her well-thumbed library books.

'Where's Ray?' I said, stalling for time.

'Bathing his stitches,' Mum said. 'Idiot. He really is an idiot.'

I tried to work out if she was saying this in an affectionate way or a critical way and I couldn't decide which it was. In any case she seemed less keen on talking about Ray and his stitches than in gazing down on the face of her brand-new daughter. She took her index finger and traced a dainty circle around both her cheeks. She touched her lips lightly and kissed the top of her head with such gentleness and sweetness, and even though she was sleeping, the baby seemed to know my mother was doing this and her ten perfect fingers stretched with pleasure.

I asked if Ray would be back soon but Mum seemed not to hear me or to want to answer the question. She beckoned me closer and placed my finger in the tiny, hot palm of the baby's hand, and her fingers curled around mine and squeezed.

'She's saying hello to you,' Mum said.

'Hello, little baby,' I said back.

The three of us sat there for what seemed like a long while and it felt to me then that Mum hardly cared if Ray did or didn't come back. She breathed in time with the bundle in her arms and could hardly draw her eyes away from its face. It only needed Margaret to have been there, it seemed to me, and she would have been fully content.

The nurse intruded, pushing a shrill-wheeled trolley, and on top of it was a pay phone whose wires she set about untangling and plugging into the wall. I rushed out a little too quickly and said, 'Nanna, did you see what they just brought? She's about to phone you. To tell you the news.'

'I won't be there,' Nanna said.

'Of course not.'

'Because I'm here.'

'Well, that's right.'

'This is stuff and nonsense,' said Nanna brusquely, standing up. 'Enough of these secrets. Secrets never did anyone any good.'

She swept her hands against one another as if she was wiping her hands of the lot of it.

'Your granddad would never have stood for any of this malarkey,' she said, correctly, as she barged her way into Mum's room.

Mum had the baby in the crook of one arm and the phone in the other. At the end of the line a tone rang into dead air. A moment of confusion was etched on her face but almost before we could speak she'd replaced the receiver, repositioned the baby on her shoulder and gingerly swung her legs to the edge of the bed.

'Where is she?' she said. 'Where's Margaret? One of you fetch out my slippers.'

52

We gathered together around her, Nanna and me, and Dad
and Pam, and my mother, in her nightie and slippers, perched
on the one soft armchair, holding the baby. The curtain that
was meant to have given Margaret's bed some privacy
wouldn't nearly stretch around the six of us, no matter how
tightly and uncomfortably we crammed together. Nanna and
I stood in the middle, separating the split wings of the family.

Ray turned up presently, a plaster on his head positioned
just above the frame of his glasses, which were bent out of
shape from his fall. When my father first clapped eyes on him,
in his sandals and wide pyjamas, I felt he wanted to laugh out
loud. Here he was, face to face with his mortal enemy, yet his
enemy seemed to have no substance at all. Nanna would say
later that Ray's role in all of this was neither here nor there
and that Dad had been his very own worst enemy.

'Hello, everyone,' Ray said, without a trace of embarrassment. 'How's our girl?'

You could see Dad's hackles rise then because Margaret
wasn't 'his' girl, until it dawned on him Ray might have been
talking about the baby. In its own way this was even worse.
The baby was fine and that seemed perfectly plain and clear
to all and sundry; it was my other sister everyone was worried
about.

'She's fine,' Mum said, sharply. 'Margaret isn't doing quite so well.'

This seemed to be an understatement. The doctors had taken Margaret off the sedatives – her bodily functions had righted themselves and her heart, which had been demonstrating some arrhythmia, appeared to have clicked back into beating out good time – but the problem was she couldn't, or wouldn't, wake up. The chemicals left in her blood were too weak to induce such a deep and steady sleep and yet she was unresponsive to all of our pleadings and our chatter, and the intermittent probing from the nurses.

Mum leant down and showed her the baby. Her face looked tearful and pinched.

'See, Margaret,' she said, 'it's your little sister. She's only just born and she wants to meet you. And everything is fine now, so if you were worried about all that . . . well, it was only just Ray being . . . being stupid.'

Ray fingered his plaster and was about to make some rebuttal to his alleged stupidity, when Nanna clicked her dentures and waded in.

'Perhaps she doesn't want to wake up and talk. Perhaps she's had it up to here with the lot of you. Who could blame her if she wanted to get some rest? The way you've all been behaving?'

Ray looked at Nanna with a new respect.

'She's absolutely right,' he said, to all of us. 'In my clinical opinion, I'd say Margaret's nanna had it just about right.'

Dad hesitated.

'What clinical opinion would that be, exactly?' he asked.

'Well, David, in my work as a psychoanalyst I've had some experience of children's—'

'Don't call me David.'

'I . . . well, what should I call you?'

'I'm telling you, don't go there, you poof.'

Ray raised his shoulders and lifted his arms to the ceiling as if to ask, Who *is* this moron? Dad's fingers tightened into a large and solidly well-formed fist and I began to see the qualities of temperament he shared with his older brother, our Uncle John.

'Now, let's all not get personal,' Pam said, hastily.

Mum tore her eyes away from Margaret and absorbed in those few seconds all there was to know about Dad's Pam: her age, her class, her agenda, her tactlessness, her recently failed but willing beauty.

'There's bad blood here,' Pam said. 'Of course there is. So there's no point in any of us pretendin—'

'Bad blood?' said my mother.

'Well, it's water under the bridge. The way you choose to bring up your children. . . . the way you choose to behave as a wife.'

Mum stood up, even though it was suddenly painful for her to stand.

'What do you know about me? Or *my* life? How dare you pass comment on my family?'

Pam's eyes hardened and shrank. A woman stood before her – the wife of her boyfriend, a woman who had just given birth – yet there wasn't a shred of softness about her, nor a moment of allowance or reflection.

'If you leave them, what can you expect?' she said. 'If you run off with the likes of *him*, making little ones at your age . . . well, you ought to take everything what's coming to you.'

'You think Margaret being ill is *my* fault?'

'Well, it doesn't take a bloody expert, does it? And no one might have noticed if it wasn't for me. Who else's fault would it be, Joy? You know full well it bloody is.'

'You miserable, gold-digging . . . witch.'

'Oh, there we are, then. Did you hear that, everybody? That's her true character coming out.'

Margaret sighed out loud and sort of coughed, puncturing the moment with her distaste. We thought she might wake and speak then, but nothing. Mum sat back down, close to tears.

'I won't do this in front of her. I just won't do it,' she said. 'Get her out of here, now. Just you get *out*! And you too,' she said, turning to Ray. 'Neither one of you ought to be here. She needs to be with us now, with her family.'

A quiet descended after that. Mum offered Dad a weak and weary smile.

'They can't force her to eat,' she said, 'can they?'

'They won't need to. She isn't that bad.'

'Not yet, then?'

'No,' Dad said. 'Not yet.'

Mum shuffled forward on her chair and its metal legs scraped sharply across the lino. She lay her hand on Margaret's and stroked it and held it, and whispered, 'Sorry.'

'I love you,' she said. 'My sweetest, lovely girl. It will all be all right soon. I promise.'

Dad reached in from his side of the bed and lay his own hand on Margaret's arm.

'We made a mess of it, Joy,' he said. 'How did we make such a mess of it?'

There was silence as an answer, save for the flushing of toilets in the corridor, the tin-can crash of bedpans and the growl of other patients' discomforts. There were soft rhythmic breaths from Margaret's down-turned mouth, and stretches and happy sighs from the baby.

'Even so,' Nanna said, after a while. 'This wouldn't have happened in my day. If you were fussy about your food then, you starved.'

I looked at my sister who lay there starving herself, punishing her body and controlling it. She was managing her weight and the weight of all of this, slipping further and further from good answers. Mum leant closer into Margaret, the baby held fast to her breast.

'I should never have left.'

'No . . . well. If you had to . . .'

'I felt I did.'

'Then you should have.'

'It wasn't fair on Margaret. She's really much too young. It was selfish . . . I had a responsibility . . .'

'Too right you did,' Pam said, barging back through the curtain with a tray of plastic cups filled with tea. 'Girls her age need keeping a close eye on. Men are no good at it, none at all. Couldn't have been healthy, her working all this through on her own. Lord only knows what she'd made of it. And I'll tell you what else wasn't helpful: her obsessing on that dead woman's letters.'

'What letters?' my mum said.

'Your neighbour's, that's what. That old lady. You want to count yourself lucky, Joy. Women like you didn't have it quite so easy back in them days.'

53

Greenland

To take:
One ink pen
One notebook
One snow stick
One bivouac
One windproof
One fox fur
One bible

Alwyne Road
Canonbury
London
October 20th 1935

My dearest Phyllis,

I hope you will not mind me, or this letter, but I could think of no one else that I might write to. With all my heart I hope it finds you safe. With all my heart I hope it finds you well.

Approaching a year now since you left us all at Northwood. For me it has been some several months. I left in early March when those blizzards hit the Downs and all is still so vivid and so fresh. My time there seems as recent as my waking and my washing just this morning. Did you find it the same way? And do you still? Of the labour itself I recall most every detail and can begin at the slightest of the pains. Of course they did not hurt then, not physically at least, and were only the tweaks and tunings before the fanfare. Matron fetched me early, as if by some sixth sense, and wore that hard glow all about her. I remember how she told me that it might well be a long one, and though I told her I was ready, she insisted it had made mincemeat of stronger girls.

In the beginning I was good, as they go. I stood up and walked and wore a path up and down the tiled corridor, though they tried to have me stay by my bed. Lie down, they would say to me, and be done with it, but I had entirely done with my lying down. I had signed their dreadful adoption papers just that morning. I kissed my girl goodbye that afternoon.

It was the day before she came, I was restless and hectic, in that way that you are, and had spent the morning tidying my room. The documents came by hand and there were many pages, and the writing was tightly packed and the language dense. I want to tell you it was a shock to receive them and yet I distinctly remember thanking the man who delivered them and my telling him I had expected them. Do you know what these are? he asked – since he had been expressly advised to do so by my sister and by my brother-in-law. Yes, I said, it is all immensely clear to me. These are the legal instructions of my disinheritance.

Of course, it was the end of all things. I had come to believe over the weeks and months that a child might be happy without a father and a father's name, just so long as its mother loved it and they were not destitute. My love for her I could be sure of. My financial provision for her, I no longer could. They sought to take away my only income. They sought to take away my only home. I might have relied on some monies from academic works or from my writing but how should I do this with a baby to look after and society the way that it is? Each woman at Northwood was insistent to me then and not even Evelyn, who I knew held strong doubts of her own, would countenance my changing my mind. Without funds or a home, or any family to rely upon, it would have been an act of cruelty to have kept her.

When the pains began in earnest there was nothing dreadfully useful to be done and in any case I would not have accepted their ministrations or their pills since the pain seemed entirely well deserved. I heard myself cry out from it, over and over, and yet seemed to be somewhere else entirely. When finally they held me down for it, strapped up and prone, I clung so hard to the bedstead I am sure I left my mark on the iron. There were towels and strong unguents and steam from the sinks, and shouts for me to push and then not to push, and nothing that sounded hopeful or like the beginning of the end. I simply remember someone saying I must be cut and then another saying I would be stitched. And then it was done. And she was out. And the pain left so suddenly that I missed it since we had come to an understanding between the two of us, and in any case the grief that took its place was so very much worse.

I had sworn I would not hold her and yet I did. My arms and my body made a space for her at once and

my heart began the love of a lifetime. She turned her
sweet face and gazed up at me with her wide eyes just
opened, and I have never looked upon a soul more
beautiful. What a dear thing she was. What happiness I
felt in those moments. To feel the warmth of her skin
next to my skin, to witness her first cry on earth. I
stroked her mouth and her belly and I kissed her sweet
head, and felt the gentlest wriggle of her toes. I know
that gentle wriggle, I told her. I have felt that same
elbow and kick. To imagine I had worried I might
wonder who she was. I found that I knew her well
already.

And then, dear Phyllis, she was gone. It happened so
very quickly and on some secret signal, and without my
ever saying it was time. My skin hurt as they prised her
small body away from mine, and she cried out in shock
and looked back for me and yelled for me, and I shouted
to them all that I couldn't do it. Ellory had them grab
me at the shoulders and said there was nothing to be
done. She carried her away from me and she carried her
too tightly, and though I begged her to turn around so I
might see her a final time she never did. I remember the
sobs in my throat, the very choke of them. I remember
the same sobs in hers. At night I burst awake to those
cries. They are my life's accompaniment.

Of course, I have tried to get her back. Everything a
person might do I have done and in the course of it all I
have told the entire world and most of the entire world
has turned its back on me. They pour scorn onto me
and at every opportunity they heap fresh reward onto
Andrew. His part of the secret I have kept to myself, in
respect for his wife and for his daughter. Even so I am
meant to feel grateful. I have declined all contact with
my sister since leaving Northwood – she made some

feeble attempt to reach me in the beginning yet was easily shaken, out of shame I presume, by my change of address – and yet I hear through our lawyers that my funds remain intact if I should want them. How should I use them, Phyllis? How could I? The very knowledge of their existence is a knife in me. I have made it quite clear that I require nothing more from them and that any further correspondence should be directed through proper channels. All contact comes latterly through Frederick's offices and so, I presume, that is that.

Time drags now, so much more than it did. There are hours when I try to raise some comfort by imagining my dearest girl well and happy somewhere. I think of a house in the country, and her with a dog or a sweet china doll like the one I once shared with my sister. Of course, such pretences do not last. As soon as I begin on the detail I am filled with the ache of not having her and filled with resentment for those who do. Just last month they sent back the ruby bracelet that I gave to her and I lay on the floor and closed my eyes. It was all I sent with her, my only gift; it was the one good thing that held her to me. Was it foolish of me to think they would let her keep it? Was it foolish to hope that one day she would discover it and wonder at its history, and that somehow it would link her to her mother? I held it safe in my hands all through that night. I tried to detect the faintest imprint of her on it, to trace the finest shadow of her touch. My darling girl, I whispered to her over and again, I wonder if they ever let you hold it.

I packed it away the next morning, along with pictures of my sister and of the boys, and felt so very low then, I am sorry to say, that I set about ending myself. I drank vodka from the cabinet and wine that was left, and then the remains of some whisky. There were powders that the doctor had given me for sleep and I dissolved all of those into my glass. The bliss that came next was the only true rest I have had. Such respite. I barely remember it.

It is hard to know yet if I am lucky or not that my friend Teddy came along and found me. He stayed an entire week while I drowned in that sleep I had made for myself and somehow in the depths of it he forced me to stand and to eat. I am not sure how he did it. He will not say and I cannot ever ask him. He has been so dreadfully kind about it all and there are still one or two, even now, who remain on my side and are willing to support small endeavours.

With Teddy's help I have come to accept there is nothing more to be done here and so it seems only right that I should leave. Tomorrow I depart again for Greenland and will not return to England for another year at least. I am sure you could not imagine a worse place to be in this world and perhaps you are right. But I long to feel the Arctic in my bones. I long to know its freeze inside my heart. This wild land of ice, scars and emptiness. It has become the very place, the only place for me.

Dear Phyllis, forgive me this letter. My sadness and yours become no simpler, nor any easier, and hardly more bearable in the sharing. It is just that I had to write it down and in doing so, perhaps you will know the truth. You are a braver soul than I. You fought for your dearest boy with all your heart and I failed to fight enough for my dearest girl. I wanted you to know my admiration, yet I can hardly stand to offer up my shame. I want you to know, too, that I believe you. I have heard so much said about Northwood since we left. I am as sorry as I can be that I ever doubted you.

I shan't assure you things will get better since I cannot imagine you would offer such dishonesty to me. Let no one tell me life will grow easier. If it did, if it ever did, there would be nothing more of her for me to keep. It is the cruellest of enlightenments. The loss of her is all that I have left.

I miss her. I miss my darling girl. For ever and always and with all my heart.

Fondly, and with admiration,
Edith

54

It turns out that house cleaners – of the Pam variety, at least – have greater access to our personal lives than you might imagine. There she stood in our house, in the empty hours before Margaret and I came home from school, nudging her way through our detritus: the dirt of our socks in their basket; the scraps of our food in the sink; the folds of our sheets beneath their bedspreads; the magazines, well-thumbed and crinkled, and carefully hidden beneath mattresses. It wasn't a difficult hiding place. If I'd thought to look myself, I would have found it.

Beneath my sister's bed was a velvet hatbox with a dozen or so letters stored inside it, each in their original envelope. These were the letters that Edith had sent to her sister and that her sister, for one reason or another, had duly sent her back. There was one addressed to a woman named Phyllis Bentley that appeared to have been folded into its envelope but never sent. The ink of Edith's fountain pen was dark blue and bold, written in a lively and elegant hand. Her notes from far-flung corners of the world were smudged here and there with unknown stains and salty imprints, but even the very last of them was crisp and neatly folded, and well preserved.

I read them all in order and as quickly as I could, and yet I didn't want to hurry them or to finish them off too soon, since it felt disrespectful of me to rush. My heart ached for Edith and everything she'd been through and I thought of a hundred questions that I wished I'd asked her. It made me sad to think of Margaret reading them all by herself and I felt disappointed she hadn't wanted to show them to me, or to share them with me, and I sensed there and then the seeds of our growing apart.

Hidden beneath the letters was a jewellery box and a last envelope that was larger than the rest. It was differently coloured, the paper thicker and more luxurious, and its flap had been carefully resealed. I wanted to tear it open and devour its words but I sensed that its contents belonged to Margaret. I began to wonder why Edith had given my sister these things. Perhaps she had liked Margaret more than she had me; perhaps she'd felt some small connection to her after bathing her cuts and restoring her after the fall. Perhaps Edith hadn't given them to Margaret at all. Perhaps my sister had stolen them.

The ruby bracelet was there at the bottom, and I reached in and plucked it from the darkness of the box, startling it with the brightness of the daylight. It was quite the most beautiful thing; wrapped in layers of crumbly, rose-coloured tissue paper, it was exactly as I remembered seeing it that first day we'd gone exploring in Edith's house. The band was delicate, finely etched and narrow, only big enough to fit a child's wrist. The stones themselves were dark red and cut to shine from all angles; the clasp was shaped as a perfect lion's paw. As I wrapped its golden warmth between my fingers I thought of Egypt and Edith and her lost baby daughter, and it didn't seem to matter in the least how my sister had come upon these treasures. The letters and the bracelet were priceless. It was a blessing they'd been saved from the fire.

★　　★　　★

Mum and Ray read them first and then Dad and then, finally, Nanna. Mum said, 'Oh dear. That poor soul, that poor woman.' Pam patted her hair and said, 'I told you.' Dad and Ray both seemed touched in their own different ways but it was Nanna who seemed especially affected by them. She had some faint recollection of Edith, of her fame, from the newspapers of the day, or perhaps from some geography lesson in school. When Nanna had finished reading the last of them – seated in her armchair in her bungalow, surrounded by the fug of ripe banana smells and the scent of old baked cake – she pulled her small cardigan tight around her. She had once known a woman just like Edith, she said, and I didn't think she meant an explorer. She shook her head slowly at the thought of it all and spoke the name Hattie, which I took to be the name of her friend.

'Things were quite different in those days,' she said, and began on some recollection about my granddad and her at a bus shelter, but she decided not to finish it. After that she asked to hold my baby sister, though she'd only just recently let her go. I watched Nanna rock her back and forth in her arms and when she began to grizzle, which she did all the time, Nanna sang her a song which soothed her and put her back to sleep. It was a nursery rhyme I hadn't heard in a while and had to do with cradles rocking and bows breaking, and babies falling head first out of trees.

One afternoon while we were sitting by Margaret's bed in the hospital I planned to ask Mum how she felt about life with Ray and what she thought about the way things had all turned out. I wondered if she agreed with Nanna's latest view of things, that Mum had stepped out of the frying pan and into the fire. I thought about reminding her of the job she was planning to get and the driving lessons she was going to take and I wondered if there might be a chance, even now, of us going on holiday to Spain.

I watched her shift her bulk from one side of the plastic hospital chair to the other and reach down to pluck my sister from her Moses basket. The pregnancy weight hung off her like a coat she was wearing through an endless winter and waiting for spring's arrival to shed. She still wore those same dresses, with their pleats and their folds and their prim, pink maternity bows but Ray said she wasn't to worry about getting her figure back for another month at least. Ray told her she still looked just as beautiful to him. As radiant as ever, he said. Mum looked at Ray like she wasn't all that bothered what he did or didn't think about her figure.

With my sister on her lap, Mum unwrapped a breast, distended and large, from the sheath of its bra and blouse and, for the twentieth time that day, stuffed a bright red nipple in the baby's mouth. Her lips gaped and puckered and then, when they had remembered what they were supposed to do, they clamped down and sucked and sucked and sucked. There didn't seem any point in asking Mum about Spain or the job or the driving lessons after that. She wouldn't have the time. Not for a while.

Ray came in as Mum finished feeding and this seemed to be a signal for her to pass the baby up to him. He stared at his daughter like she was a task or a project, or an album cover whose sleeve notes he couldn't quite decipher. She lay still for a moment and then began to struggle in his arms as if everything about the world – its air, its brightness, its colour, its noise – offended her and made her uncomfortable. She started to cry. Her mouth sprang wide open, raw red and cavernous, and her shouts grew unacceptably loud. Her little back arched and Ray's face creased up tightly until his expression looked mostly like hers did.

'Bounce her,' Mum told him. 'Bounce her, gently.'

Ray did this, and after several attempts, and Mum explaining to him exactly how it ought to be done, she began to calm down and stop crying. Ray looked happy, as if someone had pressed a gold star onto his pyjama lapel.

'She'll need her nappy changing in a minute,' Mum said.

'Well,' Ray said. 'Then I'll do it.'

Dad and Pam stopped by later that same afternoon and we waited for them to get comfortable before we started. Pam gave Mum an air kiss on the cheek to say hello and Mum stiffened in surprise but accepted it. Nanna said, 'How do you do?' and Pam said, 'Fine, thank you,' and though there wasn't any warmth or sincerity in these greetings, each woman seemed to think them good enough. The difficulty would most likely be between Ray and Dad, and I held my breath and counted up to ten as Dad pulled his hand around the curtain.

Pam was dressed in one of her good frocks and Dad had followed her lead and made an effort. His shirt was smartly pressed and he'd shaved and splashed on enough aftershave that I could smell its too-sweet mustiness all the way from the other side of the bed. Even with this armour – a dig at Ray's casualness – my father seemed lost. He shifted uneasily from the ball of one foot to the other and coughed beneath his breath as if he had something in his throat, which he clearly didn't. Ray stood up to acknowledge him but he wore a sour expression on his face, like a chess player about to announce a stalemate.

My sister, who'd emerged from her comatose state a week ago and was becoming more vocal by the day, was having none of it.

'Shake hands,' Margaret said, after their stand-off had gone on long enough. 'That might be a good place to start.'

The handshake was a firm one and it suggested all kinds of things, most of which I felt were negative, and yet it satisfied

Margaret and made her happy. As if to demonstrate her satisfaction in this matter she scooped up the remains of the ice cream the nurses had left her for her tea and ate it steadily and with some small measure of enjoyment. After the ice cream she polished off a cup of tea with half a sugar in it and exactly three-quarters of a digestive biscuit, a portion she might just as well have measured with a ruler. The nurse came by then to apologize for the lack of tea and biscuits for the rest of us but said it wasn't strictly acceptable to have this many visitors around a bed at one time. It was only allowed when a person was very sick, and Margaret, as we knew, was getting better. Of course, this was a special occasion, and so the matron had kindly allowed it.

When everyone was settled Nanna took the package of letters from her bag and sat them neatly on top of Margaret's covers. She arranged them in date order – Nanna was diligent in that way – and when she'd found the last one she held it up for all to see, clasping it between her thumb and forefinger. The address was written in a neater, less flamboyant hand than Edith's and it was addressed to Edith with a return address from her sister in Norfolk. The envelope was thick and white, and the paper that showed through a small tear in one corner was duck-egg blue. Edith had donated it to Margaret – as she had all the other letters and the bracelet – and from the way my sister told it, we surmised this final one was the nearest thing Edith had left to a suicide note. It had been delivered to her on that spring afternoon by the man with the flowers, only days before the fire in which she died. Whatever was inside it had been so upsetting to Edith that she'd carefully resealed it to hide away the dreadfulness of its contents. Margaret had been too scared to open it. Even though Edith had said she could.

'I should have read it at the time,' she confessed to us later. 'If only I had . . . I might have been able to do something.'

We told her that was nonsense but the guilt had bitten hard into Margaret by then and she never lost the feeling, even as an adult, that she might have done something to save her. After Edith's death this final letter had sat there in its hatbox, burning a hole through Margaret's psyche. After the fire, she felt sure that if she opened it, something quite dreadful would happen to the baby or to Mum.

'I'd like to hold her, if that's OK. Just while we open it.'

Mum took Margaret's plate and tea cup, and settled our baby sister into Margaret's arms.

'Do you want to be the one to read it out?' Pam asked.

'No,' Margaret said. 'I think I'd rather it was Mum.'

55

My dearest Edie,

I write to you in haste, so forgive me if this letter seems
all in pieces but I must hurry and run it to the post
and hope it catches you in time, and before the documents arrive. I expect they will look fearsome and all I
can say is read through them if you must, but then you
must promise to discard them and ignore their meaning
at once. They are all bluff and bluster and refer to our
inheritance and my control of the monies as the older
sibling. You will remember from my last letter that
Frederick had found some loophole whereby I might be
persuaded to withhold your share of the funds if your
behaviour was deemed unacceptable or damaging to the
family name. Why this clause was inserted in the first
place I can only guess, but Frederick says it is just the
kind of thing that comes as standard in these matters
and so I truly doubt it was purposely intended, or even
much considered, by our father.

What must you think of me, Edie? How have I let things go so far? I have no good excuses and you are right to call me a coward, but I beg you not to damn me completely or for good, since you cannot know how difficult it has been these last few months. I am sure Frederick does not mean to be so awkward (or perhaps he does and I am so used to defending him that I can no longer see it), it is just that, in its own way, all of this has been quite testing for him. Most people would regard marrying into a fortune as a blessing but Frederick has always been troubled by it and seems to think it makes him less of a husband and a man. He has always to be proving something or other to someone and I doubt he will rest, or give me and the boys a moment's peace, until he has his seat in the House of Commons and later his place in the Cabinet.

So you can see what this fuss of yours is doing to him, can't you? Politics is his way of being something. Something beyond me and mine. If he cannot make a go of it this time then I fear our marriage, which is hardly much to speak of as it is, will quickly be forced to an end. You might perhaps say this is a good thing, and goodness knows I would be lying if I said there were not days when I had dreamt of it. It would bring a thousand freedoms for me, and yet it cannot be good for the boys.

There is a dullness about him, Edie, a certain paleness, that I had not noticed nor appreciated before we married. If I must spend another evening hearing his same dreary views on the Spanish war or the Depression or that nasty little German, I might be forced to take a gun to my head! All of his opinions he copies from *The Times*, and though he ably pretends otherwise he knows nothing of the arts or any culture. Even so, he behaves as if *I* were a burden on *him*. How might we be expected to have Ramsey MacDonald here to supper, he wants to know, when my disgraced sister is on show to the whole of London, nursing her brand-new bastard child.

Sweetest Edie, I don't say any of this to upset you, or even to chastise you, but only so you will hear it from the horse's mouth and know exactly how it is. Did I ever mention to you Frederick's lists? At night before we sleep, when most people might think to talk or read, or write a letter, he makes fantastic lists of society people he would like to meet and invite here for long weekends of bridge and shooting. If you read those names, Edie, you would laugh: Auden and Orwell and Chamberlain and Getty and so on. I think perhaps the thing that kills him is that those selfsame men, if offered the opportunity, would very much like to meet you!

How have I not said it up to now? How proud I am of you, Edie. How stupidly, dreadfully proud. I cannot say I approved of your travels to begin with, but just look at the wonders you have achieved. I worried like a mother hen each time you went away, counting the days while you were out there on that dreadful ice, wondering how you could possibly survive it. But then, of course, I always knew you would. You were always so very much braver than I, ever the little adventurer. Do you remember that weekend up in Scotland when you were only nine, when you disappeared for hours and hours. Mummy was beside herself and ready to send the search party and then you turned up as if nothing was wrong – and in time for dinner – announcing to all and sundry that you had taken a boat out on Loch Ness. Of course you had caught sight of the monster himself and had

not been in the least bit scared to see it! How we
laughed. How very much like you.

So you see, my darling Edie, things are not all black
and white. I wish beyond all things that you had never
found yourself in this dreadful situation but I beg you
not to think that I blame you for it. Andrew has everything to answer for and it angers me more and more
each day to see him praised, most especially when I see
his wretched face on a newsreel or read his name
printed in some paper.

To begin with I had hoped you would go through
with it. You had hardly ever talked about having children
and at the start of all this, when I mentioned
Northwood to you, it was my genuine feeling you would
be comfortable there and that the decision we had come
to was good. Yet I knew in my heart just how hard it
would be and was foolish to think you would stand it.
How could you suffer it Edie? You are my sister. My
kind and loving sister. You are not at all that breed of a
woman. The kind that could give a child away.

I must hurry and come to the end of things. Violet is
back from her errands and has offered to run this to the
post so Frederick does not suspect me. She is a
wonderful girl and I am quite sure I can trust her to
deliver it. All I ask of you now is that you let me handle
things my own way where Frederick is concerned and
give me some time afterwards to smooth things over.
The important thing is that he is allowed to make a
stand and have his moment. Things will be easier when
everything is done with. The rest I will handle when the
time comes.

Do not worry about the money and not for a second;
it is not mine to take from you ever and even if I
wanted to. You could not begin to manage for a moment

without it and for you to suffer the possibility it might be taken from you at such a time is unbearably thoughtless and cruel. Forgive me, Edie, if you ever can. Mother and Father would have stood for you, and right away, I am sure of it. Damn Frederick's opinions. Damn all of them. Follow your heart and be glad of it.

You will adore her, Edie, I know it. It is hard to make plain until you see it and feel it for yourself, but the love of a child is like nothing else. Regardless of who she is or how she came to be here she will have stolen your heart in only moments. You will be a mother, Edie. You will be quite the most wonderful mother.

With greatest love and affection,
Your sister,
Broo

56

The new house they built in place of Edith's burnt-out shell never fitted well into our street. Though they tried to make it plain and dull and simple like the others, its newness and its freshness marked it out. The bricks were a brighter shade of red, the woodwork shone a brighter white and even the small iron gate that replaced her old one was blacker and stronger, and swung shut with a different depth of click. New people moved into that house and lived in it and furnished it, and Pam and my father briefly became their friends. Inside its magnolia-painted walls, among the wall units and the bean bags and the old-fashioned shag pile that these people liked, you could still catch the faintest wild sniff of her. I thought it was all to do with the flames that had licked this spot. Margaret said it was the imprint of her ghost.

When we were grown-ups, Margaret and I would some-times talk about Edith when we got together at Christmases and birthdays and celebrations. In the months in between she'd lie dormant in our memories, silent and slumbering, yet ever ready to spring forth without good warning. I'd remember her suddenly as I stood browsing in the window of a jewellery shop or if I switched on some old Tarzan film. I'd find her sitting beside me in the lounge of some far-flung foreign airport or when I caught my sister pushing a perfectly good roast potato to the side of her plate.

I last thought of Edith when I was sitting in a park that I like to go to on a Sunday morning to take a break from it all. There are children running all over the place, but they are not my children and so I don't mind them or pay them attention or even raise my eyes from the newspaper that I'm stealing an hour to read. The weeks are full and long: a jigsaw of work and errands and sweetness and sourness, and ordinariness and love. I bend beneath the mountain of all the pieces that refuse to fit, no matter how hard I try to force them, and scramble hungrily towards the pockets of fresh air that come in moments and at weekends. These Sunday morning hours are precious. They are my own and they belong to me.

He came and sat beside me by accident. He hadn't picked out my bench or chosen to sit next to me with any purpose. To begin with I tried to keep on reading, but the article I was studying annoyed me and I was only reading it in the first place because I thought I ought to, in the way that I sometimes did that summer. In any case he sat closer to me than he should have, until his leg was almost brushing against mine.

It seemed such a waste not to look at him. He was young and so beautiful, and so full of life and of energy. He had a rucksack at his feet that was layered in travel stamps, some frayed and torn, some fresh and stuck tight to the crumpled fabric. I wondered if he wasn't en route to somewhere exotic. Africa, perhaps? Or India? Perhaps he was on his way home.

I wondered what returning home was like for a man like him. I wondered how much it could mean. For me, now, it was always the selfsame journey: to the curtains I had hung; to the carpets we had laid; to height charts and hand prints and blood stains and love stains, and all the familiar scents.

To furniture we had bought and would keep for years, until it was too old or too worn, or too lacking in style to seem acceptable. Ours was a home whose lines were firmly drawn, whose boundaries had set in without me noticing. I had a family that I loved and good friends I had known for a long time, and books on my bookcase that I had owned since before I turned seventeen. Most days I longed to be close to it all. Most days it made me happy.

The man rummaged in his bag and dug out a sandwich. He wasn't careful in the least about the noise that he made or the mess that he was leaving and when he'd found his food he turned to me and offered me a bite, in that pre-cocious way some young people have. It was then I got to thinking about Edith. And Mum, and Dad and Margaret, and all of it. I wondered what had happened to Pam and her two girls and if Dad had ever loved her, and if the short years they had spent together before they realized they were strangers had helped ease the pain of Mum's leaving. I thought about Ray and made a mental note to buy a birthday card for him and a book about globalization or greenhouse gases because that was what he was into these days. I remembered that I'd promised to pick Mum up and drive her to the cash and carry to pick up supplies for the shop. After my baby sister had gone to school, Mum had found a job working in, and later running, a health-food shop, and one way or another, perhaps because she didn't have the energy to start all over again, she found herself staying put with a man whose other-ness she had lusted after but never truly loved.

The sandwich the man had made was uninspiring. It had been in that bag a long time. He held it level to my face and nodded at me and I suddenly felt hungry and wanted to reach over and take a bite of it. I wanted him to know that I had that choice and that I understood exactly the lure of those kinds of adventures. He smiled and his hands reached towards me and they were strong hands with expressive fingers, quite unlike my husband's which are narrow and long, and which I have always loved. He was challenging me then, and he was free and had nothing to lose, and he made me think of Edith since she seemed like a woman who'd lost everything.

She had suffered the pain of it right up until the death of her sister. Frederick was the wealthy visitor that Margaret and I had seen with the flowers. He'd called to break the news of her sister's passing, and in the guilt that often accompanies the death of someone close, he had thought to deliver his wife's last letter. Perhaps he and Violet had made a pact. Perhaps they were having an affair. We never found out exactly how he stopped it or why he kept it, or the methods he employed to protect his interests and keep the two sisters apart; we only know the note never got to Edith. Not until it was too late. Edith lit that house fire with a box of her own matches. That's what the fire report said.

After Margaret came home from hospital the three of us moved in with Mum and Ray in that small house, until Dad sold the old one and we could move out to somewhere a little bigger. It was easier and harder than we'd expected but the thing that made it bearable was how we doted on our new baby sister. We had begged Mum to name her Ruby in honour of Edith but she had her heart set on Elaine. Dad came up with a far better tribute in the end, a solution that I wouldn't have expected. I had thought he'd be the first to say a treasure like that should end up in a museum, but he wouldn't even hear of it, not for a minute. He said there were ways and means of finding people these days and that it might be nice for me, and most especially for Margaret, if we set about finding Edith's daughter and returning her mother's letters and the bracelet to her. It became a decade's work. But we duly did.

The beautiful man went back to his food. I went home to my husband and to my children.

Thanks to Carolyn Mays, Jonny Geller, Kate Howard, Emma Knight and to all the wonderful gang at Hodder. To Andy, as always, for everything. To Denis who was so generous with stories and outings and time. For their friendship and support, and for being there, always and without asking, my love and thanks to Hannah Griffiths, Kirsty Hanley, Olive Howe, Gabbie Asher and Becky Swift.